Abigail's Affair

(*'Looking for Love'* series)

Book One

by Pat Spence

Copyright © 2015 Pat Spence

All rights reserved.

ISBN-10: 151420388X
ISBN-13: 978-1514203880

Abigail's Affair

Cover design: Andrew Aske/Steve Carse

Back cover picture: Fridmar Damm/4Cornersimages

This book is a work of fiction. The names, characters, places, and incidents are products of the writer's imagination or have been used fictitiously and are not to be construed as real. Any resemblance to persons, living or dead, actual events, locales or organisations is entirely coincidental.

For Malcolm. Let it be.

Love is like war: easy to begin but very hard to stop.

H.L. Mencken

ACKNOWLEDGMENTS

Thank you to...

... my husband Steve for his patience in reading the early drafts, Andrew Aske and Steve for designing the cover, Amelia for technical assistance, Bel Friedman for copy editing, Danusia Hutson for proof reading, Jo Rees for story editing, Judith Weir for reading, Dona Pirozek for checking Australian detail, Tracey Smith-Band for social media and managing the Facebook pages, Tim and Linda O'Rourke for advice and guidance, Kirsty Kinmond for incredible support, and all my other friends who have offered encouragement over the past 18 months.
Not forgetting George the cat for keeping me sane!
And my mum for baking cakes!

CONTENTS

Chapter 1	1
Chapter 2	8
Chapter 3	16
Chapter 4	19
Chapter 5	27
Chapter 6	35
Chapter 7	43
Chapter 8	54
Chapter 9	69
Chapter 10	77
Chapter 11	84
Chapter 12	93
Chapter 13	98
Chapter 14	110
Chapter 15	124
Chapter 16	138
Chapter 17	157
Chapter 18	168
Chapter 19	174
Chapter 20	181
Chapter 21	187
Chapter 22	193
Chapter 23	208

Chapter 24	222
Chapter 25	226
Chapter 26	234
Chapter 27	237
Chapter 28	246
Chapter 29	253
Epilogue	260

CHAPTER 1

Frith Street, Soho. Our favourite coffee shop.

Jake and I sat at a table at the back. It had become our table, as somehow it always seemed to be free whenever we came in. We held hands across the table, gazing into each other eyes and sipping frothy cappuccinos. Jake laughed at the white moustache on my upper lip and I wiped a tissue across my mouth.

As usual, the coffee shop was busy. A woman at the next table spoke quietly and urgently in Russian into her mobile phone. The Croatian waitress cleaned away empty coffee cups from the table opposite, smiling at us briefly, quickly pocketing the £2 tip that had been left. A group of young business people stood noisily by the counter, waiting for their take-out skinny lattes and flat whites, and a couple of tables away, two elderly gentlemen, resplendent in fedoras and cravats, talked politics over their espressos.

This is why we liked our coffee shop. You could people-watch to your heart's content and still remain in an anonymous little bubble. Jazz music played soporifically in the background and the smell of warm coffee beans permeated the air.

It was a cosy, crowded, safe haven, sheltered from the outside world.

Jake was dressed, as normal, in his faded blue jeans, with an Iggy Pop 'Wild One' 87 T-shirt beneath his old black leather jacket. His unruly black hair was tied back in a ponytail and his dark brown eyes were fringed by thick black lashes. I loved it that people turned to stare when we were out, wondering if they recognised him or simply admiring his beauty. He had effortless 'Johnny Depp' film star looks and an irresistible, easy charm, but he also had a tenderness and attentiveness to his manner that made me feel I was his most precious possession. He made me feel loved, worshipped and wanted, and I adored him.

"What shall we do next?" he asked, reaching across and brushing away a strand of hair that had fallen over my cheek.

The physicality between us was like nothing I'd experienced before. Just the brush of his fingertips over my cheek was enough to make me feel undressed.

"I don't know," I answered. "What do you suggest? Culture, entertainment, or the underground car park in Tottenham Court Road?"

As the words left my lips I felt a weakness inside, as lust threatened to govern our activities for the next hour.

"Hmm, difficult decision," said Jake, and I knew he was feeling the same.

He stroked the palm of my hand, making my skin tingle and sending shooting sensations throughout my body. I took a deep breath and reined myself in. Anticipation was everything. I had to savour every moment.

"Perhaps we should save the car park for this afternoon?" I murmured.

"Whatever you want," he said. "This day is for you. Your wish is my command."

"Why don't we take in some culture first?" I suggested. "How about The National Gallery or the Tate Modern, or the Design Centre? Which is closest?"

Before he could answer, his mobile sounded and a frown crossed his face.

"Sorry, I've got to take this," he said, his voice assuming an edgy, business-like tone.

Picking up his cell phone, he walked quickly through a door at the rear of the coffee shop.

Just like that, the moment was ruined. Reality hit hard and I felt my throat constrict. It was her. Checking up on him again, giving me a timely reminder that everything I had with Jake was built on a lie. A cheap, nasty, secret lie.

I could kid myself this was the best thing that had ever happened to me, but who was he going back to every night? Who was he building a life with? Not me, that was for sure. I stared at the closed door, feeling empty.

Jake came back and slid into his chair.

"That was …" his voice tailed off.

"I know," I said curtly. "Everything all right?"

"Yes, fine."

"How does she always manage to call and ruin the moment?" I asked, with a tight smile. " Why don't you switch off your phone?"

"It might be work."

"They could leave a message."

"Please don't spoil things, Abigail," said Jake, taking hold of my hand. "You know it's you I want to be with. We will be together. I promise."

"I suppose this means you still haven't done anything about the situation?"

He looked ahead stonily.

"No."

"I thought you might have said something to Tiffany by now."

Just saying her name made me tense.

Jake grimaced. "Yes, I know. And, yes I'm a coward. I just haven't, okay?"

"Are you going to? Because, if you're not, I'd prefer to know."

He looked at me with tortured eyes.

"Of course I am. D'you think I like living a lie? Going back to Tiffany every night and having to pretend? All the time, wishing it was you? Sometimes, I'm just about to say something and I think, how can I hurt her? What's she done to deserve this? Then I look around my house and realise what I'm seeing is my past. I think of you and I'm looking at my future. But moving from past to future isn't easy. There's a lot of pain."

He stopped and looked down at the table.

"Sometimes I think she's having an affair."

"Tiffany?" I asked incredulously. "How can you think that? She's pregnant."

"I don't know that it's mine, do I? She's not interested in me any more."

"You really think she's seeing someone else?"

"Maybe if I tell her I'm leaving, she'll say 'good riddance'."

"Yeah and pigs might fly," I said scornfully. "She's not seeing anyone. Now she's having your second child, she knows she's got you. She wouldn't jeopardise everything by having a fling. You're barking up the wrong tree."

"It's all driving me crazy," said Jake, sitting back and holding his head. "Some days it seems clear and I know what I have to do. Other days, it's too complicated and I can't move. It's like this great fog is swirling round in my head. It must be horrible for Tiffany. Sometimes I barely say three or four words to her or I don't even speak. Quite often, she's asleep when I leave in the morning and in bed when I get home."

"The days you work in London?"

"Yes."

"So, why bother driving back? It's a long way. Why not stay in a hotel? Especially if you don't want to see her."

"She likes me to come home every night," he said doggedly.

"Even if she never sees you because she's asleep?"

"She's funny about me spending the night away. It causes less friction if I go home."

I looked at him in dismay.

"This is the woman who's supposed to be having an affair?"

"Abigail, this is not helping. I'd like nothing better than to sort things out, but it's difficult and you're going to have to leave it to me." He looked into my eyes. "We're going to be together. I know it. Just trust me. Okay?"

I broke away from his gaze and steeled myself to speak.

"Jake, I have something to tell you."

He was instantly alert, fear creeping into his eyes.

"What? You've met someone else? You're leaving me?"

"Not exactly," I said, "but I think it best if I went away for a while and gave you time to sort things out with Tiffany."

"Away where?"

I paused, unsure of his reaction. "Australia."

"Australia? But that's the other side of the world. You're going to find somebody else aren't you? You'll meet one of those muscle-bound surfers on Bondi Beach and not come back."

"Don't be stupid," I exclaimed. "One of the reasons I'm going is so you can sort your life out. It'll be easier if I'm not here."

He looked miserable. "How long for?"

"A month."

"How will I cope on my own for a month? I wish I could come with you."

"We both know that's not possible. Jake, I'm tired of waiting. You said you were going to tell her months ago. And nothing's happened. The baby will be here and you still won't have said anything. Then it'll be impossible to tell her for another few months and suddenly it'll be Christmas. I'm not spending another Christmas on my own. You don't understand how lonely I get."

"Not half as lonely as me," he countered. "Nothing is worse than being stuck in a relationship you don't want any more: the long silences, the constant irritation with each other. Sometimes I feel my head is going to burst. Every day I try to summon the courage to say something and I can't find the words. We end up talking about something incidental, like the cost of cauliflower. You have no idea how frustrating it is. There's nothing left between us. At night I lie in bed and there's a huge barrier between us. We're complete strangers. And yet, all the time, there's this baby bump getting bigger. You think you're unhappy, Abigail. You don't know the meaning of the word."

He paused and added: "Who are you going with?"

"I'm not going with anyone. I'm going to stay with my old friend, Rosalyn."

For a moment, the silence hung heavy between us and I was aware of Nina Simone singing "My Baby Just Cares For Me' in the background. Then, to my surprise, Jake agreed.

"I suppose you're right. It might spur me on to do something. As long as you're around, there's no incentive to sort things out." He sighed loudly. "I'm going to miss you, though."

I felt panic rising within me. I was so in love, the thought of being separated from Jake for more than a couple of days filled me with terror. Weekends were bad enough. How would I cope with a whole month's separation? It wasn't as if I was going somewhere close. I couldn't go much further if I tried, unless I joined the Mars mission. But it was clear if I stayed, Jake would never do anything. He needed to feel the pain of absence. If I'm honest, I even allowed myself to think about meeting someone else. Someone a lot less complicated than Jake. Sometimes I found the Misery Competitiveness Stakes a little dangerous. It seemed so negative, trying to outdo one another with hard luck stories. Jake usually won. He was so good at it.

The questions filled my head. What if he forgot about me and decided to stay with Tiffany? What if I got back and nothing had changed? What if I met someone else?

"When are you going?" he asked.

"Next Friday. I fly from Manchester Airport."

"In that case," said Jake, "I think we'd better go

straight to the underground car park. And afterwards, I'm going to drive you home and make love to you all over again until you beg me to stop. If I've only got till next Friday, I have to make the most of every minute with you." His brown eyes devoured me hungrily. "Come on, we have no time to lose."

He grabbed my hand and my stomach flipped as he pulled me up from the table and out through the coffee shop onto the busy Soho street.

CHAPTER 2

It was a cold, wet day in March when my friend Edith and her boyfriend, Derek, drove me to the airport. I sat forlornly in the back of the car, rain battering the windscreen and spray from lorries creating a momentary whiteout.

Edith was a no-nonsense, straightforward creature with a heavy dark fringe, black-rimmed spectacles and a permanent vermilion slash across her mouth. She was like a cross between a 1950s secretary and a gothic vampire. She and Derek survived on a diet of continual bickering and put downs, but they'd been together forever and I doubted they'd ever part. She'd been a good friend to me since Rosalyn left for Australia two years ago.

I was already regretting my decision to go away and leave Jake behind. How would I survive without him? How would I cope getting to the other side of the world? I'd never travelled this far before.

"You're very quiet," said Edith. "I thought you'd be excited."

I smiled at her weakly. "I'm not sure I want to go." I'd never told her about Jake, fearing her disapproval, and now was not the time to come clean.

"Don't be silly," she said, with matronly cheerfulness. "You'll have a fabulous time. At least you're heading for sunshine. And you'll get to see Rosalyn. When did you last see her?"

"Just over a year ago, when she came back for her sister's wedding."

"Is she the good looking one with legs up to her neck?" asked Derek, looking in the mirror.

"That's her," I answered.

"You don't forget legs like that. She was very attractive…" began Derek, but Edith stopped him in his tracks.

"Concentrate on driving, Derek. Don't get distracted."

"You're right, I suppose," I said. "I'm just nervous about the journey."

"I'd be more nervous about coping with Rosalyn," said Edith. "She's a complete pain. Totally self absorbed."

I'd forgotten the rivalry between them. They'd never got on. Edith had relished becoming my new best friend in Rosalyn's absence, but she was there by default and she knew it.

"It goes with the territory," I answered. "When you're a successful model, you can't help it. Her modelling career's taken off. She's got this fabulous lifestyle, going to parties and mixing with all kinds of glamorous people."

"Yeah, sure," said Edith sarcastically. "Seeing is believing."

I decided to leave the subject alone. By then, we'd arrived at the airport and the next half hour was spent parking the car and checking in. Then it was time to say goodbye. I gave them both a hug, feeling small and alone.

"Thank you for driving me. I'll phone or text when I get there."

"Have a lovely time," said Edith, smiling broadly. "A month will pass quickly. Just enjoy the sunshine."

"Let me know when you want picking up," said Derek, pecking me on the cheek.

"Thanks Derek. Who knows? I might not come back. I may meet the man of my dreams and stay out there."

"Yeah, sure." He smirked, clearly amused at such a ridiculous suggestion.

I waved one last time. Then passport in one hand and flight bag in the other, I stepped forward into Departures. There was no turning back.

Once in the Departure Lounge, I was filled with a strange sense of euphoria. I'd done it. I'd left Jake behind.

All I had to do now was get to Australia.

I purchased Rosalyn's favourite perfume, Daisy by Marc Jacobs, in the Duty Free area, then walked along an endless moving pavement towards the Departure Gate. I sat down in one of the plastic bucket seats and looked round at my travelling companions, hoping to find a kindred spirit or even a single man, but they were all families or middle-aged people. I briefly wondered why magazines ran articles on meeting the love of your life at airports or stations. It never happened in real life.

On the plane, I sat next to an older couple named Daphne and Reggie, who were going to Melbourne to visit their son and attend a family wedding.

"Melvyn works in IT," explained Daphne, proudly. "He went over to open the Melbourne office two years ago and soon he'll be running the Sydney office. He's such a nice boy. I can't understand why he's still single at 35. Are you single, dear?"

"Er, yes, I am. But I do have a boyfriend."

"You're not married though, are you?" She glanced at my ring finger. "You should look Melvyn up when you get to Melbourne. You'd get along with him very well. Don't you think, Reggie? She'd get along with Melvyn very well?"

Reggie peered at me with huge eyes, magnified through large, milk bottle bottom glasses.

"Oh, yes, you'd get along with Melvyn a treat. He's a smashing boy," he said enthusiastically.

"I'm sure I would," I said without conviction, deciding Melvyn from Melbourne, who specialised in IT, was probably the last man on earth I'd be interested in. He sounded too nerdy for my liking and I certainly didn't want to hook up with a sad, single computer geek. In my experience, there was usually a good reason why a man of 35 was still single.

"Who's getting married?" I asked, feigning interest.

"My sister's boy, Archie," answered Daphne. "Melvyn got him a job at the Melbourne office and next thing you know, he's met a girl and they're getting married. My sister can't come. She has a heart condition. So Reggie and I are going instead. As a bonus, we get to see Melvyn. You should look him up, dear."

Soon Manchester was beneath us, a diminishing grey blob on the landscape, quickly obscured by rushing white clouds and I experienced a flutter of excitement at the unknown possibilities ahead. Fortunately, Daphne took out a Sudoku book and Reggie started a cryptic crossword, so further talk about Melvyn was averted. I took out my phone and re-read Rosalyn's texts.

20th January
Hi Abs,
Great to hear from you. Things are pretty good in the great down under. Registered with a new, top …I repeat top… model agency and getting loads of modelling work. I am hot, hot, hot! Having a blast. Fighting off the admirers. Lost count of the number of parties I've been to. You'd love it here. Why don't you visit? Ros xx

13th March
Hi Absy,
Glad to hear you're enjoying life. What's happening with the old love life? You've gone very quiet on that front. Can't recommend Aussie men highly enough. They are such a laugh. Why didn't I come over here sooner? Getting loads of work. Swimwear last week. Catwalk tomorrow. Plus, don't fall off your chair, training to become an aerobics teacher!!!! Write soon. Love to Edith (not). Ros xxx

4th June
Dear Abby,
Sorry haven't replied earlier. Buying fab apartment with modelling money. Life is one long round of parties and yet more parties. The sky is blue and the sun shines all day. What's not to like? Get yourself over here. We could hire a car and go exploring. Do say yes. Ros xxxx PS. Does Edith still look like a bat with glasses?

20th September
Hi Abs, Can't wait to see you and show you round. So many exciting people I want you to meet. Apartment is fab, fab, fab. Melbourne is the trendiest place to be, so much happening. See you soon. Say hi to Morticia aka Edith. Ha ha! (Watched Adams family last night, made me think of her.) R xxx

3rd December
Sorry haven't been in touch. Been on location by the sea doing a swimwear catalogue. Two weeks of posing and pouting, wearing skimpy bikinis etc. etc. What a hoot! Have you booked your ticket yet? Love, Ros xxxx (You should see me in my new white shorts, the men can't believe my legs!)

17th Jan
Hi Abigail, Went on date with gorgeous guy last night. Took me to fabby new restaurant. Agent reckons I may get into film work. Only one small problemo… can't act! But they don't seem bothered about that. You have to be here. Blue sky, fluffy white clouds, lots of sunshine. Plus great bars, restaurants, loads of friends. Brill! Are you still coming over? Ros xx PS. qualified as aerobics teacher!!!!!

25th Jan
Hi Abby, Fabuloso news you're coming over. Can't wait. Just a quickie as whizzing off on modelling job. They are sending a car for me!!! Let me know date and time of your arrival so I can be there to meet you. Soooooooooo excited!!!!! You'll love it here. Ros xx PS. can you pick up some Daisy by Marc Jacobs at the airport?

1st March
Dear Abs, See you at the airport 5th March. Can't wait to show you round, Melbourne is such a fantastico place. You won't want to go home. Really looking forward to seeing you. Bet Edith wishes she were coming. (Glad she's not.) Ros xx (Don't forget my perfume!! Daisy by Marc Jacobs!!!)

That was her last message, five days ago.

I sat there with a big fat smile on my face. I couldn't wait to see Rosalyn.

After all the frustration and intensity of the Jake situation, this was just what I needed. Her life sounded fantastic, everything mine was not. She was meeting people, doing exciting things and keeping her options open. I imagined the parties we'd go to and the people we'd meet. This was just what I needed, a month of parties and fun, frolicking in the sunshine without a care in the world.

I settled back in my seat, plugged in my iPod and drifted away to the sounds of Coldplay.

Some time later, lunch was served, a delicious meal of Barbecued Salmon with Quince Glazed Tomatoes and Steamed Rice with Pinenuts. I could really get used to international travel, I decided, sipping my gin and tonic, and letting Daphne's talk about Archie's wedding and Melvyn's single life wash over me.

We had a four-hour stopover in Singapore Airport and I spent the time with my new friends, quickly realising this was as far as I wanted the friendship to go.

I'd heard enough about Melvyn to last a lifetime and when I saw his photo, I understood why his quest for a spouse was proving so difficult. He was a geek, with a large moon face, heavy black glasses and long greasy hair. No matter how clever he was, I could never find him attractive.

Still, I dutifully wrote down his telephone number and agreed to call him, time permitting.

Somehow, I had a feeling I'd be too busy.

Back on the plane, I was relieved to find I was sitting apart from Daphne and Reggie. I spent the night tossing and turning, unable to find a comfortable position, but awoke to beautiful bright sunshine streaming through my tiny window.

The aroma of cooked breakfast wafted down the aisle and I realised I was actually rather hungry. Nearly there, I thought with excitement. I looked in my hand luggage for my make-up bag, determined to present my best face to the world.

As I searched, I noticed a sealed envelope, tucked away and, intrigued, pulled it out, realising too late it was a letter from Jake.

Dear Abigail,

By the time you open this you'll either be on the plane or in Australia. Whichever it is, you'll be a long way from me. Forgive me for writing. I know you wanted to get away and put all thoughts of me out of your mind, but I couldn't do the same. I'm the one you've left behind.

For me, life goes on, with all its drudgery and greyness. You are the only colour in my life and my heart is breaking at the thought of not seeing you.

I know you are doing this to make me sort things out, and I truly hope I am able to. I wish I could press a button and be teleported out of my existing life into a future with you. It's all such a mess and I have so many obligations. I wouldn't blame you if you met someone else and didn't come home, although I couldn't bear it.

I truly believe we will be together. It's what I want more than anything. I want to build a life with you, discover the world with you, grow old with you. I believe it's my destiny. I know we said we wouldn't email or phone. That's why I've written a letter. I hope you don't mind.

I love you Abigail, more than I can ever express. You alone have the power to see inside my heart, and it is breaking without you.

All my love,
Jake xx

Tears came into my eyes, as the pain of separation seared through me. Then anger surfaced. How dare he write? The rules of our separation were no contact for a month. Within just a few hours, he'd broken his word. And to what end? To make me miss him all the more.

Angrily, I scrunched up the letter into a small paper ball. He was weak. How could I ever trust him to make the break from Tiffany? As usual, it was all about him; what he wanted, how he was feeling, how much he was missing me. I hadn't realised just how much I needed to get away from him. Somewhere along the way, I'd lost sense of who I was. I'd become an extension of Jake's messed up world. He saw me as his escape route, but was that any basis on which to build a relationship? And now, just when I needed to focus on myself, he was getting inside my head all over again.

But old habits die hard and before long I found myself thinking back to the days when I first met Jake.

CHAPTER 3

I'd just joined the radio station as Commercial Copywriter and was sharing a small office with Jake, who was Commercial Producer. Obviously, I wasn't involved with him at that point and, if I'm honest, I didn't even fancy him. He was too pretty and self-indulgent for my liking.

I'd been there about a month when he let the cat out of the bag.

"Tiff's pregnant. I'm about to become a father," he said with a funny, half-smug smile. "It's due in three weeks."

"Three weeks?" I quipped. "That's the fastest conception I've heard of. Must be a record!"

He grimaced. "I'm not sure how I feel about it. That's why I never said anything."

He didn't appear to feel anything.

The week the baby was due he spent every night working late. I felt sorry for Tiffany, at home on her own, waiting for the baby to arrive, waiting for Jake.

Thankfully, she went into labour early one morning. Jake drove her to hospital and two hours later, his son entered the world. From the moment Nat arrived, Jake was a changed person. He was entranced. There was nothing he wouldn't do for his boy. It was total love.

He took to calling Tiffany in the middle of the day to hear the baby gurgling into the phone. He told me he wanted to have hundreds more children. It was the ultimate test of manhood. It made sense of everything. It made him feel like a god. It made me want to slap him. He was gaga in every sense of the word.

The star of the show, of course, was the baby. Not Tiffany. She quickly assumed a back seat. Both parents doted on the new arrival and took little notice of each other.

Cracks already present began to widen.

Tiffany wanted nothing to do with Jake physically. Her hormonally driven, overwhelming desire for sex at any time of the day had waned completely. Now she had no desire for sex at any time. Being a man, this bred great frustration in Jake. He'd taken to masturbation, he informed me.

"Really?" I said, mildly disgusted at this confidence. "Don't wear your arm out, you might not be able to operate the mixing desk."

Secretly, I was delighted at this rift between the nauseatingly perfect couple.

Call it plain, good old-fashioned jealousy. I was envious of their large country house, their money, their baby, their horses, their weekend dinner parties, their holidays abroad.

Jake's father had been a minor pop star in the 1960s, but more importantly he'd penned a number of successful hits, resulting in a tidy inheritance when his lifestyle finally caught up with him in the early 90s. His estate financed the good life for Jake and Tiffany, and it meant Jake could indulge his fantasies to be a pop star, promoter, voice-over artist and now producer, without having to worry too much about actually earning a living.

The golden couple had everything they wanted. Although I doubted they appreciated it. People like that rarely do. They tend to take it for granted. It certainly didn't make Jake happy.

Over the next few months he began to confide in me. First I was curious, then interested. Gradually I became obsessed. After a while, there was nothing I didn't know about his life.

He told me about his childhood, his father's success, his parents' divorce, meeting Tiffany, getting married, renovating their manor house, his growing unhappiness, his love for his son and his confusion about life. Our little office became the master confessional chamber, with Jake the confessor and me administering absolution.

Some days, we talked so long, it was nearly 5 o' clock before we started work. That would mean working late into the evening.

He never seemed to worry about getting home to Tiffany.

CHAPTER 4

"Madam, you want cooked breakfast?" demanded an oriental voice.

"Oh, yes. Thank you," I said, momentarily disorientated.

Nothing beats the smell of bacon, eggs, beans and tomato, even served in-flight on a plastic tray, and I tucked in heartily, putting thoughts of Jake to one side.

I'd been travelling for the best part of twenty-six hours when the captain announced we were approaching Melbourne. At last, the journey was ending and my adventure was beginning. We landed in brilliant sunshine and I stepped on to Australian soil, hardly believing I was there. It seemed nothing short of miraculous that one day you could be on top of the world and the next down below, an analogy that was soon to become all too true, although I didn't yet know it. For the moment, my wonder and awe were unscathed.

I passed through immigration control, excitement building at the thought of seeing Rosalyn. Passport control was carried out amidst much laughter and joking. A handsome, tanned man in shorts and socks examined my passport, winked at me and asked how long I was staying, giving me the distinct impression I was being chatted up. Everything felt sunny, warm and friendly and I fell in love with the country there and then.

I walked through Customs and into a sea of brightly coloured, smiling people shouting and waving. For a moment I was overcome by the colour and confusion, then heard my name called loudly.

"Abigail, Abigail…"

It was Daphne and Reggie, emerging behind me.

"Don't forget to call Melvyn," called Daphne enthusiastically, her face flushed with excitement.

"You've got his phone number, haven't you? He

should be here to meet us. We could introduce you."

"Er, yes," I started to say, when my attention was distracted by another voice.

"Abigail, Abigail! Over here. Thank God you've arrived. I can't stand this crowd much longer."

Rosalyn's clipped British accent, now with distinct Antipodean overtones, cut through the clamour like a laser. I turned to find the friend I hadn't seen for a year emerging from the melee and embraced her warmly.

"Rosalyn, good to see you. You're looking great."

I turned to say goodbye to Daphne and Reggie, hoping I wouldn't have to undergo the humiliation of meeting the moon-faced Melvyn and introducing him to Rosalyn, but they'd already gone.

"How was the flight?" asked Rosalyn and without waiting for an answer, continued chatting. "There's a bus due in a few minutes, so we'll catch that. I've got a Travel Pass, so it doesn't cost me anything. You'll have to pay, but don't worry, it's only a few dollars. You're looking rather tired, Abigail. Not used to the long flight, I suppose. I've done it four times, so I'm quite used to the old long-haul trek."

I'd forgotten how much she talked. Feeling suddenly weary, I followed her to the bus terminal, dragging my case behind me.

"I hope you don't mind," she said, as we reached the bus stop, "but there's something I have to do before we get back to the house. I'll explain en route. Oh, here's the bus. What good timing. Hop on."

She leapt up the steps, while I struggled with my case, feeling out of place. I paid my bus fare, glad I'd ordered some Australian dollars and sat down next to Rosalyn.

She looked amazing. At 6'2" she stood head and shoulders above most other people and, whereas some tall people tend to stoop and feel a little self-conscious, Rosalyn was full of confidence. She relished her height and enjoyed the attention it brought her. As well as height, she'd also been graced with a slender, well-proportioned figure and long, slim legs. Her olive skin was smooth and firm, and after the hot Australian summer, now a deep Mediterranean bronze. Her features were fine, symmetrical and regular, the result of good breeding and handsome parents. She turned heads wherever she went and I couldn't help but stare at her. She was a picture of glowing health and rosy-cheeked beauty, a stunning advertisement for the Good Life Down Under. Miss Great Outdoors, Queen of the Barbie. Her blonde hair was bleached nearly white, tied back in an adolescent ponytail, with a few small tendrils escaping here and there, giving her a 'thrown together' outdoors appeal. Today she was the epitome of 'Vogue model posing as country girl', complete with lacy cotton blouse, tight faded Levis and open sandals.

I felt pale and insignificant in comparison.

There was no question as to which one of us was attracting passing glances from more than a few passing men and it was equally obvious who they would have made a pass at, given half the chance.

Still, I'd managed the long journey on my own and here I was in the Land of Dreams. I felt a great sense of achievement. I was on holiday for a month and all I had to do was enjoy myself. I looked forward to Rosalyn's luxury apartment, having a long shower and slipping into fresh, clean clothes.

"Okay," said Rosalyn, sitting back in her seat and looking at me with a grin, "Before we get back, I just have this teensy little marathon to run. It shouldn't take any longer than a couple of hours. You can sit on the sidelines and cheer me on. Might put a bit of colour in your cheeks. You look very pale."

"A marathon? Today? What about my suitcase?"

"Oh, don't worry, you can pull it behind you. Come on Abigail, I've been looking forward to this for weeks. It's just unfortunate it clashed with your arrival. It'll be a blast. You'll see me in action. I'm pretty fit, you know. Aerobic classes four times a week. Jogging every morning. I've never been fitter. And when I get my Lycra shorts on, you should see the men's faces. They've seen nothing like it."

"No, I bet they haven't," I said forlornly. "Can't I go back to yours first and freshen up? I've been travelling for a day and a half."

"Sorry, there's no time. The marathon starts in twenty minutes. You could always run it with me." She looked at me hopefully.

I stared at her as if she was mad.

"I don't think so. Running's not my thing."

I felt a sudden pang of longing for Jake. God, how I missed him. I thought of his irreverent humour and wicked laugh, his dark eyes and sheer physical presence, and for a second, the pain was almost too much to bear. I craved his touch with the desperation of an addict needing a fix. How was I going to get through the next month? Never mind that, a voice in my head pointed out, how are you going to get through the next few hours?

The bus dropped us off at the gates of a large park, but I was too intent on lugging my heavy suitcase behind me to take in much detail. All around were happy and excited people, laughing and cheering. Bunting festooned the trees and a carnival atmosphere pervaded the air. A large banner announced the Fitzroy Fun Run, in aid of Breast Cancer Awareness.

"These are the Fitzroy Gardens," Rosalyn informed me proudly. "One of Melbourne's most beautiful parks. You could always take a walk around while you're waiting."

"And do what with my suitcase?" I asked her tightly. "I can't just leave it, the police would blow it up."

"Abigail, you seriously need to chill," said Rosalyn. "You are so uptight. Good job you've come to Oz."

"I'm not uptight," I said defensively. "I just wasn't expecting a marathon, that's all."

"Actually, it's not a marathon, it's a Fun Run. It won't

take long. Particularly with my legs. I can go twice as fast as anyone else." She glanced at her watch. "I need to go and change. Don't want to miss the start. I can't tell you how much I'm looking forward to this. I've got $500 dollars of sponsorship money riding on this. See you back here in a couple of hours. Don't forget to cheer me on."

She bounded away through the crowds, leaving me standing with my large, black suitcase, feeling out of place and too hot in my fleecy blue tracksuit. With difficulty, I positioned myself near to the start line, where a number of people in vests and running shorts were stretching and limbering up. After a few minutes, Rosalyn appeared, towering above the other competitors, looking magnificent in Day-Glo green Lycra shorts, matching trainers and a skimpy crop top. I watched in admiration as she pushed her way to the front of the runners, making sure she had the best possible starting position. I saw her scanning the crowds looking for me, and waved, calling her name, but she didn't appear to hear me.

Suddenly, a disembodied voice announced the beginning of the Fitzroy Annual Fun Run, the crowd cheered and a pistol cracked. They were off, Rosalyn taking an early lead, her long legs moving like tanned, shapely sticks of dynamite. I tried to cheer her on, but my voice was lost in the crowd and soon she was a rapidly diminishing bright green blob in the distance, moving at terrific speed. I watched her disappear out of sight, the rest of the runners following, and then looked around, wondering what to do for the next two hours. This wasn't quite the arrival I'd expected. The crowd began to disperse and, with relief, I noticed a cafeteria adjacent to the start line. Moving through the thinning crowds as quickly as the impediment of my suitcase would allow, I made my way across.

Inside, it was noisy, hot and overcrowded. Babies cried, children shrieked and adults laughed. Harassed, red-faced waitresses did their best to mop up spilt drinks and clear tables piled high with dirty crockery. Somehow, I managed to buy a cup of tea and find a small table to the rear of the café. I gratefully parked my suitcase by the wall, wishing, not for the first time, that I'd travelled light.

Once I was seated, I couldn't help myself. I pulled out Jake's letter and re-read it, allowing myself the self-indulgence of feeling bereft and miserable. Then, hardly knowing what I was doing, I texted him.

Hi Jake,
Arrived safely. Gone straight from airport to Rosalyn's fun-run. No time to shower or change. Sitting with suitcase in a cafe, waiting for Ros. Feeling hot and jet-lagged. Wish you were here. Missing you. Love, Abs. xxxx

I figured as he'd already broken the pact, the agreement was null and void, which meant I could contact him whenever I wanted. I half expected a message to come straight back, but nothing appeared and my travel-weary brain couldn't work out what time it might be in the UK. I texted Rosalyn, telling her she'd find me in the café. Then, desperate to talk to someone familiar, I dialled Edith's number. She answered almost immediately.

"Hello, Abigail, what's the matter? It's midnight here."

"Sorry, Edith, I never thought."

"What do you want? I was fast asleep. Are you okay?"

"Sorry, I just wanted to speak to you. Rosalyn's driving me mad."

"But you've only just got there."

"I know. We've come straight from the plane to a marathon. I've had no time to unpack or freshen up. Now I have to wait till she's run the bloody thing."

"Quelle surprise! She doesn't change, does she? What do you want me to say? You know what she's like. There's only one way and that's Rosalyn's way. You'll just have to get on with it, Abigail."

"I know. I just wanted to hear a friendly voice. I'm

sitting here in this café on my own, with my big heavy suitcase."

"Look, there's nothing I can do. Why don't you get a coffee and read a magazine. It's not a great start, but I'm sure things will get better. Please try to enjoy your holiday. You're in Australia for God's sake. You'll soon be back in rainy old England. Make the most of the sunshine. See the sights. Go off on your own."

"You're right. Sorry to call."

"Call any time, just not in the middle of the night."

"Okay, thanks Edith. Bye."

I sat in the noisy café, feeling miserable. Then despite the noise and my best efforts to stay awake, my head fell forward and I drifted into a black dreamless sleep.

I was awoken some time later by a loud piercing voice.

"So here you are. I got your text."

I cautiously opened one eye and looked up to see the day-glow queen standing before me. Removing the remains of an egg sandwich that had stuck to my face, I sat upright.

"Hi Rosalyn. How did you do?"

"A new personal best," she exclaimed. "Overtaken in the last few yards, which was damned annoying, but I was the fastest woman on the circuit. You should have seen me. I was like grease lightning." She looked at me reproachfully. "I thought you might have been at the finish line to cheer me on."

Energy exuded from her body and I felt even more exhausted.

"Sorry, I fell asleep. Feeling a bit travel weary. But well done. You did really well."

"It's not a good idea to nap as soon as you get here," said Rosalyn pointedly. "You need to stay awake and get in the time zone as quickly as possible. It's the only way to cope with jet lag. Anyway, come on, we need to get going. There's a bus in five minutes. I'll change when we get back."

She strode across the café and I followed, lugging my suitcase. Once again we sat on a bus.

"Tell me about your apartment," I said. "It sounds fabulous. Can't wait to see it."

"Ah yes, I was going to tell you about that."

"Tell me what?"

"I'm not actually living there. I couldn't keep up with the mortgage payments. It's rented out."

This wasn't what she'd said in her text messages.

"So where are we going?"

"Back to the house I'm renting."

"Do you share with anybody?"

"Yes. Two others, Miranda and Ken."

"Do they know I'm coming to stay?"

"Oh, yes, they're cool with that. They're looking forward to meeting you."

"Is there room for me?"

"Yes. Sort of."

"What do you mean 'sort of'?"

"Well, there's a small area at the back of the house and we've made it into a kind of bedroom for you."

Thoughts of the luxury apartment, the trendy friends and the fabulous lifestyle disappeared. This didn't sound good. In fact, it was sounding decidedly bad. A month suddenly seemed an awfully long time. I stared ahead, too weary to ask any more questions.

CHAPTER 5

It wasn't as bad as I feared. Not at first glance, anyway. Rosalyn's house was a sweet little Victorian single-storey terrace, with wrought iron balustrading that reminded me of antique lace. It nestled in a street of similar houses, all with black or white lattice railings and an abundance of brightly coloured flowers. In the warm, sleepy sunshine, everything felt slow and hazy, as if we'd slipped into the past.

"Welcome to Acacia Avenue," said Rosalyn.

"It's lovely," I said, as we walked up the pathway. "Okay, it's not quite the luxury apartment with views over Melbourne I was expecting, but it's very pretty."

"I knew you'd like it," said Rosalyn, "and it's really handy for everything. I love it here."

Inside, the house wasn't quite so pretty, and I realised it hadn't quite arrived in the present. A long hallway led down the centre of the house, with all the rooms leading off. The communal lounge and kitchen showed the typical signs of shared living. Tired-looking mustard curtains hung at the lounge window and the multi-coloured carpet was a remnant from the 70s. A battered old brown leather sofa stood against one wall, with two ancient green floral armchairs opposite, and an old mahogany coffee table, inlaid with mosaic, between them. A pile of old newspapers lay on the floor, alongside some grubby trainers. The only tributes to modern living were a large flat screen TV in one corner of the room and an iPod docking system on the coffee table.

It was a similar story in the kitchen. Unwashed dishes stood piled high by the sink, ants ran along the work surfaces and grease spots covered the once-pretty linoleum floor. An old fridge shivered and shook in one corner, and the cooker had clearly seen better days.

Bijou and trendy it was not, but even these rooms

paled into insignificance compared to my room.

"It's a shed," I said, as Rosalyn led me into the timber attachment at the back of the house. Its flimsy walls looked as though the slightest breeze would blow them away.

"It's an extension," said Rosalyn, "and we've put a lot of hard work into making it nice for you. I bought that duvet cover and Miranda donated this rug. Ken dragged in the cupboard from the kitchen so you'd have somewhere to hang your clothes. You could be a little bit grateful, Abigail, after all the trouble we've taken."

"Okay, it's great." I tried my best to look thankful and chose not to look too closely at the big spiders' webs stretching between the wooden panels. "At least I've got my own space. I don't suppose you could get rid of the tins of paint and garden tools? Or some of these old boxes?"

"Unfortunately, there's nowhere else to put them," said Rosalyn, running her finger through the dust on the lid of the nearest paint pot. "Just step over them, you won't notice them after a while. I think it's a jolly nice little shed, er, room."

"If you don't mind, I'd really like to unpack and take a shower." I sat down on the bed, which felt alarmingly hard and box-like. "Perhaps afterwards we could sit in the back garden and catch up over a cup of tea? I'm sure you've got loads to tell me."

"You won't catch me in the back yard," declared Rosalyn looking horrified, as if I'd just suggested bathing in a river full of crocodiles. "Ozone layer, melanomas, wrinkles… need I say any more? Sunbathing is an absolute no-no as far as I'm concerned. Factor 70 every time I go out for a run. Of course, I'm blessed with skin that turns instantly bronze if I so much as step outside, so it doesn't bother me not being able to sunbathe. But with your freckles and fair skin, you're a prime candidate for skin cancer, Abigail. The last place you want to be is in the sun.

You need to cover up."

"I thought you said I looked pale."

"You do, but sitting in the back yard will only give you wrinkles. And you have enough of those already.'

I couldn't be bothered to argue.

Okay, so no luxury apartment, no nice room, no sunbathing. So far my holiday was not shaping as planned, and Rosalyn appeared to have turned into a self-obsessed fitness freak. I smiled at her weakly.

"Can I use the shower? I really need to freshen up."

"Great idea," declared Rosalyn. "That's just what I need after all that running. Tell you what, I'll take a shower while you unpack. Then while you shower, I'll make us a nice cup of tea. How does that sound?"

"Perfect," I said morosely, feeling as if I'd fallen into an alternative universe.

I handed her the bag containing her bottle of perfume.

"Here, Rosalyn, a present for you. I bought it at the airport."

She peeked in the bag.

"Ooh, Abigail, how nice of you. Daisy by Marc Jacobs. How did you know that was my favourite?"

"Er, you told me."

"Did I? I don't remember. Well, it's very kind of you."

I unpacked and sat on the bed, feeling waves of fatigue wash over me. It was more than I could say for the shower. By the time Rosalyn had finished, not only was there no hot water, there was no water at all. A couple of meagre drops dribbled out of the showerhead and disappeared down the plughole. That was it. The shower was miraculously dry. I turned my attention to the washbasin and was relieved to find cold water gushing from the tap. Telling myself that people in Third World countries made do with less, I set about having a cold wash. Glancing in the mirror, I recoiled in horror at the freak that looked back at me. Was that lank-haired, pale-faced, panda-eyed apparition really me? Why hadn't Rosalyn told me my mascara had run? I looked like something from Night of the Living Dead.

Make-up repaired and feeling refreshed by the cold water, I went in search of Rosalyn. I heard voices in the lounge and opened the door to see a large, pretty blonde girl sitting on the sofa next to Rosalyn, both doubled up in laughter.

"Honestly, Rosalyn, you get worse," said the blonde girl, giggling helplessly.

"It's true, Miranda, she had an egg sandwich stuck on her face…"

Apart from the fact they were obviously laughing about me, which was humiliating enough, I felt a stab of jealousy. Rosalyn and I had been like that once, laughing all the time. Now it seemed I'd been replaced. Perhaps that was why we hadn't fallen straight back into our old friendship. I coughed loudly and they looked up, trying to control themselves.

"Hi, you must be Abigail," said the blonde girl, wiping her eyes. "I'm so sorry. I'm Miranda. How are you?" She leapt up, holding out her hand.

"Fine, thanks, now the egg sandwich has been removed." I shook her hand. "Pleased to meet you."

Despite my jealousy, I liked her immediately. Unlike Rosalyn, she was very pale, without a trace of suntan, giving her blue eyes a watery quality and her face an English look. Her ash blonde hair was cropped close to her head and she wore a lot of make-up, with heavy mascara and bright red lipstick. She was also very well upholstered and I gazed with envy at her magnificent cleavage. Compared to Rosalyn's natural 'country girl' prettiness, Miranda was a femme fatale with a boarding-house homeliness. She was the sort of woman who'd look after you, make you feel at home and give you a good time.

"Sorry, Abigail," said Rosalyn. "We shouldn't laugh,

but you did look funny. Come and sit down and I'll make you a nice cup of tea."

I noticed she'd changed into Day-Glo pink Lycra shorts with a matching crop top.

"You're not going running again?" I asked her incredulously. "You've just done a half marathon."

"No, don't be silly," she answered. "I'm not superhuman. I've done my run for the day. But I do have a double aerobics class to take." She looked at her watch. "Crikey, look at the time. Sorry chaps, I'm going to have to dash. Miranda, can you look after Abigail?"

She leapt off the sofa, all long brown limbs and Lycra-clad torso.

"Why don't you bring Abigail down to The Hub for the second half?" she suggested. "See me in action. It'll be fun and it's only down the road."

Without waiting for a reply, she bounded across the room and out of the door, calling from the hallway: "Second session starts at 3 o'clock. Don't be late."

We heard the front door slam behind her.

Miranda looked at me.

"That is so not going to happen," she said. "I'd rather have my teeth pulled."

I grinned at her, realising I may have just made a friend.

Miranda led the way into the kitchen, her black skirt swaying over her generous hips. Over a steaming mug of tea, she told me about herself.

She was twenty-six and an actress, working as a tour guide between jobs.

"Anything you need to know about Melbourne, I'm your woman," she said brightly. "Dandenong Mountains, Fairy Penguins, Goldfields at Sovereign Hill, City Sights, just ask me. I can tell you exactly where to go and what to see."

"Great, I'd like to see the sights while I'm here. Sounds like an interesting job."

"It pays the bills," she said, wrinkling her nose. "I just hope my agent calls soon with some acting work. The problem is I only moved down from Brisbane six months ago and it's difficult breaking into a new area. You have to get your face known, meet the right people. It takes time. If you're lucky you get a break. If you're not, you work as a tour guide."

"What sort of thing are you looking for?"

"Film, TV, theatre. Truth is, darling, I'd take anything. Even a TV walk-on part."

My mouth dropped as she lit a cigarette.

"I thought it wasn't allowed. Rosalyn's anti-smoking."

"Rosalyn's not here, is she?" replied Miranda, grinning. "When the cat's away... Besides, I pay rent, same as she does. D'you want one?"

"Yes, please."

I took a cigarette from the pack and she lit it with an ornate gold lighter.

"That's pretty," I commented.

"Thanks. It was a present from my last boyfriend. Bastard. He went off with someone else."

"Sorry to hear that." I made a mental note not to tell her about Jake. I could hardly expect her to be sympathetic. "Had you been going out long?"

"Nearly six months. He was the first person I met when I got here. I thought it was serious, but he had other ideas. Just a couple of weeks ago I found out he was two-timing me, the slimy shit. So that was it. I told him to sling his hook."

"Is he still with her?"

"Quite frankly, I don't know and I don't care. But if I ever find out who she is,

she's gonna need hospital treatment."

No, I would definitely not tell her about Jake. I changed the subject.

"Perhaps Rosalyn could find you some work through her modelling agency."

"Modelling agency? I don't think so. She's an aerobics teacher. Doesn't do modelling as far as I know."

I looked at Miranda in confusion. "She told me she was a model. She said it was one long round of celebrity parties and modelling jobs."

"If she's a model, then I don't know about it. And if she's going to celebrity parties, she's not taking me."

"It's just like the luxury apartment," I said bitterly.

"Oh, that exists," said Miranda. "I've been there. It's beautiful, views over the river, very swanky. She couldn't afford the mortgage on her own and there wasn't room for lodgers. So she rented it out and came here."

"She didn't tell me," I said. "I thought I'd be staying in the lap of luxury. Not that this isn't great," I added, trying to be polite.

"It sucks, let's not pretend," said Miranda. "Guess I'd be upset if I thought I was staying in some up-market pad and ended up in this shit-hole for a month. There again, you wouldn't have met me, darling, so every cloud has a silver lining."

I smiled at her, liking her immensely.

"Why did you leave Brisbane?" I asked.

"Man trouble. Why else?" she said, inhaling deeply on her cigarette. "Got too involved with my agent. It didn't work out. Time to move on. Brisbane wasn't big enough for both of us, so thought I'd try the bright lights of Melbourne. Plus, my cousin lives here."

"Do you see much of him or her?"

"Her. Paula. No, not much. She's getting married soon, so she's been pretty busy. Which reminds me. I need to get a dress for the wedding. I've been hanging on, trying to lose weight. But it's next week, so I can't leave it any longer."

"I can come shopping with you, if you like," I offered.

"Might just take you up on that," said Miranda, stubbing out her cigarette, "I'm crap when it comes to posh frocks. Must be the actress in me, I go for the leopard print or frills every time and end up looking like a dog's dinner. I wish I had taste… and I wish I could lose a couple more pounds."

"You know what you need," I said, grinning. "Rosalyn's aerobics class."

She looked aghast. "No fucking way. There's more chance of me flying to the moon."

I looked at my watch. "If we go now, we'll just make it. Got any trainers?"

CHAPTER 6

We stood at the back of the aerobics class, wishing we weren't there. Miranda had poured herself into an ancient black leotard that may once have fit her but was now seriously indecent. Black fish net tights, shiny black Doc Martens and a black bandanna around her head added a certain attitude. Unfortunately, any hint of urban cool was seriously missing in my apparel. Thin white legs, dirty white trainers, baggy white shorts and a polo shirt made me look like a twelve-year old.

At the front of the class, Rosalyn was speaking into a microphone fitted around her head.

"Okay chaps, can everybody hear me? Yeah? Then let's get going. I'll put the music on and we'll kick off. Any injuries I should know about? No? That's great."

Loud, thumping, high-energy music filled the exercise studio and I felt the pumping bass reverberate through the floor. I realised very quickly this was a bad idea. Apart from the jetlag making me woozy, I had no natural co-ordination and was incapable of moving in time with the others. Miranda seemed to be suffering from the same disability and she didn't even have jetlag as her excuse.

"Okay, chaps…to the left, step, step, step… to the right, step, step, step, step.

And plié, step, step, step…… Let's warm it up now, get those bodies working. Arms in the air girls, sweep round, two, three, four, and sweep, two, three, four."

Rosalyn was mirroring us, so when she said left, she actually went right, which confused my brain even further. I started mirroring Rosalyn's mirror, which meant I was doing everything in reverse and crashed into the woman next to me.

"Oops, sorry. Are you okay?"

She had no time to reply. Her gaze was firmly on the pink-clad figure at the front. This was serious stuff.

"Lunge right, two, three, four, and left, two, three, four."

Now I was getting left behind. When I lunged right, they lunged left, and when I was mid lunge, they were mid-step. I looked at Miranda in despair and that was my undoing. She giggled, went left instead of right and crashed into the woman to her left.

"Whoa, sorry, mate, my fault."

The woman looked daggers and I felt a giggle building in my throat.

"Okay, girls, let's really step it up now. I want to see those muscles working. Let's pump up the volume, and follow me. …Over, step and plié, two, three four… hold …and again. Over, step and plié, two, three, four…"

The sight of Miranda holding down her plié when everyone else was stepping became too much. I felt a laugh bubbling up within me and couldn't contain it any longer. I collapsed into giggles, and Miranda, seeing me giggle, gave up the ghost.

"Fuck it, I can't do this."

"Plié at the back," came the instructor's annoyed voice. "Get back into line. Let's keep it going. In time with the music. Step forward, to the side, to the back, to the side and front. And again."

I stepped to the side. The same side as Miranda and we crashed into each other.

"She didn't say which bloody side," said Miranda. "How am I supposed to know which way to go?"

She stood with her hands on her hips, looking indignant.

"Pick it up at the back," came the instructor's fevered instructions. "Get back in the rhythm, girls. And marching, two, three, four. Swing those arms, two, three four. Pick it up, two, three, four…"

"Fuck, fuck, fuck, fuck," said Miranda under her breath, in time with the music, swinging her arms the wrong way. "Fuck it up, two, three, four… fuck it up, two, three, four… Oh fuck it! I'm outta here. Come on, Abigail."

She grabbed me and together we made a beeline for the door, which fortunately was at the back of the room, just behind us. We fell into the corridor, doubled up with spasms of laughter. In the studio, the sound of Rosalyn's annoyed voice wafted through.

"Carry on, girls, you're doing great. Ignore the disturbance. If they can't keep up, it's their loss. No pain, no gain, now, step it up…."

Miranda and I clutched each other, tears running down our cheeks, hysterical with laughter. I don't know what Miranda's excuse was, but mine was one of sheer release. After my anxiety about the journey, heartache at leaving Jake and exhaustion at the park, I needed to let go. And that's what I did. I laughed until I had nothing left inside and Miranda followed suit.

God, I haven't laughed so much in years," she said through her tears. "Heaven help us when we get back to the house. Rosalyn is not going to be happy. But you know what? I don't give a flying fuck. Come on, let's get a drink."

She led the way out and I followed. Outside was her bright yellow Volkswagen Beetle and we piled in.

"Where are we going?" I asked.

"Ken's bar," she answered. "It's only a few blocks away and you'll get to meet your third housemate."

Ken's Bar it turned out was not actually Ken's Bar. It was the place where Ken worked. In reality, it was the Fleur de Lys, an attractive Victorian building, with small leaded light windows, dark blue and gold paintwork, and a large white fleur-de-lys on the sign. A profusion of planters and pots outside, brimming with petunias, lobelia and geraniums, gave it a pretty, urban feel.

"Welcome to Melbourne's best gay bar," said Miranda, as we walked through the double doors.

"Gay bar?" I asked, raising my eyebrows, "You

mean…?"

"That's right, Ken's as gay as a lord," answered Miranda. "And here comes the pearly queen now."

"Darling," said a tall boy, in his mid-twenties, with dyed pink hair and an ear full of piercings. He wore a striped T-shirt in white and blue, a leather waistcoat and pale blue jeans. "What the fuck are you wearing?" He eyed up her leotard.

"It's a fucking leotard, what do you think?" said Miranda. "We've just done a runner from Rosalyn's aerobics class. Fucking disaster. May I present the adorable Abigail Aske, newly arrived from the United Kingdom of England."

"United Kingdom or England, but not both, darling," he said in a camp voice, picking up my hand and kissing it. "Abigail. Enchanté. Je m'appelle Ken."

"Enchantée, monsieur," I said, smiling at him. "Comment allez vous?"

"Fuck it, you don't speak French do you?" he asked in horror. "I can't keep this up, as the cardinal said to the pope."

"No, that's the extent of my French, don't worry."

"Phew. That's a relief. Thought I was going to need French lessons. Ooh er." He winked at me. "Okay, lovely ladies, what can I get you? Apart from a change of clothing. On the house …"

"In that case, a Jeroboam of your best Cristal champagne, 1959 vintage, please, barman," said Miranda.

"Fuck off, you can have a glass of Liebfraumilch and like it."

"Fuck off, at least give us a decent Chardonnay."

"Okay, two glasses of my best fucking Chardonnay coming up. That all right for you, Abigail?"

"I should fucking think so," I answered and that was it. I was in. A die-hard member of the Fuckin' Aussie Club.

Ken placed three glasses of wine on the bar.

"Here's to never going to a fucking aerobics class ever again," said Miranda, raising her glass.

"Or doing a fucking plié or lunge," I said raising my glass. "Bottoms up!"

"I'll drink to that," said Ken, raising his glass. "You're going to be in fucking trouble with Rosalyn when she comes in."

"She doesn't know we're here, darling," answered Miranda. "We didn't tell her where we were going."

'Correction. She didn't know until I texted her," Ken said, looking at his watch. "Should be here in about twenty minutes and I've got a ringside seat for the showdown. Bring it on."

"Bitch!" said Miranda. "You never could resist a bit of voyeurism, could you?"

He beamed at her.

Twenty minutes later, an irate Rosalyn walked in to the bar, spoiling for a fight. She still wore her Lycra pink aerobics gear and looked fabulous. Her blonde hair was tied back in a ponytail and she glowed with the oxygenated energy of the severely fit.

"Hi Ken, soda water, please, with ice and a slice. And as for you two," she glowered in our direction, " don't ever darken my aerobics class again. It's no wonder you can't lose weight, Miranda, you don't have the discipline. How d'you think I manage to look like this? Not by dicking around at the back of the class and making a fool of the instructor. This is the result of hard work, exercise and discipline."

She paused to take a sip of her drink and Miranda raised her glass to Ken in a mock gesture. "Cheers, mate," she muttered under her breath.

Ken raised his glass back to her, grinning widely.

Now Rosalyn turned on me: "I expected better of you Abigail. You've changed. You're not the fun person you used to be. You're uptight and horrible. I'm not surprised you're the shape you are, either. You're just as hippy as you ever were, broad round the beam and small up top. Typical British pear shape. Not like me. No hips to speak of. Straight up and down."

"I see," I said, stung by her rudeness. "It's all about body image, isn't it, Rosalyn? Don't you think it's slightly odd to greet someone off a long-haul flight and take them straight to a marathon, lugging a great heavy suitcase behind them? Didn't it occur to you I might need to freshen up and have a shower? Not that I managed that. There was no water in the shower. I had to use cold water from the tap."

"Okay, ladies, first round over," said Ken, seeing we were attracting an audience among the Fleur de Lys's clientele, who were, unsurprisingly, all male and of one persuasion. "Time to kiss and make up."

Rosalyn turned on him. "Back off, Ken, this isn't your fight."

Miranda tried to intervene. "Look we're all tired. Why don't we have a drink and bury the hatchet?"

'In whose back?" quipped Ken. Rosalyn ignored him.

"That's your answer to everything, isn't it Miranda? Have a drink? Well, I've got news for you. I'm not an alcoholic like you. I look after my body, unlike you. And I know you've been smoking in the house, I can smell it."

I was horrified. This was getting out of hand and things were being said.

"Rosalyn," I said contritely. "I'm sorry, okay? Sorry we messed up your aerobics class. We kept going wrong and the worse we got, the funnier it seemed. It was nothing to do with your teaching. It was us."

Now she turned on me. "It was disrespectful, Abigail. I invited you to my class and the least you could do was show me some respect. Like I say, you've changed. You used to be attractive. Now you're just a washed-up old has-been with a caved in face and wrinkles."

"What d'you mean caved in?" I demanded.

"Your face used to be round and pretty. Now you're

thin and bony. You used to have flesh on your cheeks, now your face is gaunt."

"Yeah, well, I've had a lot to contend with over the last couple of years," I said. "It kind of takes its toll. Not that you'd know. You weren't around. You came here."

"Yes, and look how well it suits me," said Rosalyn. "No wrinkles to speak of. Someone thought I was in my mid twenties the other day. You need to take a good look at yourself, Abigail. You might not like what you see. Anyway, I have to be up early for my run in the morning. I'm going home to get my beauty sleep. I suggest you do the same. You could certainly do with some."

With that, she turned and, head held high, walked diva-style out of the pub, leaving the doors swinging in her wake. A round of applause broke out across the bar.

"Meow," called someone in a very camp voice. "Great entertainment, Ken."

I turned to Miranda. "Wonderful! I've been here less than a day and I've already upset Rosalyn. Doesn't bode well for the rest of the holiday."

Miranda smiled laconically. "Look on the bright side, darling. You could be on your own with her in the luxury apartment. At least you've got Ken and me to look after you."

Back at the house, I crept into my shed room and lay on the hard, box-like bed, staring up at the spidery ceiling, thinking of Jake. Being in love was a state I wouldn't recommend to anyone. Its glowing intensity had long since waned, replaced by a dark, dangerous addiction that held me in its grip. I'd thought I could escape it, huddled down in my Australian bunker. But the war was in my head and you can't escape what's inside you. I'd been foolish to think I could. And now Rosalyn's thoughtless words brought all my insecurities to the surface. I missed Jake more than ever and before I knew it, I was texting him again.

Hi Jake,
A horrible first day. Too tired to explain. Wish you were here. Wish I'd never come. Miss your arms around me. Please send me a message. Yours, Abby. xxx

I knew I was being weak and it was the wrong thing to do. I knew it wouldn't spur him into action. But at that point even the crumbs he was offering seemed better than nothing.

CHAPTER 7

I was awoken the next morning by my mobile phone ringing. Feeling groggy and disorientated, I struggled to find it beneath a pile of discarded clothes. I vaguely remembered falling into bed the previous night, leaving my clothes in a heap on the floor, the effects of wine and travel quickly anaesthetising me

"Don't hang up, don't hang up," I pleaded silently. It had to be Jake. Who else would call me?

"Hello?"

"Abigail, darling, is that you?" My mother's voice sounded loud and clear.

"Yes." I felt disappointed and relieved at the same time. "Yes, it's me."

"Did you get there all right?" asked my mother.

"It was a long journey, about twenty-six hours, but I'm here."

"How's Rosalyn? Still twittering?" My mother remembered Rosalyn of old.

"Yes, worse than ever. But it's okay," I lied.

"I can't believe I'm talking to you so loudly and clearly. You could be in the next room. What time is it there? It's 10.30 in the evening here."

I looked at my watch. "9.30 in the morning."

"Hang on a moment, Dad wants a word."

My father came on the line and proceeded to ask exactly the same questions.

"Hello, darling, how was the journey?"

"It was fine, I had to change planes in Singapore, but I met a nice couple and tagged along with them."

"What time is it over there? It's 10.30 at night here."

"It's 9.30 in the morning."

"How's Rosalyn? Still talking the hind legs off a donkey?"

"Yes, same as ever. No change."

"Hang on, your mother wants a word."

"Hello, darling, I don't know how you're going to survive a month with Rosalyn. I know I couldn't. She's very pretty, but she's not exactly what you'd call thoughtful, is she? I don't think I've met a more selfish girl. Remember that time you broke a bone in your foot and all she was concerned about was whether she'd have someone to go to the school disco with? She didn't give two hoots about you."

"Mum, that was years ago."

"And then there was that time when you broke up with your boyfriend, and what did she do? Started going out with him herself. Didn't give your feelings a second thought."

"Why are you bringing all this up now? If you felt that strongly, why didn't you say anything before I left? This isn't helping."

"Sorry, darling. I'm just worried about you. I want you to have a lovely holiday, but you always seem to be disappointed by Rosalyn. She's never risen to the occasion in all the years you've known her."

"Mum, she's fine. I've met her housemates, Miranda and Ken, and they're great, too."

"House-mates? I thought she was living in a flat?"

"It's an apartment and it's gorgeous," I lied. "With views over the river. Now, please stop worrying."

"Sorry, darling, Can't help it. Not since…. you know…." She tried, but failed to keep the strain out her voice. "Gracie would have loved to visit Australia."

"I know, Mum. But you have to let me live my life. You can't wrap me in cotton wool. I'm fine. I'll be back before you know it. Anyway, I'd better go, this call will be costing you."

"What's money, Abigail?" said my mother bitterly. "We've got plenty of that. I just wish we still had Gracie."

"Okay, I really have to go. Love you, Mum. Give my love to Dad."

"Love you, darling. Bye."

I dropped my phone on the bed, trying to keep thoughts of Gracie out of my head. Gracie, my beloved older sister, who had died in a car crash two years earlier.

My parents had never got over the shock and I was still learning to cope. The pain was never far from the surface. It just didn't break through as often as it had, which meant life for me had become bearable again. Not so for my parents. Every journey I took was a source of anxiety.

And now I'd gone to the other side of the world.

All this worry about Rosalyn was simply a displacement activity, taking their minds off bigger issues over which they had no control. I understood and sympathised, but I had to live my life. And my mother's opinions about Rosalyn were not without grounds. Rosalyn was selfish. She'd always been self-centred, but she'd been fun with it, and that had always tipped the balance in her favour. Now, I wasn't sure. Last night, she'd been cruel and hurtful and I'd seen a different side of her. Her glamorous lifestyle was all fantasy and it seemed she had her own demons to face. Maybe my arrival was bringing them to the surface.

"Why does life have to be so bloody complicated?" I said to the wall. "Why is it all so painful? I just want things to go back to how they were."

The wall was silent and before I knew it, I was dialling Jake's number.

After two rings, he answered.

"Hello, Abigail."

"Hi, Jake. Sorry for calling. You're probably busy."

"No, it's okay. I was working."

"What, at nearly 11 o'clock at night?"

"Anything's better than being with Tiffany."

"Oh, I see."

"How are you?"

"I'm fine. Just missing you."

"I know. I miss you too."

"I'm beginning to wonder why I came here, Jake. Well, I know why I came. It's just not how I imagined it would be. Rosalyn's a complete pain, there's no luxury apartment or celebrity lifestyle, my bedroom is a shed and I had to watch Rosalyn run a marathon straight off the plane, lugging my suitcase behind me."

"Yeah, I saw your text."

"Why didn't you reply?"

"Well, you know, I wasn't sure it was a good idea."

This wasn't going as well as I'd hoped. He obviously hadn't said anything to Tiffany and every time I made contact, the chances of it happening became more remote. Our conversation felt stilted and distant. I tried again.

"I wish you were here Jake and we could explore Australia together. Can you imagine what that would be like?"

"We probably wouldn't see much of Australia."

"Why's that?"

"We'd be in bed the whole time. God, what I wouldn't give to be lying in bed with you now, feeling your skin beneath my fingertips, parting your lips with my tongue…"

My insides started to churn. This wasn't why I'd phoned him and it didn't feel right, but it was certainly doing things to me.

"I wish you were here right now, Jake."

"And what would you like me to do to you?"

I bit my lip. "Make love to me, make me feel safe and wanted."

"D'you know what I'd like to do to you?"

"What?" My voice was faint and breathless.

"I'd like to fuck you. Over and over till you begged me to stop."

His voice was low and gravelly and I felt the familiar thrill go through my body. This is what he did to me every time. This is why I went back time and time again. He had total power over me and I was addicted. I couldn't break this attraction no matter how hard I tried. Distance only made it worse. I'd gone cold turkey and now I was feeling the withdrawal symptoms.

Jake's voice suddenly changed.

"Gotta go. Speak to you soon."

The line went dead and he was gone. I stared at my mobile phone. He'd done it again. Led me on, got me where he wanted, then disappeared. Dancing to Tiffany's tune, no doubt. Bastard. How could you hate someone yet love them so intensely at the same time? No wonder my head was all over the place.

There was a knock at my door and Rosalyn came in, carrying a cup of tea. She smiled and sat on the end of the bed.

"Peace offering. Can we start again? It all got a little out of hand last night. I said some things I shouldn't have. I am really glad to see you, despite how it looks."

I looked at her warily. "Of course, Rosalyn. I never wanted us to fall out. I guess it was a bit ambitious to do an aerobics class the same day I arrived…"

"Yeah, these long-haul trips can take it out of you."

"…and to be honest, the sight of Miranda trying to do those pliés was the funniest thing I'd ever seen."

"I know. I was trying not to laugh myself. I can't see how she's going to lose weight before the wedding next week. She wants us to go into Melbourne this afternoon to help her choose a dress, is that okay?"

"Yes, that's fine. It'll give me chance to look around."

"Who was that you were talking to when I came in?"

"Oh, just my Mum and Dad. They send their love."

"Great. How are they?"

"Fine, absolutely fine, considering all that's happened, you know."

"Yeah, it's been tough on them. Tough on you too, Abigail. I'm sorry I left you to face things by yourself, it's just, you know …"

Now we were getting into difficult territory and I wasn't sure I wanted to go there.

"Look it was a hard time for us all after Gracie died. I probably lent on you too much. I wasn't thinking straight."

"It was tough. I just couldn't give you the support you needed. I'm sorry. It was easier to run away."

"Is that the reason you came to Australia?"

"One of the reasons. Not the only one. I needed to start again, begin a new life. And you'd changed. You were sad and serious all the time. I'm not saying you should have been different after what you'd been through. I just felt you were dragging me down with you, and I had to get out before I suffocated."

She paused and played with the duvet cover. Neither of us knew quite what to say. This was a big revelation and I needed time to take it in. I thought of the times I'd blamed her for leaving me alone, when I'd felt more lonely than I ever thought possible. Then I thought how difficult it must have been for her. To keep blaming her was counter-productive. We had to move forward.

"You're right," I said. "We need to start again."

"Thanks, Abigail, I really am pleased to see you." She leaned over and gave me a big hug.

Later that morning, Rosalyn bounded into the kitchen dressed in bright blue Lycra.

"Right chaps, time for a run!"

"Don't look at me," said Miranda. "You're on your own. I still haven't recovered from yesterday."

"I wasn't expecting you to come with me. I'm just telling you I'm going for a run. I'll see you in an hour." She left the house in a flurry of energy, leaving Miranda and I sprawling on the sofa like a couple of couch potatoes.

"Rosalyn and I made up," I told Miranda. "She apologised and we've put the disagreement behind us."

I didn't tell her about Gracie or Rosalyn's confession as to why she'd come to Australia. It seemed too personal.

"Good, I'm glad," said Miranda. "Although Ken will be disappointed there won't be any more showdowns, the old drama queen."

"Where is he?" I asked.

"Don't know," said Miranda. "He didn't come back last night. Obviously got lucky."

"I like him," I said. " He's funny."

"He livens things up," admitted Miranda. "We'll go and have another drink with him later." She leaned forward conspiratorially. "But first, while Rosalyn's out, there something I want to ask you."

She led the way out of the lounge, down the corridor and into Rosalyn's room.

Surprisingly, it was all pink and frilly. Everywhere I looked there were pink satin flowers, pink ruffles, pink frills, pink lace mats and pink drapes. I'd never known Rosalyn to be romantic and this was a side of her I hadn't seen before. I began to wonder how well I really knew her. Miranda picked up a framed print from the dressing table and held it out to me.

"This is what I wanted to show you. You know her family. Are they as aristocratic as they look?"

It was a Victorian-styled sepia print showing Rosalyn's mother lying on a chaise longue beside a large aspidistra in a pot. Her father stood behind, holding an air rifle, and at the front sat a large gundog.

"This is a staged photo," I said. "But the answer to your question is yes. They're very upper-class and extremely eccentric."

"Ha, I knew it," exclaimed Miranda. "Tell me more."

"They live in a massive house set in its own grounds. It's quite spooky, full of antiques and shadows. Her father is very dapper and absolutely charming. Drives an old Bentley. Her mother used to be a mannequin for one of the fashion houses in the 1960s, Chanel or Rive Gauche or something like that. She was once quite stunning, although she's more like a wilting lily now. Spends most of her time lying on a chaise longue, like the one in the photo. When she speaks, she barely moves her lips, as if it's all too much effort. And she looks at you askance, as if she can't be bothered to turn her face to you. Sometimes, a half smile crosses her lips, as if she's thought of some amusing thought that she can't quite be bothered to share with you."

"Wow," said Miranda, her eyes round. "How about the dog?"

"She's called Missy. Only has one eye. Lost the other one when Rosalyn's dad was cleaning his gun and it accidentally went off. Missy was in the line of fire."

"Oh my God. Is that true?"

"Who knows? Both parents are mad as sticks."

"Oh my God," said Miranda again. "It's like something out of a film."

"The first time I went to the house I stayed over in her sister's room while she was at boarding school. Mrs Greville-Whyte - you'll notice Rosalyn's shortened her name to plain old 'White' by the way - glided along as if on casters, like something out of a horror movie, and took me into a room full of old-fashioned furniture. There was a great four-poster bed in the middle. I went to put my bag on a chair in the corner and she practically leapt on me, shrieking: "Don't touch that chair. It belonged to Clive of India. Nobody touches it.""

"Who?" asked Miranda blankly.

"Clive of India. Some old general," I answered. "Committed suicide, apparently."

"While he was in the chair? No wonder no one wants to touch it. It's probably haunted. If there is such a thing as a haunted chair. One thing puzzles me. If there's so much money, why is Rosalyn always broke?"

"Typical aristocracy. Land rich and cash poor. Rosalyn was always telling us hard luck stories. About having no food in the cupboards and getting an orange and bottle of tomato sauce in her Christmas stocking. Before I left, I went round to see if her parents wanted to send anything. Her mother gave me an old sweater full of holes and her father a five-pound note. Like I say, completely batty."

Miranda put the photograph back on the dresser.

"It's another world. I feel sorry for her."

"There was a lot of pressure on her to get married," I said. "Find a good-looking upper-class chap and settle down, like her mother and her sister. She wants her family to be proud of her, but she can't fulfil their expectations, so she feels like she's failed."

"Poor kid. That's why she came to Oz."

"Something like that. Initially, she got work as a nurse. But it didn't work out. And then the modelling took off. Or so I thought."

"Ah yes, the imaginary modelling career." Miranda made a face. "I'd say that girl's got a few issues."

In the kitchen, Miranda made coffee and took the biscuit tin off the shelf.

"I know I shouldn't," she said, "but what the hell. I'll buy a bigger dress size.'

She peered in to the biscuit tin and frowned. "Sorry to ask, Abigail, but have you been eating the biscuits?"

"Not guilty. I can honestly say I haven't eaten a single biscuit since I arrived."

"That's strange. There were loads and now it's empty. This isn't the first time it's happened."

"Maybe it's Ken," I suggested.

"No," said Miranda firmly. "Ken doesn't eat biscuits - not unless they're ginger creams. And he's rarely here."

She dropped her voice. "I think it's Rosalyn. She seems to have a major preoccupation with food. Always talking about her diet, her figure, her exercise routine, and commenting on what other people are eating. She makes me feel guilty having one piece of chocolate. I think she's a secret binger. Probably throws up afterwards. Was she like this when you knew her?"

I paused before answering, wondering how much to say. "She had a few problems. But it was a long time ago."

"What kind of problems?" asked Miranda.

"It started one summer, when we were students working in a fast-food restaurant. We ended up putting on a lot of weight. Actually, we grossed out. I put two stones on, Rosalyn more. I couldn't get my jeans over my knees. We were like two roly-polies. That was the start of it."

"What happened?"

"I went to uni and the weight fell off gradually. It wasn't so easy for Rosalyn. She couldn't bear people commenting on how fat she was, so she stopped eating. I didn't see her for a while. When I did, I was shocked. She was stick thin, always cold, living on low calorie drinks and biscuits." I stopped and looked at Miranda. "I probably shouldn't be telling you this."

"Cross my heart, I promise I won't say anything," Miranda assured me. "What happened next?"

"She wouldn't listen to me. I was really worried about her, but there was nothing I could do. Eventually, she got a new boyfriend who was very supportive. She listened to him and gradually he got her eating more. Over time, she put the weight back on and got on with life. She took a job in a hospital, split up with the boyfriend and seemed happy on her own. Within a couple of years, she seemed back to normal. She was fun to be with, we always had a laugh together and I kind of forgot about it."

"Until now. And you're wondering if it's happening again," said Miranda.

"Well, yes. The signs are there."

"Let's keep an eye on her," suggested Miranda. "She looks healthy. And she's very fit. Maybe it's not as bad as it was before. D'you know what I think we should do this afternoon? Go into Melbourne, find me a dress, have a drink at Ken's Bar, then have a lovely meal. Melbourne's got some of the best Italian and Chinese in the world. You have to try them. What do you say?"

"I say great, let's do it," I beamed at her. "With Rosalyn, of course. She really was trying to make amends this morning."

"Of course," said Miranda. "I wasn't going to leave her out."

I smiled, cheered up at the thought of going to a restaurant and eating good food.

I realised I'd hardly eaten since I'd arrived in Melbourne.

CHAPTER 8

Later that afternoon, Miranda, Rosalyn and I took the train into Melbourne in search of 'the dress'. With its mix of contemporary and Victorian architecture, Melbourne city centre was chic and pretty, full of picturesque alleyways and arcades, quaint street lamps and flower displays. Ornate trams trundled along, people leaping on and off at every junction, giving the place a European, old-fashioned feel.

"That's it," shrieked Miranda as we walked past a small boutique. "See that black dress in the window? That's exactly what I'm looking for. Come on."

She charged in to the shop and we followed.

"Looks tarty to me," whispered Rosalyn. "Too low cut for a start. Not what you'd wear to a wedding."

"Reserve judgement," I suggested. "Let her try it on."

Miranda stepped out of the changing room and our jaws dropped.

"What do you think, guys?" she asked. "Is it too over the top?"

The black linen dress fitted her with the snugness of a glove two sizes too small. Miraculously, Miranda had poured herself in, exaggerating the contours of her voluptuous figure to the point of no return. Her magnificent cleavage reached staggering proportions, gloriously displayed by the dress's plunging neckline. Its nipped in waist gave her an hourglass figure rivalled only by Marilyn Monroe in The Seven Year Itch and its A-line skirt gave a Lambada-like sway as she walked. It was a dress that would be noticed, not so much for itself, but for the body that filled it.

"You look incredible," said Rosalyn. "It emphasises your curves."

"It's stunning," I said enthusiastically. "Definitely you."

"It feels like a second skin," enthused Miranda. "I love it. Shall I get it?"

"Absolutely," I said. "You'll stun them all and probably attract a gorgeous man into the bargain."

She beamed at us. "I can't believe I've found a dress so easily. Hang on while I take it off."

No sooner was she in the changing room than Rosalyn laid into her.

"Second skin? It's tighter than her actual skin. And talk about it being over the top. Her breasts are practically falling out. It's far too tight and tarty. If I was that large, I'd do something about it."

"But you're not, so best not say anything," I cautioned.

"I can be diplomatic, you know," said Rosalyn in a tight voice.

I was beginning to get the feeling that this three-way friendship was not going to be easy, especially with Rosalyn as the lynchpin.

Miranda came out of the changing room and went to pay for her dress, almost swooning when she realised the price.

"How much? Jesus, that's more than I earn in a month. Oh, what the hell, stick it on my card. It's not every day your cousin gets married. But I am going to need a drink after this… I feel Ken's Bar beckoning."

Within twenty minutes we were in the Fleur de Lys and Miranda was showing Ken the dress.

"Looks fabulous, darling," he said with his hands on his hips. "Like I always say, if you've got it, flaunt it. You'll wipe the floor with them. Wait till you see what I'm wearing. I've got this divine pink waistcoat, matches my hair perfectly. I've got high hopes of pulling…."

"You're going to the wedding?" asked Rosalyn sharply. "Is that right, Miranda?"

"Yes, he's coming as my plus one. I didn't want to go unaccompanied. I thought I'd told you."

"No, I think I would have remembered that."

"Ah, are you feeling left out, darling?" asked Ken, in mock concern. "Only the stylish get invited to weddings."

"Fuck off, Ken," said Rosalyn. "That's got nothing to do with it."

"I wasn't going to mention it," said Miranda, "but I texted my cousin yesterday to see if you and Abigail could come. I haven't heard back from her yet."

"You might be going to the ball after all, Cinderella," said Ken. "There's always room for an ugly sister."

"If you weren't the other side of that bar, I'd throttle you," said Rosalyn. "You're a complete bitch."

Ken blew her a kiss and went to serve another customer.

On cue, Miranda's smart phone pinged and she scrolled down her messages.

"She's replied," she informed us, reading from her phone. "Hi Mandy, great to hear from you. No prob if you want to bring two more guests. Had a couple of cancellations. See you on the day. Paula. xx"

Miranda beamed at us. "That's my cousin. Laid back to the last. So, we can all go. Happy now Rosalyn?"

"I wasn't that bothered," began Rosalyn.

"No back-tracking," said Miranda sharply. "You wanted to come and now you've got an invite. What are you going to wear?"

Rosalyn smiled. "I've got this gorgeous full length white halter-neck dress. I haven't had a chance to wear it yet. This will be the perfect opportunity."

"How about you, Abigail?" asked Miranda.

"I don't know. I didn't exactly bring wedding clothes with me."

"Don't stress," advised Miranda. "We'll find something for you."

She called over the bar. "Ken! Ros and Abigail are coming to the wedding too. Won't that be fun?"

"A girls' outing? Can't wait!" he called back. "I'll be a

rose surrounded by thorns."

"What time d'you finish, Ken? Fancy coming out to eat with us thorn birds?"

"Half an hour and I'm done," he answered. "Unless anything better comes up, I'm all yours. Where are you going?"

"Giovanni's," said Miranda.

"Ooh, haven't had an Italian for ages," he answered. "Nothing nicer than a bit of chorizo sausage!"

Miranda raised her eyes. "I think you'll find that's Spanish. But we get the joke."

He gave her the finger.

We followed Miranda onto one of Melbourne's oldest streets into the heart of the city's cosmopolitan café society. The pavements bustled with people. Music drifted out of open doorways and the whole place had a carnival feel. Eateries of every nationality leapt out from a confused blur on the sidewalk. Italian, Chinese, Indonesian, Turkish, Greek, Vietnamese, French and Caribbean restaurants offered all kinds of exotic cuisine, and the aroma of freshly cooked food wafted on the air, making my mouth water. It was alive, busy and intoxicating.

Giovanni's was a cheerful little Italian bistro, sitting snugly behind white wicker tables and chairs, carefully arranged on the pavement. Red and white checked tablecloths danced in the early evening breeze. Inside, candles in Chianti bottles gave off a low, flickering light and a smiling fat man, who I guessed to be Giovanni, showed us to our table with a flourish.

"This way, signorinas, you are all looking lovely tonight. Please, 'ave a seat. Oh, and a signor. It is signor, is it not? I wasn't sure with the pink 'air."

"Just call me signorina. Suits me fine," said Ken in his best camp voice. "A carafe of your best house red, sir, and make it snappy."

"Franco, house red," called out Giovanni.

Within seconds we were drinking the best red wine I'd ever tasted and looking at enormous menus. I'd had nothing but Vegemite and rice-cakes since I arrived and my stomach growled hungrily. I ordered garlic bread, lasagne and mixed salad with a selection of cold meats, almost salivating at the thought of a proper meal! Miranda ordered rigatoni carbonara and Ken went for spaghetti bolognese, while Rosalyn had a side salad to accompany her glass of water.

Soon, our meal arrived, steaming and bubbling in earthenware dishes, served by Franco with the grandiose style of a true showman. He swirled the pepper grinder lasciviously, spooned out the Parmesan cheese with gay abandon and charmed us with his amorous smile and mobile eyebrows.

The wine and conversation flowed, the food tasted divine and I felt good. This was just what I needed. Adding to the entertainment, Franco took a real shine to Rosalyn.

"You are beautiful lady," he crooned. "Such long legs and beautiful figure. Bellissima! I think you are married?"

"Not yet," smiled Rosalyn, enjoying the attention.

"Why not, I ask myself? Surely, the men, they queue up for you," he draped himself across the empty chair behind her. I moved my chair further away from him. He had a body odour problem.

"Oh, I'm not short of admirers," she admitted. "It's just a question of finding the right one."

"So many men for such a beautiful signorina. I am not surprised. I think maybe you would like to come out with me later?"

He raised one eyebrow seductively and smiled out of the corner of his mouth. I concentrated on my lasagne.

"You'll have to join the queue, I'm afraid," said Rosalyn playfully.

"Franco, my name is Franco," he moved a little closer to her, fortunately away from me. "And your name?"

"Rosalyn," she simpered.

"Rosalyn! A beautiful name. I kiss your 'and.'"

Before she could protest, he had seized her hand and planted his fleshy red lips on it with the ferocity of a limpet. I bit hard into a piece of tomato. Miranda smirked.

"You're a bit forward, Franco," said Rosalyn flirtatiously.

"No, not forward. Just amorous. It is my Latin blood. It makes me very passionate. When I see a beautiful lady, I cannot resist her. It makes me want to make love. You know I feel an urge... down here."

I took a huge bite out of my liver sausage.

"You can keep your urges to yourself, young man," said Rosalyn, pretending to be stern.

"No, I cannot keep them to myself. Not when there are lovely ladies around."

He beamed at Rosalyn and a piece of greasy black hair fell across his forehead. He tossed his head back but the lock of hair stuck where it had landed.

I poured fresh olive oil over my salad.

"You meet me later tonight? We go for a drink, we go dancing, we make love, beautiful Rosalyn?" He ran his finger playfully up her arm. I picked a piece of pepperoni off my salad and sank my teeth into its textured surface.

"I don't think so," said Rosalyn, at last beginning to weary at this display of Mediterranean testosterone. "Sorry, I'm seeing my boyfriend tonight."

"Franco!" Giovanni called. "Table number four. Needs serving."

"Okay, okay!"

He turned to Rosalyn and spoke in a low, urgent voice.

"If your boyfriend doesn't come tonight, you come here to see me? I finish 11.30. I wait for you."

"He's going to have a long wait," she said, as she watched him go.

"Honestly, who'd be heterosexual?" asked Ken. "The nerve of the man thinking you'd be interested. Now, if he'd chatted me up it might have been a different story."

"Tart," exclaimed Miranda, flicking her napkin at him. "You don't care, do you, Ken. As long as it moves, it's worth humping."

"Excuse me, I have standards. I'm not the one picking up waiters."

"Oh please," said Rosalyn. "D'you really think I'm interested? Anyway, Stuart's coming round later tonight."

"Stuart?" I asked. "Who's he? Your boyfriend?"

"He'd like to be," said Miranda. "Stuart is gorgeous and has been after Rosalyn for ages, but she's not interested. I think she has some secret lover hidden away. Why else would she refuse him?"

Rosalyn flushed. "He's a lovely guy. He just doesn't do it for me."

"He could do it for me," said Miranda.

"And me," said Ken. "Any time."

"In your dreams, gay boy," said Miranda. "Come on, let's pay up and go."

We settled the bill, leaving a dejected looking Franco staring after us, his greasy forelock still clinging to his brow.

"If you don't mind darlings, I'm moving on," Ken informed us. "Not that I don't find you fascinating, I just need more suitable company. If I don't come back, you know I got lucky! Ciao!"

He gave each of us an air kiss, then minced down the street, turning to wave before disappearing from view.

"He must get lucky a lot," I said. "He's never at the house."

"Don't even go there," said Miranda. "Ever since he broke up with his long term boyfriend a couple of months back he's been terrible. On the pull every night. I just wish he'd find somebody."

"What happened?" I asked.

"The usual," she explained. "He found Paul in bed with another man. It'd been going on for months and he had no idea. Broke his heart, poor boy. All this camp stuff, it's just an act, you know."

"Relationships!" said Rosalyn scornfully. "What's the point? You only get hurt. You're far better playing the field."

We arrived back at Acacia Avenue to find a tall, dark-haired man waiting on the doorstep.

"Hi, Rosalyn," he said, stooping to kiss her. "Hi Miranda." He kissed her cheek. "I guess you must be Abigail. Pleased to meet you." He planted a kiss on my cheek and I gawped at him. He was gorgeous. A complete charmer.

"Hi, I guess you're Stuart," I said in a squeaky voice, wondering why Rosalyn wasn't interested in such a hunk.

We sat in the lounge and Miranda produced a bottle of Chardonnay from the depths of the ancient fridge. An old Sade album played in the background and I sat back, watching Stuart carefully. He was clearly besotted with Rosalyn.

"You're looking great, Ros," he said, sitting close, unable to take his eyes off her. "How did you get on in the Fun Run? I'd have come to cheer you on but I was working."

"I won the women's race," said Rosalyn. "A new personal best."

"Fantastic. Wish I'd been there. Let me know when you're doing the next."

"Where do you work, Stuart?" I asked.

"Oh, it's boring. I work in the family business," he said. "We have a factory that manufactures components for supermarket trolleys."

"Boring but lucrative," Miranda pointed out.

"Well, yes, we're doing okay," said Stuart casually. "I can't complain."

Gorgeous and rich, I could hardly believe Rosalyn

wasn't interested in him. He was every girl's dream. I watched her, wondering what was going on. While Miranda devoured Stuart with her eyes, tongue practically hanging out, Rosalyn kept her distance, showing just enough interest to keep him dangling, but no more. He was kind, sexy and intelligent and had the most beautiful deep blue eyes.

It simply didn't make sense.

"I can't stay long," he said. "I just wanted to pop over with an invitation. I wondered if you girls would like to take a trip up the coast to Port Fairy next week. My family has a small chalet up there and it's such a beautiful stretch of coastline, I thought Abigail might find it interesting."

"Thanks, Stuart," I said eagerly. "That sounds fantastic."

"I'm working, so count me out," said Miranda. "But thanks for the offer, Stu."

"How about it, Rosalyn?" he asked. "We could drive up on the coast road, stay two or three days, do some sight-seeing, have a barbie, maybe take a boat out."

"You'd be coming as well, would you?" said Rosalyn rudely.

"Well, yeah, that was the plan. Is that a problem?" He looked momentarily confused.

"No, of course not. We might have something on, that's all," said Rosalyn dismissively. "Can I let you know?"

"Of course. Tell me tomorrow? I've got lots of meetings, so probably best to text me." He looked at his watch. "I must go. I've an early start in the morning."

"Okay, nice to see you," said Rosalyn disinterestedly. "I'll show you out."

Stuart rose from the sofa, smiling at Miranda and me.

"Bye, girls. Nice to meet you, Abigail."

"Likewise, Stuart," I answered. "Hope to see you next week."

"Yeah, hope so. You can't visit Melbourne and not see the Great Ocean Road."

Rosalyn showed Stuart out, a bored expression on her face and I couldn't help but feel sorry for him.

"What's all that about?" I asked Miranda.

She shook her head. "Beats me."

When Rosalyn came back into the room, we leapt on her.

"What is wrong with you?" asked Miranda. "He is drop dead gorgeous. He's smart, he's rich and he's totally smitten."

"You could do a lot worse," I pointed out.

Rosalyn shrugged.

"Treat 'em mean, keep 'em keen," she said with a shrug. "Like I said, I just don't find him attractive. You can't manufacture it."

"What about the coast trip?" I asked. "Can you take the time off, Rosalyn?"

"Depends if I can get cover for my classes," she said. "I suppose it might be fun. I just don't want to give him the wrong idea."

"Oh, come on, Rosalyn," I said. "Say yes, please?"

"I'll think about it," she said, annoyingly.

My cell phone rang suddenly, nearly giving me a heart attack. I looked at the screen.

It was Jake. The last thing I'd expected.

"Need to take this in my room," I muttered to Rosalyn and Miranda, and headed down the hallway towards my shed room.

"Hi Jake, how are things?" I asked, shutting the door behind me.

"Missing you." He sounded miserable. " I had a row with Tiffany last night. She wanted to know why I'm not looking forward to the baby coming."

I felt my throat constrict. "What did you tell her?"

"Nothing really. What could I say?"

"The truth! This was your opportunity."

"I couldn't do it, Abigail. It wasn't the right time."

"Jake, there is never going to be a right time. You

have to bite the bullet and do it. Every day you don't say anything, it gets more difficult."

"I'm sorry. I just miss you. I drove past your flat today and was convinced you'd be at home if I rang the bell. I feel like my right arm's been cut off. I can't function without you."

As usual, Jake was saying all the right things but doing nothing.

"Are you having a nice time?" he asked.

"Well, yes, I am, actually. We've been out for a great meal and a friend of Rosalyn's has offered to take us up the coast next week. After that, I've been invited to a wedding."

"You're going to meet somebody else, aren't you?" he said flatly.

"Er no, why would you think that?"

"Because you're all bubbly and excited."

"That's because I'm on holiday and I've had a nice day. You don't begrudge me that, do you?"

"No, of course not. I just miss you, that's all."

"I miss you too, Jake, but you have to do something about your situation, otherwise we have no future, you know that."

"Yes, I know," he said in a choked voice. "I have to go. I can't talk any more. I love you. Bye."

He hung up and I sat for a moment, looking at the phone.

Then I put it in my pocket and walked back into the lounge, my mind in turmoil and my cheeks flushed.

"Who was that?" asked Rosalyn. "Obviously someone who means a lot to you, judging by the look on your face. You've kept this quiet."

"That was Jake," I answered. "He's a guy I've been seeing for the past year."

"Come on, spill the beans," Rosalyn persisted. "Age, looks, job. Give us the low down."

I grinned, self-consciously.

"Okay, He's thirty five, about five foot ten, black hair, dark brown eyes. Looks a bit like Johnny Depp. He's a Commercial Producer, freelance now, but we used to work together. That's about it, really."

"So, it's serious," said Rosalyn with glee. "Are we going to hear wedding bells?"

A warning bell sounded in my head, but I chose to ignore it. I decided to tell them.

"Actually, he's with somebody else. He's trying to extricate himself."

"You mean, he has a girlfriend?" asked Miranda.

"A wife." I immediately regretted my decision to tell the truth.

"Children?" asked Miranda.

"Yes, one. A little girl." I swallowed. "And another on the way."

"OMG," cried Miranda. "Let me get this straight. You're involved with a married man, who's already got one child and is expecting another?"

"Yes," I replied miserably. "Look, don't rub it in. The last few months have been hell. It's one of the reasons I came away. To give myself some breathing space and give him the chance to sort things out."

"Are you in love?" asked Miranda.

"Yes, I am," I admitted.

"And is he in love with you?"

"Yes. The second baby wasn't planned. It just happened. He'd stopped sleeping with her ages before."

As the words came out, I realised how gullible I sounded and how awful I'd made Jake appear. He was coming across as a bastard, who was messing around behind the back of his pregnant wife.

Which I suppose he was.

"If you want my opinion," said Rosalyn, "he sounds like a man who's having his cake and eating it. I can't believe you've got yourself into something like this. Have you thought about his wife and what she's going through?

Or what it will do to her if he leaves. Not that he will, of course. I doubt very much he'll leave her."

I felt sick. This reaction was all too familiar. Why did everyone feel they had the right to judge?

"You wouldn't catch me getting into anything like that," continued Rosalyn. "Too much common sense. I'd want the full attention of my man. I certainly wouldn't want to share him. Either he's with me or he's not. No half measures. No thank you."

This was not what I wanted to hear. But how could I ever expect Rosalyn to understand? To my surprise, Miranda leapt to my defence.

"I'm sure you didn't get into this situation by choice. And I'm sure you wouldn't be sticking around unless you were sure of your ground," she reasoned. "If you think things will work out, then maybe they just will. Hey, what the hell, I'm on your side. Let's hope he leaves the witch. She probably deserves it. Probably turned into a frump with no make-up, a stone overweight and prone to wearing floral dresses. She'll come off okay in the divorce settlement."

"Think of the suffering you'll cause if he does leave," said Rosalyn. "You'll ruin her life."

"Excuse me," I said, rising to my defence, "but what about my suffering? It's no fun being a mistress. It's hideous. All those nights, weekends, Bank Holidays alone, just waiting for a phone call that doesn't come. If you think I'd willingly subject myself to that, you must be mad."

"Then get out of it," said Rosalyn logically. "Sounds horrendous. If I were you, I'd cut my losses and send him on his way. Honestly, men like that want castrating. They take everything and give nothing back but a whole lot of heartache."

There was no denying it. She was right.

From an outsider's point of view, it was a no win situation. What was Jake actually giving me? Some empty promises and little else.

I sighed and looked into my wine glass.

"The fact is, Rosalyn, I can't leave him. I'm in too deep. I have to see it through, win or lose."

"Sounds like a no-win situation to me," said Rosalyn.

"You can't help who you fall in love with," I pointed out. "Have you never been in love? Truly, madly, deeply in love. Like you couldn't live without them?"

"No, I don't think so. Just give me a nice chap, with good prospects, who's good in the sack and I'm quite happy. None of this soppy stuff. Doesn't make for a good marriage, you know. You're far better to go into marriage as a partnership. The less feeling there is, the better. Otherwise one of you is always going to be jealous of the other. Better to keep it business-like."

"If that's your attitude, then why aren't you with Stuart?" asked Miranda.

Rosalyn flushed. "Oh, let's not start that up again. I need to go to bed. I'm running in the morning. "

She stood up and walked to the door.

"See you in the morning. Good night."

"There's something not right there," said Miranda after she'd gone.

"What d'you mean?" I asked.

"Well, you've been honest about your situation. Rosalyn, on the other hand, is being secretive."

"D'you think so?" I asked.

"Yeah, there's definitely something she's not telling us. I've had my suspicions for a while, but I think our friend Rosalyn is having an affair."

"Really? You saw her reaction to my situation."

"Exactly. Methinks the lady protesteth too much. What better way to throw us off the scent?"

"But who with?" I asked.

"Well, I guess he's married. She gets these phone-calls at odd times and goes rushing back to her room to take them, like you just did. Sometimes she goes out and doesn't say where she's going. She's not interested in any of the eligible men around, and some of them are drop-dead gorgeous. Sometimes she's on top of the world and other times in a pit of depression."

Miranda finished her wine.

" I may be wrong, but I think something's going on."

CHAPTER 9

Saturday morning arrived. It was rainy, overcast and cold. I gazed mournfully out of the lounge window. Instead of blue sky and fluffy white clouds, a cast-iron grey expanse threatened to empty its contents at any moment.

A baby next door began to cry and I felt tears of my own start to fall. Tiffany's baby would be due in three months. Lucky cow! She was expecting Jake's second baby and looking forward to a life of domestic bliss, deep in the countryside, in their eighteenth-century manor house. She didn't work. She didn't need to. Jake's inheritance took care of everything. Her job was to look after the house, make his meals and take care of their child. She was quite happy that way. She had no desire to work. She had no real desire to do anything, according to Jake. She pottered about the house, tended the garden, had her roots done, met other yummy mummies for lunch.

"Has she ever worked?" I once asked Jake, as we were lying in bed, with the morbid fascination of a prisoner asking the executioner how sharp his axe was. I had to know, even though I knew the answers would be unbearably painful.

"When we lived in London, she was my P.A.," answered Jake. "I was working as a voice-over artist and she answered the phone, looked after the books, that sort of thing. Then we moved to Warwickshire and I started working as a sound engineer. I was earning decent money and with dad's inheritance, she didn't need to work."

"So, she gave up, just like that?" I demanded, thinking how pathetic she sounded.

"Yes. I must admit I thought she'd do something. Maybe charity work or start up a business. I offered to set her up with her own riding stables. She loves horses."

So would I be, if I had the time and the money, I reflected bitterly. "What happened?" I asked.

"She wasn't interested. Said she wanted to ride for pleasure, not business. She never had much 'get up and go'. Always needed a kick up the pants. Not that she's stupid. Not by a long way. She's more intelligent than me."

Got a funny way of showing it, I thought.

"So, she got pregnant?" I asked.

"Not straight away," said Jake. "When we first moved, we were renovating the Manor. So, she spent her time project-managing the renovation, looking round antique shops and auctions, finding interesting pieces. Then she took charge of decorating the house. A year ago, she finished the last room, my study."

"And then she got pregnant?" I pressed on with my interrogation.

"I remember the day she told me," Jake sighed ruefully. "I knew she'd come off the pill three months earlier and that she wanted a baby. It wasn't what I wanted, so I hid my head in the sand and pretended not to notice. Then one day, she took me out for a meal. We were sitting in the restaurant and she told me. I felt sick. I felt the prison door slam shut and knew that she'd trapped me."

"But how could you feel trapped, when you had the lifestyle and the beautiful house?" I persisted. "Surely starting a family was the next logical step?"

Jake grimaced. "It's never been right with Tiffany. I always felt something was missing. She wasn't my soul mate. I was making do, until the real thing came along. I always thought things would get better."

He sat up and looked out of the window.

"But it never did. We were just papering over the cracks. It never changed the relationship. Deep at the heart of it, the rot had set in and there was nothing we could do. It was easier to cover it up than face it. So, we muddled along, always believing one day things would pick up."

He turned and smiled at me sadly.

"Don't get me wrong. We're not unhappy. We're

actually very compatible. It's just there's no passion, no soul. I hate to use the old cliché, but she's never really understood me or taken an interest in me. So, all along, we've compromised, buoyed up by our lifestyle. Deep down, I knew I wouldn't end up with her. Sooner or later, the cracks get too big to cover up. When she told me about the baby, I panicked. Although I'd suspected for some time she was pregnant."

"You had?" I asked incredulously. "What d'you mean?"

Jake's face softened as he remembered. "She looked so beautiful. She was blooming, exuding energy. Her face was radiant. And she was in another world. Take it from me, when a woman is pregnant, she changes. She becomes like a stranger, all wrapped up in herself. When you think about it, all those hormones racing about her body, she's bound to become different. And, of course, I was excluded. Once I'd played my role, I was redundant. I'd supplied the goods, done my bit, and that was it. Mind you, when she got into the second trimester, it all changed. She suddenly got into sex. Couldn't get enough of it. Any time of day or night. That was a plus point."

I listened, feeling sick. Well, I'd asked for it. I'd bombarded him with questions and he'd answered. I just hadn't realised how much it would hurt.

The baby in the house opposite began to cry again bringing my thoughts back to the present. I thought about Tiffany's impending birth. Another baby. That just showed how wrong things were between Jake and Tiffany, I thought bitterly. How could he have deceived me? Led me on. Given me hope. Let me fall in love with him. I hated him. But I missed him.

I missed his arms curled around me, holding me tight. I missed his long, deep, romantic kisses. I missed his sad, brown eyes looking into mine, and his long, silky dark hair. I missed his jokes, his laughter, his silly voices. I missed his crumpled shirts and tattered, old jeans. I missed his battered old leather jacket. I missed his fingers touching my face. I missed him telling me how beautiful I was. How could separation hurt this much?

With a superhuman effort, I pushed thoughts of Jake out of my head and focused on the day ahead. I took a shower, thankful it was working and relishing the comfort of the hot water, falling over my shoulders like a warm, protective cloak. I stayed in until the water ran cold, then brusquely towelled myself dry, forcing myself to be strong and independent. Pulling on jeans and a sweatshirt, I wandered into the kitchen and found Miranda sitting at the table, reading a magazine.

"Morning," I said briskly, filling the kettle with water.

"Good morning to you, too. You look like you've had a rough night."

You could always rely on Miranda to say it as it was.

"Took me a long time to get to sleep," I admitted. "After Jake called everything was going round in my head."

"I'm not surprised," said Miranda. "You shocked us with your, er, confession. And now, of course, I'm intrigued. You have much to tell me."

"I didn't think you'd be on my side," I said, "after what you've been through. I thought being the 'other woman' would make you hate me."

"Every situation's different, I guess," said Miranda philosophically. "But hey, I'm over what happened to me. Good riddance and all that."

"Thanks, Miranda, it means a lot to have you on my side. Unlike Rosalyn. Where is she?"

"Out for a run. Do you have a photo of Jake you can show me before she gets back?"

"Yes, in my purse."

I showed Miranda my favourite photo of Jake. I'd taken it one hot, sunny day when we'd been to Oxford. We'd found a quiet place down by the river and had just made love in the open air. Afterwards, we'd sat dreamily watching the river go by, his fingers lightly caressing my shoulder.

"When we're together," he'd said, looking into my eyes, "we're going to travel and I'm going to make love to you in every European capital city." It was the perfect moment and I hardly dared breathe for fear of disturbing the air around us. I wanted to capture it forever so I'd taken a picture of him, never wanting to forget his white linen shirt and olive skin, his smouldering eyes and burning passion. Of course, I didn't tell Miranda that. I just let her look at the photograph.

"Oh my God," she said, her eyes opening wide. "He is drop dead gorgeous. Johnny Depp or what? I can see why you've fallen for him. Film star looks or what?"

"I know," I said. "He's got everything. Good looks, sensuality, intelligence, wit, sense of humour…"

"Just a wife and family in the way," said Miranda "Do you think he's really going to leave?"

"I don't know," I admitted. "He says he will."

Miranda laughed. "What a man says he'll do and actually does are two different things in my experience."

"He says it's over between him and Tiffany."

"Of course he does," interrupted Miranda. "But when this baby is born, he's going to find it difficult to walk away. I bet Tiffany doesn't think it's over."

I stared at her. "D'you think?"

"We could always check out her Facebook page," she suggested.

"I don't know," I said, a feeling of panic starting to rise inside me. "It's not something I've ever wanted to do. I need to keep her at arm's length."

"You need to find out the truth," said Miranda, reaching for her laptop. "I don't want to see you throw your life away. Film star looks can cover up a multitude of sins. Let's see what Tiffany's got to say for herself. What's her surname?"

"Wetheroak," I answered, feeling nervous. I wasn't sure I wanted to do this.

Miranda logged into Facebook and typed in the name Tiffany Wetheroak.

Suddenly pictures of Jake and Tiffany filled the screen. I looked at them in horror. The most recent picture had been taken two days ago. It showed a pregnant Tiffany, looking blonde, beautiful, and slender, with a neat little bump showing beneath her designer tunic. She was smiling broadly, her eyes shining and excited. Jake stood by her side, her arm around her.

I read the comment: *'Two months to go. Jake and I can't wait to introduce baby Joey to the world.'*

"Baby Joey?" I said in disbelief. "She knows it's going to be a boy? Jake said they didn't know what it was going to be. And two months' time? Jake said it was due in three months. Either he's a total liar or she's making this up."

Miranda gave me a wry smile and continued scrolling down.

Next came a photograph of Jake and his son, Nat, each holding up a guinea pig, with the caption:

'Jake and Nat on a family outing to Hatton Country World yesterday. Just after this picture was taken, Jake's guinea pig weed all over him. Hilarious!'

Underneath, Jake had commented:

'Not so perfect ending to a perfect day. Took ages to dry out.'

"I bet it was hilarious," I said bitterly. "This is the man who never goes on family outings, who's not interested in doing things with his family. And yet he describes it as a perfect day."

Miranda scrolled further down. There were more pictures and the more I saw, the worse it got.

There was another showing Jake with one arm round

Tiffany and the other round Nat, obviously laughing at some joke, with Tiffany's caption: *'Family love… you just can't beat it'* and Jake's comment: *'Love y'all'*; then another of Jake grinning with his brother, captioned *'Brothers in arms'*, liked by Jake; and another showing a close up of Tiffany's pregnant stomach, captioned *'Not long to go'*, with a comment from Jake *'Can't Wait. Love you Tiff'*.

Strangely enough, the picture that hurt the most was a close-up of a shelf on a wall, with Tiffany's comment: *'At last, Jake has put up my shelf. The renovation is complete!'* and Jake had commented: *'It's the little things that mean the most.'*

I'd seen enough. I felt completely sickened. What did it all mean? Was Jake playing a game with Tiffany? Was this all show and the reality me? Or was Tiffany the reality and he was playing a game with me? If so, where did I fit in? I didn't want to know the answer to that question.

I thought of the sadness and the love that shone out of his eyes whenever he looked at me. Why was he always so sad? Was it because he knew deep down we'd never be together? I knew he was unhappy with Tiffany, that theirs was a relationship built on habit and compromise, and he found it unfulfilling and unrewarding.

I knew she didn't touch his soul the way I did. She didn't inspire him to great love and passion. Otherwise, why would he be with me? But she'd been his partner for such a long time and the bonds that had been formed were difficult to break. The biggest bond of all was his son. I knew he couldn't face leaving him and that he was the real reason he stayed.

I felt the knife of jealousy twist in my heart.

Jake had built his life with the wrong woman, he was having children with the wrong woman.

I didn't know what I'd do if he decided to stay with her. I felt ill at the thought of Jake living with Tiffany, Jake eating with Tiffany, Jake sleeping with Tiffany, building a house with Tiffany, buying a new car for Tiffany, taking care of Tiffany, having a son with Tiffany and now having another child with Tiffany.

The bitterness felt like a great curling worm within me, twisting and turning, eating away my peace of mind.

"Are you all right?" asked Miranda.

"Yes," I said sharply. "It just hurts to see these family pictures. That's why I've never looked on Facebook before. I knew what I'd find. And now I don't know what to think. I want him to leave her, but I don't want to be the person who breaks up a family. I couldn't have that on my conscience. And those comments Jake has made. They seem like the perfect happy family, but he says they're not."

"It's not for me to advise you," said Miranda, "but it strikes me life would be a whole lot easier if you could get out of this situation."

"I know," I said miserably. "But that's easier said than done. I was half hoping I'd meet someone on this holiday and I could go back and tell Jake it's all over. But what's the chance of that happening?"

I heard the sound of a key being turned in the front door.

"Rosalyn's back. I can't face seeing her yet. Can you tell her I'm having a lie-in? I need to compose myself."

"Of course," said Miranda. "Why don't you come on my City Tour this afternoon? I'll get you a free place on the coach?"

"Yes. Great idea."

I picked up my bag and made a hasty exit from the kitchen.

CHAPTER 10

Once back in my room, I texted Jake. I couldn't help it.

> *Hi Jake,*
> *How are you? Good to talk to you last night. Sorry we couldn't talk longer. Done anything interesting in the last few days? Missing you. Text me or call. xxx*

Almost immediately a message came back.

> *Hi Ab,*
> *Missing you too. Sorry couldn't talk for long. Haven't done anything all week except work. It's the only way I can take my mind off you. Can't wait to see you.*
> *All my love, Jake xxx*

I looked at his words, knowing they were lies. He hadn't been working. He'd been enjoying family days out. How could I believe anything he said?

I texted back:

> *What about trip to Hatton? Facebook tells a different story.*

This time there was no immediate message. He was obviously digesting the information and thinking of a fresh lie to spin. Five minutes later my phone pinged.

> *That's all Tiffany's doing. Best not to read it. You know the truth. We're not a happy family. You are the one I want to be with. I will tell her soon. I promise.*

I texted him:

> *Promises and lies. The question is, which to believe? Why put up a shelf if you're not planning on staying there?*

Straightaway, he replied:

> *Why are you doing this? I've told you it's over between Tiffany and me. You have to believe me. Why do you keep on asking these questions? You have to trust me.*

This was not the response I wanted. But I didn't know what response I did want. It was all getting too confusing. The thought of being second best to Tiffany was unbearable, but the thought of never seeing Jake again was even worse.

I quickly texted:

> *Sorry. Don't know what to think. Going to the coast for a few days. I need some thinking time. A. xxx*

The message came back:

> *Okay, make sure you don't meet anyone else. I want you for myself. Love you. xxx*

I put my phone back in my bag and took a deep breath. Now I had to face Rosalyn. Luckily, she'd had a good run and was buzzing.

"I've just done my best time ever. 47 minutes. The best I'd achieved before was 51minutes. You should have seen me go. Mind you, having long legs gives me a real advantage. And these new aerodynamic shorts make a huge difference. You should come with me, Miranda. Might help you lose some weight."

I caught Miranda's eye and spoke before she could answer.

"Actually, Rosalyn, I was thinking of doing Miranda's City Tour this afternoon. Do you want to come with me?"

My question threw her off course.

"Oh hi, Abigail. City Tour? Er, probably not. I've seen it all before and besides I need to visit a friend this afternoon."

Miranda gave me another look.

"Who's that, Rosalyn?" she asked. "Anyone we know?"

"No, it's someone from aerobics. She wants me to run through a routine with her. I said I'd pop over."

"Too bad, Abigail," said Miranda. "You'll have to do the City Tour on your own."

"I think I can manage that," I answered. "I'll have an excellent Tour Guide."

"Straight from the Lonely Planet Guide Book," said Miranda and beamed. "Thought any more about your trip up to Port Fairy?" she asked Rosalyn.

"Actually," said Rosalyn, surprising us both. "I texted Stuart this morning and told him we'd go. It's all arranged. We're going tomorrow."

"Excellent news!" I said in genuine surprise. "I'm really looking forward to it. What changed your mind?"

"I was always going to say yes," said Rosalyn. "I just didn't want Stuart to know. You have to keep them dangling. That's what keeps them interested."

"But you're not interested in him," I pointed out. "Why play games?"

Rosalyn's cell phone buzzed, saving her from answering.

As soon as she saw the name on the screen, she flushed and disappeared into her bedroom, calling behind her: "Sorry guys, gotta take this in private."

I glanced at Miranda.

"See what I mean?" she said triumphantly. "She's hiding something."

The afternoon went by pleasantly enough. Miranda's coach was comfortable and air-conditioned and her City Tour very informative.

"Right folks, here on the left is Old Melbourne Gaol, the place where Ned Kelly spent his last days. You can see the mask he used to wear and the scaffold where he was hanged, and every twenty minutes or so, they stage a particularly gruesome reconstruction. You'll also see a display of creepy death masks belonging to various bushrangers and convicts. Apparently, more than a hundred men were hanged here between 1841 and 1929. It's a dark, dank place, with strange shadows and ghostly echoes, providing an unpleasant reminder of the brutality of Australia's early convict days."

She paused for dramatic effect.

" Some say Ned Kelly's ghost still walks. You certainly don't want to be in there after dark."

Miranda relished the role, and the actress in her added a whole extra dimension to the tour.

"On a more positive note, folks, if you're into culture, you can visit Melbourne's National Gallery, coming up here on the right. It has a fabulous collection of Aboriginal art and a great collection of paintings, including some fabulous Impressionists. It might not be on a par with what you European folks have in your countries, but don't forget, Australia is a young country with very little history or culture to draw on, so we're very proud of our Art Gallery."

I thought back to a recent trip Jake and I had made to the Tate Gallery in London and suspected Melbourne's offering would be rather tame in comparison. Not that Jake and I had concentrated on the Caravaggios or Botticellis or Rubens or Rembrandts, we had another agenda and I blushed at the thought of it.

"Well, I hope you've enjoyed the City Tour," came Miranda's voice. "Don't forget we have lots of other exciting tours. You can book at the Information Centre, folks. I look forward to seeing you again."

The tourists vacated the coach, some leaving tips, although not enough in Miranda's opinion.

"Five dollars!" she exclaimed, making a face. "Let's hope the next lot are more generous. D'you want to stick around, Abigail? It's only more of the same."

"No. I think I'll go exploring," I said, relishing the thought of having time to myself. "I'll meet you at the house later on."

For the next hour, I ambled around Melbourne, soaking up the sunshine, looking in the shops and buying souvenirs. For once, I found I was enjoying my own company and hardly gave Jake a thought.

It was late afternoon when I took a train from Melbourne's main station and returned to the house. Walking up the pretty tree-lined road, I saw a car parked outside Rosalyn's house. It was facing towards me and I peered in, trying to see who was inside.

It was Rosalyn and a man.

The reflection on the windscreen obscured his face, and I didn't want to get any closer in case they saw me. I hid behind a large tree and watched. I saw Rosalyn lean over and kiss him, a long lingering kiss that seemed to go on for some time. Then she opened the car door and got out. She leant back into the car to say something, kissed him again, and shut the door. The car pulled away. She waved, watched it disappear down the road, then walked up the path and let herself in the front door.

I stood on the pavement, not sure what to think or do. I didn't want to follow her straight into the house, but I couldn't hang around on the pavement for much longer. My behaviour was beginning to look a little odd. I decided to walk up the road and back down again, giving her a lead of around seven or eight minutes so she wouldn't guess I'd seen anything.

Then I knocked on the front door, waiting for her to answer.

"Hi Rosalyn, sorry, I don't have a key."

"Lucky I got back before you."

"Yes, it is. Have you been back long?"

"About half an hour, my friend dropped me off."

"Oh, okay. How was the aerobics routine? Did your friend appreciate your help?"

"Yes, she was really glad I could make it."

"She?" I asked. "Did she drop you off?"

"Yes. Why all the questions?" She looked at me curiously.

"Sorry, no reason. Just wondered how your afternoon had gone."

"It was great, thanks. How was your City Tour?"

"Great," I answered. "Miranda's very professional. I learned a lot."

I could hardly wait for Miranda to come home. It looked like she was right. Rosalyn had a secret lover and for some reason she didn't want us to know about it.

I told her later that evening when Rosalyn popped out of the room.

"Miranda, I think you were right," I said in a whisper. "I saw a man drop off Rosalyn just as I got back this afternoon. They had a long snog in the car, then he drove off and she went into the house. She told me her girl friend dropped her off."

"Did you see what he looked like?" asked Miranda.

"No, I couldn't see. Why, do you know who it is?"

"Not really. Rosalyn has dozens of admirers. It could be anyone, but it's strange she's keeping it secret. Why would she hide it?"

Rosalyn came into the room and Miranda assumed a casual tone.

"How did your aerobics session go this afternoon?" she asked innocently.

"Really good," answered Rosalyn. "We did a great workout."

"Who's your friend, do I know her?" Miranda pushed the point.

"No, it's someone who used to come to my classes, who's taken up teaching."

"Did she come over here?" asked Miranda, a little obviously, I thought.

"No," said Rosalyn, sounding mildly irritated. "I went

to her house and when we'd finished she brought me back. Why all the questions? You're as bad as Abigail."

"Sorry. I just wondered if we'd met her."

"No. You haven't met her. Okay?"

"Okay," said Miranda and glanced at me briefly.

I saw a glint of determination in her eyes. That might be all for now, but she wasn't going to let this drop.

She was determined to find out the identity of Rosalyn's mystery man.

Chapter 11

Stuart put the top down on his Mercedes sports car and the wind whipped through our hair as we sped along. The coast road wound its way along the cliff tops, providing stunning views of white crested ocean below and it felt wonderful to be alive.

It was a beautiful day. Everything appeared magical and vibrant, the colours more vivid than I could ever have imagined. The sky was clear blue, the sea deep aquamarine and the cliffs almost red in the bright sunshine.

I savoured every moment, willing the journey not to end, enjoying the freedom of the open road and the car's throaty growl as it ate up the miles.

Within an hour we'd arrived in Port Fairy.

"It's an interesting place," Stuart informed us. "Founded by whalers and sealers. They built great mansions with the fortunes they made. By 1840, they'd hunted all the whales and the town went into decline. The beach was littered with great white whale bones."

"Sounds grim," I said. "How come you know so much, Stuart?"

"My family's been coming here for years," he explained. "My father's an avid bird watcher and it's an ornithologist's paradise. There are pelicans, swans and fairy penguins, even a mutton-bird colony."

"Very interesting," said Rosalyn in a bored voice. "I hope there's more to do than watch birds."

"It's pretty wild and unspoilt," said Stuart, "a real chill-out place. That's why I love it here. It's a good antidote to the world of business."

Chilled out it may be, but nothing prepared me for its faded glamour.

Driving down the main street was like being on a film set. Each of the buildings had ornate balconies and verandas. Rusted old signs swung in the breeze, bearing such names as 'Granny's Ice Cream Parlour' and 'Milk Bar', and I saw a run-down old cinema and a shabby hotel, once grand, now peeling and cracked. Further along, set back from the road, stood a line of beautiful old houses, once white, now yellowed and grubby with the passing of time.

"It's a strange place, Stuart," said Rosalyn. "Like something out of a horror movie. A bit creepy."

"I think it's romantic," I said warmly. "Like time's stood still and nothing's changed."

"It hasn't," said Stuart. 'I've been coming here for years and the main street's still the same. They used to have a slogan, 'Port Fairy, where past is present', which just about sums it up."

"I hope there's running water and electricity in your chalet," said Rosalyn, looking concerned.

"There's an old tin bath in the yard and plenty of candles," said Stuart frowning. "Don't worry. You'll get used to it."

"Are you serious?" began Rosalyn, then saw he was laughing. "OMG, Stu, I had a vision of some old shack in the woods."

"That's not a bad description," said Stuart. "But it has been modernised. There's central heating, power showers, flat screen TV. You won't be slumming it, Ros."

The road led out of Port Fairy and alongside a desolate, windswept beach. Gulls swooped and soared, and huge breakers broke along the shoreline. It was magnificent in a bleak kind of way.

"Up this road here," said Stuart. "There's the chalet facing us."

At first glance, it looked exactly like a shack in the woods. Like the old houses, the once splendid chalet had been ravaged by time and was now faded and peeling. Ivy ran up the posts of the wooden veranda and one of the window shutters hung loose, banging against the frame in the blustery wind.

"Are you sure it's habitable?" said Rosalyn, wrinkling her nose in disgust.

"It'll be fine," said Stuart, leaping out of the car. "I'll take a look at that shutter. Come inside and take a look."

He unlocked the front door and we walked in to a large, spacious lounge. Unlike the exterior, it was contemporary and stylish. The walls were painted in pastel shades and the beige carpet was new. The cream sofas were modern and expensive and a huge home entertainment system stood to one side of the room. Huge pieces of modern art were hung on the walls and someone had been cleaning, judging by the faint aroma of pine disinfectant.

We quickly explored. There was a lovely bathroom with a roll top bath and large walk-in shower, and we each had our own bedroom, decorated in pretty pastel shades, with freshly made beds and crisp, white linen sheets. The kitchen was well equipped with a large black range cooker, a microwave and enormous fridge, and fresh flowers had been placed in a vase on the kitchen table.

"Looks like Mrs Harding's been in," said Stuart. "She's our caretaker. I called her yesterday, asked her to give the place an airing and put food in the cupboards."

"How wonderful to have someone like Mrs Harding at your beck and call," I murmured to Rosalyn, as we explored. "You have to admit it, Ros, Stuart has style!"

"What do you think, Rosalyn?" asked Stuart, putting his head around the door.

"Very nice," she answered brightly. "Stunning."

I noticed photos on the dresser showing a smiling man and woman, surrounded by grinning, happy children.

"Is this your family, Stuart?" I asked.

"Yes, that's us," said Stuart. "We used to come here for the summer. Dad would leave us here with my mother during the week while he ran the factory. They were happy times."

I imagined Stuart's family coming over the years and

the many holidays they'd enjoyed. There was a happy feeling to the place and I liked it. Unlike Rosalyn, who pulled a face as soon as Stuart went out to the car to get the bags.

"I thought we'd be staying in a luxury harbour-side pad, not some old shed in the woods," she whispered. "Thank God we're only here for three nights."

"Shush, he'll hear you," I warned. "It's gorgeous. It's beautifully furnished and it's free. Make the most of it."

I could cheerfully have stayed for a week. I had a proper bed, with linen sheets, in a real bedroom and a bathroom with a power shower. It was a vast improvement on my shed room at Acacia Avenue.

Soon, Stuart had a barbecue going and we sat in the back garden, drinking beer and eating the most divine food I'd ever tasted. The Eagles' 'Desperado' wafted out of the open French window, giving the afternoon a lazy, unhurried feel and I could see why Stuart called it his chill-out place. He dragged some ancient recliners from a rickety shed on to the old stone patio and we lay in the sunshine looking out over the garden. A central lawn was surrounded by trees and shrubs, and although someone had made an attempt to keep the weeds at bay, it was semi-wild.

"It's brilliant here, Stuart," I said, sipping my beer and feeling relaxed, "I can imagine you here as a boy."

"See that rope hanging from the tree over there, with the old tyre attached?" grinned Stuart. "We had hours of fun swinging on that. My mother used to put a hammock up between those two trees over there and she'd lie, reading a book, while we went on expeditions."

"Reminds me of my mother on her chaise longue," said Rosalyn, from beneath a huge parasol. She'd plastered herself with Factor 70 and wrapped a shawl around her shoulders. There was no way the sun was going to touch her body, although I noticed she couldn't bring herself to cover her legs.

"That's my abiding memory of my mother," she continued. "Lying in a darkened room with one of her 'heads' on, while we all had to be quiet. Probably the total opposite to your childhood, Stu."

"Can't remember my mother ever having a headache," he said. "More often than not, she'd join in our games. We had perfect childhood summers here."

"Sounds fun," said Rosalyn, wistfully. "I used to hate our family holidays. I never got on with my sister. She was always making fun of me. I was glad to get home."

"What are we doing tonight, Stuart?" I asked, not wishing to hear any more of Rosalyn's stories. I'd heard them all before.

"I'll take you to an Ocker bar in Port Fairy, if you like."

"Is that a good idea?" asked Rosalyn. "Won't it be a bit rough?"

"Not with me as your chaperone," answered Stuart.

I wondered yet again why Rosalyn wasn't interested. He was a dream come true. I'd have snapped him up months ago.

"Okay. As long as you're with us," said Rosalyn, looking worried. "I won't drink, so I'm happy to drive back, if you can trust me with your lovely car."

"Excellent," said Stuart, beaming. "That means I can have a drink."

Later that evening, we drove into Port Fairy. Stuart looked good in jeans and a dark blue polo shirt that matched his midnight blue Mercedes and Rosalyn was stunning in white leather shorts, revealing her long brown legs, and a white halter neck top, revealing her bronzed back. I wisely decided not to compete and opted for jeans and a sweatshirt.

Although they weren't a couple, Rosalyn and Stuart looked good together and I couldn't help but feel like a gooseberry.

The sun was setting over the beach, creating a wild, dramatic seascape and Stuart stopped the car for me to take some photos. I clicked away, wishing again that Jake was there with me. How romantic to walk together, hand in hand, along the desolate shoreline, with the gulls screeching and the wind buffeting us, then go back to our chalet in the woods and make love until dawn. I vowed one day I'd return with him.

"Ready to go, Abigail?" asked Stuart. "You were miles away."

The bar was sparse and utilitarian. Peeling posters hung off the chipped walls, the bare wooden floor was beer-stained and a few ancient tables and chairs were placed around the room.

As we opened the door, the smell of stale beer hit our nostrils. A group of men stood at the bar, while others watched an ancient TV at the back of the room. A general low murmur filled the bar, interspersed by outbursts of laughter.

As soon as Rosalyn and I walked in, everything stopped and I felt a dozen pairs of eyes on us. The atmosphere was immediately hostile and I looked around for Stuart. Thankfully, the minute he appeared behind us, everything returned to normal.

"Good job you're here, Stuart," I said in relief.

"Typical Ocker bar," said Rosalyn under her breath. "Sexist and macho."

"All part of the Port Fairy scene," said Stuart, laughing. "They're quite harmless. Come on, I'll get you a drink."

We were soon sitting at one of the tables, drinking beer from the bottle, chatting to the locals.

"How ya doin' Stu?" asked one of them thumping Stuart on the back, "Haven't seen ya for a while."

"Fine, Gerald," said Stuart, thumping him back. "I've a factory to run these days, mate. Don't get much time to come up here any more. Let me introduce you to Rosalyn and Abigail, from England."

"England, eh?" said Gerald, eying us up. He looked at me closely. "You a Whingeing Pom?"

"I hope not," I said playfully, but his eyes had already gone to Rosalyn, or rather her legs. He appeared mesmerised.

A couple more of Gerald's friends joined us and a lively conversation struck up as they regaled us with tales of the outback.

"Some folks live their entire life out there," said Gerald.

"Yeah? What's it like?" I asked.

"Miles from anywhere. Nearest neighbour's a hundred miles away. If you get sick, you call the Flying Doctor. School's done by transmitter telephone and you get water from artesian boreholes. It's salty and full of minerals. Okay for cattle but not for people. All your provisions have to be flown in from the coast."

"You seem to know a lot about it," said Rosalyn.

"Lived most of my life in the bush, rounding up cattle," explained Gerald, "till I came to Port Fairy and became a fisherman."

"Do many people get lost in the bush?" I asked.

"Get lost in the bush and you die," said Gerald flatly. "Simple as that. Couple of teenagers perished last year. Lost their way and died of thirst and starvation."

"Great," said Rosalyn.

"I saw a film in England, before I left," I said, "about a huge beast that lives in the outback called a Razorback. It's as big as a house, with enormous tusks, thick rhinoceros skin and great snorting nostrils. It runs faster than a car and once it has your scent it hunts you down relentlessly. Have you ever seen one?"

"Yeah, I know a guy who saw a Razorback," said a friend of Gerald's, introduced as Mick. "Said it was as big as Sydney Opera House. Had a long razor-sharp fin right down its back. Rolled on top of the guy he was with. Cut him in half. Said it ran faster than an Express Train."

"Really?" I said gullibly, not knowing if they were winding me up and seeing too late Mick wink at Stuart.

"What about that film, Picnic at Hanging Rock?" I asked.

"True story," said Gerald. "Hanging Rock's a hundred and fifty kilometres north west of Melbourne. You've seen the film?"

"Yes, a couple of times."

"It's pretty true to life. A party of schoolgirls went for a picnic. Some went climbing over the rocks. Three of them disappeared. A couple of days later, one of them mysteriously came back. Didn't know where she'd been or what'd happened to her. The other two never came back. Searched high and low but they were never found. They'd vanished."

"What d'you think happened to them?"

"Hard to say. There were all sorts of theories. Aliens, kidnappers, some said the aborigine spirits had got 'em. Guess we'll never know."

"Have you ever been there?" I was fascinated.

"Sure. It's a popular picnic spot. But you wouldn't get me spending the night there. When the sun goes down it's an eerie place. Feels like someone's watching you."

"You mean the ancient spirits?"

"Who knows? Australia's a young country but its old land. Holds lots of mysteries and we don't know half of it. The aborigines understood better than we do. And they respected it. We arrived with our cities and businesses and transportation and called it progress. I'm not so sure. We're not in tune with the land anymore and that's a bad mistake to make. Nature's more powerful than we realise."

I could have sat there all night.

Their tales brought Australia alive in a way that walking around Melbourne hadn't. All too soon it was time to go.

"Take you out on the boat tomorrow, if you like, Stu," said Gerald, picking tobacco out his teeth.

"And the girls?" asked Stuart.

"Specially the girls," answered Gerald, leering at Rosalyn. She rolled her eyes, but I could tell she was enjoying the attention.

"10 am sharp at Fisherman's Wharf," said Gerald. "Bring your sea legs. There's gonna be quite a swell tomorrow."

"What d'you think, girls?" asked Stuart. "Fancy a boat trip?"

"Sounds good," I said enthusiastically.

"Especially if there's going to be a big swell," said Rosalyn, giving Gerald the eye.

He winked at her. "I think I can promise a pretty large swell tomorrow, darlin'."

I stared at Rosalyn, amazed by the lewd innuendo. And she wasn't even drinking. She studiously avoided my gaze.

Gerald staggered off into the night and Stuart threw Rosalyn the car keys.

"Drive carefully, Rosalyn," he warned. "She's brand new. I'd hate anything to happen to her."

I stared at Stuart. What was it with men and cars? Why were cars always 'she'?

It reminded me of the time I'd accompanied Jake to buy his new car.

CHAPTER 12

We'd gone up to Blackpool, to a place that specialised in American cars. Jake wanted to buy an old Lincoln or a Cadillac or even a Pontiac, but soon found they were hopelessly impractical for distance driving. His other option was a more up to date model and he suggested we drive up for the day to see what was available.

I didn't have a great interest in cars, but I would have gone anywhere with Jake just to spend a day in his company.

Eventually, we found the place, up a back street in the shadow of Blackpool Tower. It looked grotty and run down, but there in the makeshift showroom stood four enormous cars, their polished chrome-work gleaming brightly. I thought they looked ugly, with their long square bonnets and wide front grilles. I ran my hand along the bonnet of one, feeling its hard metallic surface beneath my touch.

"What's this?" I asked, feigning interest.

"A Ford Mustang Convertible," said Jake, dreamily. "What a car. And this is a Buick Convertible. Aren't they something?"

"Mm," I said non-committally. "You can't be serious about buying one of these, Jake. They're okay in films, but not real life. This one's really ugly. It looks like a crouching animal that's about to pounce." I ran my fingers along the bulbous wings of a shiny red car.

"These headlights look like two malevolent eyes. What is it?"

"Classic Corvette," answered Jake. "Beautiful car. Anyway, I haven't come to see these."

"You haven't?" I frowned. "Then why are we here?"

Jake pointed at a car that was being driven onto the front driveway.

"That's what I've come to see."

"That's more like it," I said, looking at the golden machine that had suddenly appeared.

It had a completely different body shape to the classic models. The boxy shape and sharp angles were gone, replaced by low, sleek, streamlined curves. It was altogether more sophisticated and sporty.

"Mr Wetheroak, is it?" said a large man with a red face, climbing out of the driving seat.

"Yes."

"Well, here she is. A 2005 Ford Thunderbird, two-seater convertible. What d'you think? A beauty, eh? And does she go? Boy, does she go. Come and have a look."

Jake walked around the car. "She's magnificent," he said.

I felt mild distaste at their conversation. Surely the car was an 'it' not a 'she'? And why talk in such a sexual way? It was pathetic.

"What d'you think?" Jake asked me.

"She's fantastic," I said dryly. "I bet she really goes".

My sarcasm was lost. Jake's eyes were glazed. It was love at first sight. He ran his tongue over his lips with uncontrolled lust.

"Can I take her out?" he asked the sales man.

"Course you can, sir. I take it you've got a current licence?"

"Yes, here."

"Right, in you get then, sir. I'll have to come along with you, if you don't mind, sir."

"That's fine, no problem. See you in a bit," he said, turning to me.

"Don't hurry back on my account," I said, but my words were lost.

He was too busy climbing into the car and chatting with the salesman. He started up the engine. The next minute, the car zoomed off the forecourt and up the road, leaving a cloud of exhaust smoke in its wake.

Jake didn't hurry back and I spent the next twenty

minutes walking round the classic cars until I was sick of looking at them.

"Beauts, aren't they?" said another salesman, coming out of the back office.

"Yes. Stunning."

"Course, they don't look like that when they come in. That's all our handiwork. They're mostly clapped out when we first get 'em."

"Where do they come from?"

"The States, generally. We have them shipped over. Quite a market for them in Britain, you know."

"Is it generally the classic cars you sell?" I asked, trying to be interested.

"As a rule, we don't tend to go for the new shapes. Not the same, you know. Not in my opinion. I mean, take that one your husband's driving. It's a beautiful car, but to me, it doesn't have the edge of the classic model."

Husband. I liked the sound of that. I supposed to an outsider we did look like husband and wife. If only. That seemed like an impossible dream.

"Where are you from?" asked the man. "You're not from around here are you?"

For a moment, I panicked. What should I say? I debated whether to say: "Actually, we're not married, we're having an affair. This is an illicit day out and he's trying to impress me by looking at sports cars." But I didn't. Instead, I joked: "No. We're from 'darn sarf'. Just come up for the day."

Fortunately, at that moment the golden wonder zoomed back on to the forecourt and I was spared further embarrassing questions. Jake got out, looking like he'd just spent the last twenty minutes making love to the most gorgeous creature on God's earth.

"Good, was she?" I asked.

"Unbelievable."

"Going to have her then, are you?" I asked.

Again my sarcasm was lost. Jake was too in love to

notice. He walked round the car, stroked her, opened her door and caressed her dashboard.

"Careful, Jake, I think you're getting her aroused," I said, drily.

"What?" he said, distracted. He turned to the salesman. "How much did you say you wanted?"

"Twenny grand, sir. Real bargain, sir. You won't get a car in better condition than she's in, sir. An absolute beauty. And what a drive! So smooth. Effortless, sir, effortless! You felt it yourself."

"What do you think?" he asked me, looking longingly at the golden creature's beautiful body. She glinted back at him, a true temptress.

"Well, it's not really my decision, Jake. What would Tiffany say?"

"Oh, she'd hate it," laughed Jake. "A two-seater's totally impractical for family life."

That did it for me. If Tiffany was against it, I was all for it.

"Well, if you can afford it…." I left the sentence hanging.

"You don't think it's a bit pretentious? A bit flash?"

"Not at all, I think she's beautiful. You can drive me round in her any time."

Jake gazed at the car, his eyes glazed.

"It's a lot of money," he said, trailing his fingers along the golden creature's bonnet. "Tiffany's going to kill me."

"I think you should go for it," I said firmly. "They don't come up that often and you'll regret it if you don't buy it. You only live once, Jake."

"You're right," he said. "Carpe diem and all that."

He went into the inner office and spent the next twenty minutes huddled away with the large, red-faced salesman. Eventually, they emerged and the salesman shook Jake's hand. "Pleasure doing business with you, sir. You won't regret this. She's a beauty. Isn't that what we said the minute she came in, George?"

"Absolutely, Frank. The classic cars are good, but you can't beat the modern models. So much more style and class. You've made the right decision sir."

Jake shook each of their hands fervently and beamed.

"Thanks, Frank. Thanks, George." He took the keys from George and opened the passenger door.

"Your chariot awaits, madam."

"We can just drive away in it now, can we?" I asked in astonishment.

"Absolutely. They've taken my old car in part exchange."

I got in, feeling very close to the ground in the low-slung seats. The smell of newly polished leather hung in the air. Jake climbed in and started the engine, and immediately I felt the low, throaty growl of the engine vibrate between my legs. There was something very primeval and sexual about this car. So potent was its effect, we only made it to the nearest multi-storey car park. Jake drove up to the top level where it was quietest and we spent the next half hour making wild, furious love on the back seat.

One up to me, Tiffany, I thought in satisfaction.

Of course, he didn't keep it. Tiffany blew her top when she saw it and a week later Jake advertised it on eBay. He sold at a loss and ended up buying a Volvo Estate. Far more practical and family orientated. I should have realised then. Jake always did as he was told where Tiffany was concerned.

One person clearly held the reins in their relationship. And it wasn't Jake.

CHAPTER 13

The next day was glorious, if a little windy. The sun shone brightly, white clouds scurried across the sky and at 10am we were on the quayside. Gerald was already there, sitting on the deck of his fishing boat, mending nets.

"G'day'," he called out. "Ready for a sea trip?"

"You bet," called Stuart. "What about the wind, Gerry? D'you think it's a bit strong for going out?"

"No worries. As long as you sway the same way as the boat, you'll be fine," said Gerald nonchalantly. "G'day, ladies. Let's get you on board."

The boat was an old trawler and smelled of engine oil and fish. When Gerald started the engine, it reverberated throughout the boat and I began to wonder whether this was a good idea. The smell and the noise, combined with the after effect of drinking too much beer the night before, was beginning to make me feel queasy. And we hadn't even left the harbour.

Rosalyn, on the other hand, was in fine fettle. She was beautifully turned out in tight fitting jeans and a checked shirt, with a pale blue sweatshirt draped casually over her shoulders and blonde curls escaping from the matching bandana around her head. Stuart too, looked impeccable, in a pale blue polo shirt and jeans, and I thought what an attractive couple they made. Yet again I wondered why she was so reluctant to get involved with him. As if to prove the point, Rosalyn appeared to be actively flirting with Gerald and I couldn't help but feel sorry for Stuart. She seemed impervious to the smell and the noise, and I had to admire her poise and style.

Gerald guided the boat out of the harbour and we were soon on the open sea, the boat leaping over the waves and crashing into the troughs, making my stomach turn. The wind whipped my hair and flurries of white spray caught my face so that I was soon wet and cold, as well as sick. This was going to be a long journey. I sat on a seat, looking out over the sea, feeling miserable. Rosalyn meanwhile stood in the cabin with Gerald, sharing a joke, unaffected by the drone of the engine and the motion of the boat. Stuart looked sick for a totally different reason. He wasn't happy with the amount of attention Rosalyn was lavishing on Gerald.

After what seemed like an age of being buffeted and wind-blasted, Gerald steered the boat closer to the coastline and cut the engine alongside some rocky formations. Life was suddenly calm again. The wind dropped, the sun shone and the boat bobbed gently on the waves.

"These here are The Twelve Apostles," he informed us, pointing at the twelve pillars of rock that rose majestically out of the surf at regular intervals. "Very famous rock formations."

"Are you sure there are twelve, Gerald?" asked Rosalyn flirtatiously. "I can only count ten."

He stood behind her, a little too closely, so he could follow her line of sight.

"There's two at the end there," he said, placing one hand on her shoulder and pointing out the missing Apostles with his other hand. "See?"

"Oh, silly me. Yes I see them."

She leant back into him and I glanced at Stuart. His lips were pressed tight in a thin, straight line. There were more undercurrents on board than in the sea I thought wryly, wondering what on earth Rosalyn was doing. Gerald was hardly God's gift. He was decidedly unattractive.

"Okay, let's press on," said Gerald, glancing briefly at Stuart and moving away from Rosalyn.

He resumed his position at the helm and started up the engine.

Once again, the boat was bouncing over the waves and the wind was whipping my face. I caught Rosalyn's eye and she winked at me, moving to stand closer to Gerald again. I would have attempted conversation with Stuart, but I was too busy throwing up over the side.

Our next step was Loch Ard Gorge, Gerald informed us.

"It was named after a clipper called Loch Ard that ran adrift here in 1878," he told us. "Only two people survived, an apprentice officer and an immigrant Irish woman, both aged eighteen. They were swept into the gorge as the ship was driven on to the rocks."

"How romantic," breathed Rosalyn.

"I don't suppose they found it too romantic," said Gerald drily. "Not exactly a party being thrown into a stormy sea while your ship's smashed to pieces."

"Are there any other ship wrecks round here?" I asked Gerald.

"Sea's littered with 'em'," he replied. "These are treacherous waters. There's at least thirty wrecks we know about. You can still see some of 'em on the East beach."

"There used to be 'Shipwreck Walk'," said Stuart. "Do they still do it, Gerry?"

"Yeah, in the summer months. I reckon there's dozen more wrecks waiting to be discovered down there." He looked down into the dark waters.

His words gave me a thrill and made me think of Jake. He would love it here. Together we could go searching for wrecks. When we came back together.

"Further inland, there's an amazing formation called the Blow Hole." Gerald informed us. "It's a massive hole in the rock where the sea bursts out with tremendous force from an underground tunnel. Absolutely spectacular, but you have to drive to that one."

"Perhaps you could show me the Blow Hole later," said Rosalyn suggestively. "I'd love to see the sea bursting out with force."

Gerald looked as though Christmas had come early and I thought Stuart was going to explode. His glowered at Rosalyn, his face bleak.

"I'm sure we can arrange something, darlin'," said Gerald.

Our final sight on the 'Unusual Rock Formation Tour' would have been equally as mind-blowing as the Blow Hole if it had still been there.

"See that stump of rock?" asked Gerald, pointing to another pillar rising from the sea. "That was once known as London Bridge. Used to reach over to the mainland and people would walk over it. Fell into the sea one day, leaving a load of folk stranded."

"Were they rescued?" I asked in alarm.

"No, they couldn't get to them. The gulls picked them clean. Their bones are still washed up today."

"Yeah, right." I was beginning to get Aussie humour at last.

Gerald grinned at me. Then we were off once again. This time to a secluded cove where we could drop anchor, have a swim and barbecue fish. It would have been magical, if one event hadn't overshadowed everything.

We nosed gently into the cove and I stared down into the deep blue sea. It was crystal clear. You could see right down to the sand, with shoals of brightly coloured fish darting here and there. As soon as Gerald dropped anchor, Rosalyn needed no bidding. She pulled off her clothes, revealing a skimpy white bikini, and the eyes of both men came out on stalks. They were transfixed. Her toned olive skin contrasted perfectly with her white lacy bikini. Her legs appeared endless, her stomach flat and her cleavage magnificent. I was glad I'd brought my Speedo one-piece. At least it would hold in my stomach, if anyone was bothered, that is.

"Watch me," shouted Rosalyn, climbing on to the roof of the cabin and doing a perfect dive into the blue water. She barely broke the surface and came back up, laughing, to the sound of applause.

"Come on Abigail," she called, "It's gorgeous in here."

"Okay," I said, "but I'm not diving in."

I went into the cabin and began to undress, quickly pulling on my swimsuit. I heard a loud shout of 'Geronimo' followed by a loud splash and, looking out, saw that Gerald had joined Rosalyn in the water.

"Are you going in, Stuart?" I asked, but he shook his head.

"No, I'll crack on with the barbie."

I felt desperately sorry for him, but there was little I could do to make things better.

Carefully, I climbed down the metal ladder at the back of the boat, gasping at the coldness of the water. I inched in slowly until I was finally submerged, then started to swim around the boat.

"Rosalyn," I called. "Where are you?"

I soon found her. She was in the shadow of the boat, clinched in an amorous embrace with Gerald. With one hand, he was holding on to a buoy secured to the hull. The other was around Rosalyn's waist. They were snogging furiously and hadn't heard me. Even worse, Stuart had heard my call and was looking over the side to see what was happening. It didn't take him long to see the entwined couple. He looked furious. I bobbed around, not knowing what to do, then quietly swam back the way I'd come and climbed up the metal ladder. There was no question about it. Rosalyn had ruined everything.

Stuart prepared the barbecue in silence and hardly ate a thing. I tried my best to make conversation, aware that he was upset. But it was to no avail. He would only respond with monosyllabic answers. Rosalyn and Gerald, on the other hand, seemed blissfully unaware that they'd been seen, and carried on laughing and joking without a care in the world.

Fantastic barbecue, Stu," said Rosalyn, picking at her fish.

"Yeah, you've done us proud here, mate" said Gerald, eating with relish.

"Thank you," said Stuart tightly, sipping at a beer. I could only assume politeness prevented him from punching Gerald's lights out.

I sat watching, wondering how this was going to affect our holiday. I couldn't understand Rosalyn. Why was she throwing herself at a gnarled old Aussie, when a gorgeous guy, clearly besotted with her, was so readily available? It didn't make sense.

Within a couple of hours we were back at Fisherman's Wharf. Stuart coldly helped Rosalyn off the boat, while Gerald tied the ropes, eyeing her from the deck.

"Nice ass," he murmured appreciatively, as she stepped onto the quayside.

"Less of that, young man," said Rosalyn, playfully, "or you'll be in trouble later."

Gerald grinned and winked.

"Thanks, Gerry, great trip," called Stuart from the quayside, obviously meaning the complete opposite. I jumped on to the quayside, offers of help noticeably absent.

We walked back from the sea front along the riverbank, coming unexpectedly upon a magnificent yachting marina. Tall white masts rose majestically in the late afternoon sunshine, contrasting with the dark green spruce trees silhouetted on the shoreline, and imposing Victorian mansions nestled on the riverbanks. To one side of the marina, construction was taking place and a sign informed us this was an "Exclusive marina development of luxury apartments, with stunning sea views, high level spec and mooring rights."

Now I saw a different side of Port Fairy.

"Looks expensive," I said to Stuart.

"It is," he answered. "This is what I wanted to show you. How d'you think it compares to the chalet?"

"No comparison," said Rosalyn enthusiastically. "This is amazing. You should get one of these, Stuart."

"I already have, Rosalyn," he said coldly. "I've bought the penthouse. Should be ready in a couple of months. This is my new summer holiday home."

If I wasn't mistaken, he was pointing out to Rosalyn exactly what she was missing, and I didn't blame him.

Later that afternoon, back at the chalet, Stuart informed us he was going back to Melbourne.

"Sorry, girls, there's a problem at the factory and I have to get back. You're welcome to stay here as long as you want. You can walk into Port Fairy and to the beach, and there's food and drink in the chalet. Text or call me when you want to come back and I'll send a car."

Within ten minutes, he'd gone, leaving Rosalyn and me alone.

I turned on her.

"Okay, Rosalyn, what's going on?"

"What d'you mean?" she asked indignantly.

"I mean leading Stuart on, then flirting outrageously with Gerald and even having a snog with him. Right in front of Stuart's eyes. He's been so kind and this is how you repay him. There's no problem at the factory. He just couldn't bear to be under the same roof as you a moment longer. You must know he's crazy about you. Why d'you treat him like this?"

I could barely keep the anger out of my voice.

Your 'treat 'em mean, keep 'em keen' approach has backfired spectacularly. You won't see Stuart again. Is that what you want?"

To my surprise, she sat on the sofa and burst into tears.

"I don't know what I want. I'm in a mess Abigail. I like Stuart, but I can't offer him anything and he was getting too close. I thought by flirting with Gerald, Stuart would pick up the message and I wouldn't need to have a heart-to-heart with him. I didn't expect Gerald to grab me in the sea and I didn't realise Stuart could see."

"Surely you know what happens if you lead a guy on," I said. "You're not that naive. Gerald thought he was on to a good thing."

"Sometimes I just can't help myself," said Rosalyn. " I didn't mean for Stuart to get hurt. I really like him. I just can't commit to him."

"But he's gorgeous. He's kind, he's sexy and he's good looking. He's even wealthy into the bargain. He's besotted with you and could give you the most fantastic lifestyle. Couldn't you even try?"

"No," said Rosalyn through her tears. "I can't. I just can't."

"Why not?" I shouted at her in exasperation.

"Because I'm involved with someone else, that's why," she shouted back.

I stared at her.

"You mean the man who dropped you off that day you were supposed to be helping your friend with the aerobics routine?"

"Were you spying on me?" she asked suspiciously.

"No. I was coming back to the house and you were there. I didn't know what to do, so I hung back."

"What did you see?" she hissed at me.

"Nothing. There was too much reflection on the car windscreen. I just saw you kissing someone."

She seemed to relax a little.

"It's a tricky situation," she began.

"What like mine?" I asked.

"Sort of. But at least he hasn't got a pregnant wife in the background," she snapped.

"Below the belt. We're talking about your situation, not mine. What's going on?"

"When I met him he was with someone else," she said. "But that's over now."

"So what's the problem?"

"He won't commit to me, but I can't stop seeing him. The sex is amazing. I'm addicted. But that's all it is to him.

Just sex. There is no relationship. Not yet, anyway. He says we have to keep it secret."

"Doesn't sound like he wants a relationship. You'd be better off without him."

"I seem to remember telling you that."

"Easier said than done, I know."

"And you're right. Stuart is a fantastic catch," she continued. "I know he adores me. I'm just not in a position to respond. But how do I explain that to him? I really like him and I don't want to lose his friendship. I just can't give him what he wants."

"Miranda thought you were seeing somebody," I said.

Rosalyn looked horrified. "Why would she suspect?"

"Er, you've been secretive, taking phone calls in your room, showing no interest in Stuart… D' you want me to go on?"

"No. Just promise me you won't say anything to her. I have to live with her. I couldn't bear her barbed comments. Especially after what she's been through."

"Okay. I won't. But you have to get out of this relationship. It's not going anywhere."

"And yours is? Is it so different from mine? Yours is a secret. Yours is held together by sex. You don't really think Jake's going to leave, do you? Not with another baby on the way. You're even more deluded than I am, Abigail."

She was on dangerous ground and this was a conversation I didn't want to have. I changed the subject rapidly.

"While we're having a truth session, Rosalyn. Why don't you tell me about your modelling career. The one you mentioned in your emails. The fashion shoots, the parties, the celebrity events. What's happened to them?"

Rosalyn looked into the distance and chose her words carefully.

"There is no modelling career," she said slowly.

"I gathered that."

"There was to start with. After the nursing job didn't

work out, I signed up with a modelling agency and I was getting lots of work. I really did that swimsuit shoot on location and all the brochure work I told you about. And I did go to the parties. But gradually the work dried up and so did the party invitations. They said I wasn't relaxed in front of the camera, not photogenic enough. They said I had the height and the figure for catwalk work, but they didn't get much call for that. They offered me promotional work selling perfume in a department store. But I was so bored, I only lasted two days and walked out. They never contacted me after that. And the new friends I made all seemed to disappear. Never returned my calls or were 'too busy' when I spoke to them. That's why I took up aerobics. At least that's working for me. But it doesn't pay as much as modelling, which meant I couldn't afford the mortgage on my apartment."

"Yeah. Miranda said the apartment was real."

Rosalyn looked at me closely.

"I haven't told you any lies, Abigail. I've just been a little economical with the truth here and there."

"Like not telling me I'd be staying in a shared house."

"I thought you'd be staying at the apartment with me. Then I realised I couldn't afford it, so I had to rent it out and find somewhere cheaper to live."

"Who did you rent it to?"

"That's where it gets tricky."

She looked down and started playing with her fingers. "Initially, it was a young couple, but they gave notice. So I've rented it to the man I'm involved with."

"Oh great," I said, in disbelief. "The one who doesn't want a relationship with you. When did it all start? Before or after he moved into your apartment?"

"I was seeing him already," she said miserably. "He was looking for somewhere to live, so I offered him the apartment. I thought we might end up living there together, but it wasn't what he wanted. He said he didn't want anything too serious, couldn't offer me a monogamous relationship."

I looked at her horrified.

"So he rented your flat, then told you he was sleeping with other women? What a schmuck."

"There wasn't much I could do about it," she said forlornly. "No matter how hard I try, Abigail, I just can't get him out of my system. I thought you, of all people, would understand. It's not so different from what you have with Jake."

"Except Jake wants a relationship with me. He wants a future with me."

Rosalyn laughed. "Yeah, sure. Of course he does. He's just got a pregnant wife and child stopping him. Wake up and smell the coffee, Abigail. You're in an addictive relationship just like me, with a man who won't commit."

I pursed my lips, not wanting to get into an argument. My emotions were too fragile.

"At least I'm considering having another relationship," I countered. "I half hoped I might meet someone else when I came to Australia. Couldn't you just give Stuart a try?"

She wrinkled her nose.

"Stuart's just too nice. There's no spark…"

"Like there is with the mystery man. Does he have a name by the way?"

"Of course he does, but I can't tell you. Don't ask me anything else. And don't breathe a word to Miranda or Ken. It's not your secret to tell. Okay?"

"Okay. I've already told you I won't."

In the evening I tried to text Jake, but there was no signal, so I gave up. I lay awake thinking about the day, about Stuart and his new apartment. Now I understood why he'd brought us to Port Fairy. He wanted to show Rosalyn his new holiday home, but she'd wrecked things before he had the chance.

I was sure he'd bounce back and meet someone else.

Men like him were never on their own for long. But I worried about Rosalyn.

Her life seemed to be falling apart.

CHAPTER 14

The next day, we walked into Port Fairy and followed directions to the South Beach. It was lovely. There was nobody around, just an expanse of white-yellow sand extending around the bay and blue sea, fringed with small white breakers.

We smoothed down our beach towels and lay on our backs looking up at the sky. Rosalyn wore a stylish blue and white striped bikini and lashings of Factor 70. She seemed to have got over her aversion to lying out in the sun. I wore my bra and knickers and a brief covering of Factor 10. For some reason, I'd forgotten to pack my new bikini, but I was determined to go home with some vestige of a tan. Neither of us spoke about the conversation we'd had the night before.

For the rest of the morning we lazed around, dozing and chatting about nothing in particular, digging our feet into the sand and feeling it trickle between our toes. It was a perfect day.

Further down the beach I noticed a lone figure walk into the sea and take a swim. I watched his head bobble around like a dark cork in the distance. Eventually, he came out and started to jog along the shore in our direction. When he was nearly adjacent with us, he stopped, threw a beach towel on the sand and sat down.

"Typical," I whispered to Rosalyn. "Just as soon as you've got some peace and quiet, some jerk comes along and moves into your space."

Rosalyn laughed. "Er, hello. Have you taken a look? He's fit."

I looked again. She was right. He was tall, tanned, muscular and gorgeous, with sun bleached blonde hair and long surfer's shorts. I guessed he was in his late twenties.

"Wow. I take it back. That is a nice bit of beach candy."

I watched him take out an iPod, put in earphones and lie down, seemingly oblivious to our presence. Eventually, bored with watching his prostrate figure, I lay on my front, undid my bra and slipped it off, determined to get a nice, even tan on my back. I let myself drift away, the hot sun carrying away my thoughts, leaving me empty and relaxed. After a while, I was aware of a presence standing over me, blocking the sun. I guessed it was Beach Candy Boy.

"G'day," he said, with a strong Australian accent. "Here on holiday?"

Hi," said Rosalyn. "Yeah, we're staying in a chalet up the road."

"Where are you from?"

"Melbourne. How about you?"

"Geelong University. Studying for a PhD. I have a beach house just down the way."

Nice work, I thought, mentioning the PhD and beach house all in one go.

"Mind if I join you?" he asked, crouching down. "I'm Pete, by the way."

"Er, no, feel free," said Rosalyn, a touch unsure. "I'm Rosalyn and this is Abigail."

I lay there, unable to move without giving him a full frontal view, now that I'd removed my bra. I pretended to be asleep.

After ten minutes, curiosity got the better of me and I couldn't pretend to be asleep any longer. I reached across and grabbed my T-shirt, holding it over my front as I sat up.

"Hi," he said, staring at my chest. "My name's Pete." He offered me his hand.

I shook it, holding up my T-shirt with my other hand. "Hi. I'm Abigail. Pleased to meet you."

He was even more attractive up close, although slightly older than I'd thought, with deep-tanned skin, regular features and a brilliant white smile. His eyes were hidden behind his shades, but I guessed they'd be clear blue. His bleached, unkempt hair was tied back in a ponytail and his six-pack was so well formed, it took all my control not to reach across and touch it. No doubt about it, he was hot.

"Gather you're here on holiday," he said.

"That's right. Did I hear you say you're doing a PhD? What's your thesis on?" I was hoping to catch him out.

"Political history of Vietnam and Cambodia."

"What was your main degree?"

"Which one? I have four."

"Four degrees! You must have been at university for at least twelve years."

"Fifteen if you include the PhD," he smiled in a lazy sort of way. "Full-time student. Political Science, Economics, Third World Studies and Australian Literature."

"Australian literature? That's interesting. My subject was English Literature. You can tell me which Australian authors to read."

"Look, what are you guys doing for lunch?" asked Pete, clearly wanting to change the conversation. "My beach house is just over there and we're having a barbie this afternoon. I've got some mates coming over. Why don't you pop in?"

I looked at Rosalyn. "What d'you think?"

"We could, I suppose." She looked at Pete. "What time does it start?"

"An hour or so. See that little blue gate down there? That leads to my back garden. If you fancy coming, I'll see you later."

He picked up his towel and beach bag and walked back down the beach.

"D'you think we'll be all right?" I said to Rosalyn.

"Yeah, he seems fine. And if his mates are half as gorgeous as he is, we'll have a great time."

An hour later, we were pushing open the blue gate and walking along a paved pathway through the trees.

The scene that met our gaze was breathtaking. A white clapboard two-storey beach house stood in a beautiful garden spilling over with flowers and greenery. The window frames were pale blue with white slatted window shutters and blue checked curtains, and the roof was pink sugar-candy. A bright green creeper covered with pink flowers grew up white trelliswork alongside the pale blue front door.

It was a Hansel and Gretel house, more at home on top of an iced cake or inside a snow globe.

The aroma of barbecued food filled the air and the sound of laughter and voices came from somewhere in the garden. Uneven steps led up to an open door.

"Hi, girls. You found it then?" Pete appeared in the doorway, looking like a sun bronzed god in a Crew sweatshirt, Bermuda shorts and open Converse trainers.

"Hi, Pete. This is so pretty. Is it your house?"

"No, I'd be lying if I said it was. I'm housesitting for a mate who's abroad for a few months. Come into the kitchen and I'll fix you a beer."

We followed him into a quaint country-style kitchen, with a large cream range and hand-painted Quaker-style cream units. It would have been stylish, except for the profusion of dirty dishes, books, papers, half drunk coffee cups, empty cigarette packets and full ashtrays on every surface.

"It's a bit of a mess," said Rosalyn. "You need to tidy up."

Pete gave us a lazy smile. "Yeah, sorry. Tidiness isn't my strong point."

He took two cold cans of beers out of the fridge and handed one to each of us.

"Good to see you, girls. Come into the garden and I'll introduce you."

He led the way down a side path and into a small courtyard. Trailing creepers crept up the walls, roses climbed the trelliswork and a profusion of yellow, gold and pink flowers mingled together in the flower bed. About ten or so people sat around a stone barbecue, laughing and drinking. Someone was playing a guitar. The food smelled wonderful.

"Hey guys, this is Abigail and Rosalyn," he announced.

They turned to look, smiling and waving. A few called 'hi'.

"Come and get some food," said a tall dark-haired girl. "Better get stuck in while there's some left."

It was an idyllic afternoon in a perfect setting. The beer, the music and the friendliness all contributed to the atmosphere and I began to enjoy myself. This was what I'd come to Australia for. To meet people, see a different way of life and forget my problems. I sat on a warm stone bench, drinking a beer and feeling at one with the world.

Rosalyn was having a fantastic time, surrounded by group of four or five admirers, flirting for England. After a while, Pete came and sat by me.

"Got any cigarettes?" he asked. I handed him a fresh packet from my bag. Since arriving in Port Fairy I hadn't even thought about smoking and the packet was unopened.

"Thanks," he said, breaking open the seal and taking out a cigarette. He lit it and inhaled deeply. "Where are you from?"

"The UK. I'm visiting Rosalyn. That's where she's from as well."

"What d'you think of Oz?"

"I love it. So far I've seen Melbourne and Port Fairy. It beats the rainy UK any day."

"You should go to Sydney," he said. "That's where I come from."

"I hope to," I said. 'One of my Mum's old friends lives there and I have an invitation to stay if I want to. She's an artist. Has a studio in The Rocks area. Edna Corvaggio. Apparently she's quite well known."

"Edna Corvaggio?" repeated Pete, looking impressed. "I know her. Every one knows her. She's really successful."

"Wow, I didn't realise."

"I've met her a few times at parties. She's fantastic, getting on a bit, must be about 75 now, but a real character. She's got her finger on the pulse. Knows all the right people, musicians, poets, artists. She paints these amazing abstracts with vibrant colours. You'll have a fantastic time if you stay with her."

"That's it, you've decided for me, Pete. I'll look her up. I thought she was just one of my Mum's fuddy duddy old art friends from way back when."

"No way," said Pete. "She's one of the coolest people I know. You should definitely go stay."

"I will," I said, seeing my holiday take an interesting new direction. "Thanks, Pete. Glad I bumped into you."

"Perhaps you could do something for me?" he asked, hopefully.

"What's that?"

"Put a word in for me with your friend Rosalyn. She is one good-looking sheila, but I can't get a look in with all the guys around her. I really fancy her."

I looked over at Rosalyn, laughing, joking and surrounded by admirers.

"A word of advice, Pete. Steer clear. Rosalyn is …er, complicated. She doesn't need any more men in her life right now, believe me."

"Really? You don't think she'd be up for a shag?"

"Er, no. I don't think she would." I was taken aback by his directness. These Australian men weren't backward at coming forward. "Definitely not."

"Ah well, no harm asking," he lay back against the warm stone wall and turned his face to the sun, seemingly none the worse for the knock-back.

"Where's the loo, Pete?" I asked, suddenly aware of how much beer I'd drunk.

"I'll show you," he said, jumping up. "The downstairs one isn't great. There's a better one upstairs."

He led the way back into the house, through the kitchen and up the stairs. Various doors led off a central landing.

"There, second door on the left," he pointed out.

I walked into a large, airy bathroom decorated in white and pale blue, with pieces of driftwood displayed as ornaments. Once I'd relieved myself, I looked in the mirror. Not too bad, I thought. I'd got a slight tan, my hair was behaving itself and I looked relaxed. I applied some lipstick, rearranged my hair and opened the door. With hindsight, I should have realised what was going on.

Pete was there, waiting for me.

"You look great," he said, standing in my way.

He put one hand on my neck and the soft touch of his fingers on my skin felt fantastic. He drew my face close to his and before I knew it he was kissing me. It felt wonderful and I couldn't help myself. I responded. His tongue found its way between my lips and I opened my mouth so he could kiss me harder.

I felt a familiar tingling between my thighs and knew this was having a similar effect on him by the hardness he rubbed against me. Somewhere in the dim recesses of my brain, common sense prevailed and I pushed him back.

"No, Pete, I can't do this."

"Yes, you can."

He brought his knee up between my legs and massaged my neck gently with his fingers. There was no denying it, this felt good. And Pete was very attractive.

'Why not?' asked a little voice in my head. I opened my mouth and let him start kissing me again. He pushed me back against the wall and his other hand was suddenly up my T-shirt with alarming speed. I felt my breath quicken and responded, putting my arms around his shoulders and drawing him closer. His tongue explored my mouth, making me feel wanton and desirable. I hadn't felt like this since Jake and I were last together. Jake. Jake. His name thundered in my head and once again, I pushed Pete away.

"I have a boyfriend. I can't be unfaithful to him."

His voice was low and breathy. "We're not doing any harm. No one will know. Come on, you know you want to."

"I thought you were interested in Rosalyn," I said playing for time.

"Right now, you're the only one I want," he whispered into my ear.

I swallowed and before I could think of my next move, he'd pulled up my T-shirt and undone my bra. This was moving too fast, but I couldn't deny how fantastic it felt. I felt him loosen the button on the waistband of my shorts and undo the zip. My shorts slid down a little and now I knew I was in trouble. It felt divine and it felt wrong, which only made me respond to him all the more. My head was telling me to stop but my body was desperate for more. I was aware of him starting to pull down his Bermuda shorts and now, common sense really did come to the surface. I couldn't let this go any further.

"I'm sorry, Pete, I really am, but I can't do this."

Thankfully, voices at the foot of the stairs caused a momentary distraction and prevented him from arguing with me. Someone was coming up the stairs and I seized the opportunity. I quickly pulled up my shorts and pushed past him.

"Sorry, Pete. I have to go."

One of the other girls appeared at the top of the stairs, swaying drunkenly and holding on to the bannister. She eyed me curiously, then turned to Pete.

"I need a shag, Pete. Is the bedroom free?"

I stepped around her and went down the stairs as quickly as I could, breathing a sigh of relief. Pete obviously wouldn't be coming after me. I walked into the kitchen and met Rosalyn coming through the door.

"So there you are," she exclaimed. "I wondered where you'd got to."

"I went to the loo," I said quickly, wondering how much to tell her. "D'you think we could make a move? I'm getting tired."

"Yeah, I was beginning to get bored with those guys. They aren't exactly the most switched on in the world. Come on, let's get our stuff."

We collected our beach bags and towels and were soon walking along the beach, back towards to the chalet.

"Pete tried it on when I came out of the loo," I told her.

"What happened?"

"Nothing really. Another girl came up the stairs and said she wanted a shag, so I made my escape."

"Good looking guy," said Rosalyn, thoughtfully. "Weren't you tempted?"

"Of course. He's gorgeous. But I kept thinking of Jake."

"Like he's been faithful to you," pointed out Rosalyn, unnecessarily.

Later that evening, we sat on the patio, watching the sun go down behind the trees and enjoying our last evening in Port Fairy. We'd decided to go back the next day. Rosalyn had texted Stuart and he'd arranged to send a car.

"These Aussie men are really up for it, aren't they?" I said to Rosalyn, trying to make a joke out of it.

"More than you know," she replied, sounding serious. "I had a bad experience last year. I've never told anyone about it, but it really upset me."

"What happened?"

"I'd gone on holiday by myself," she said. "I was staying in a beautiful hotel complex, near Sydney. You know me, I'll chat to anybody. I was having a drink at the bar and got chatting to a couple of Aussie guys. They seemed friendly enough. One of them was really dishy. After a while, they went off to a club and I went back to my room. I decided to have an early night. About midnight there was a knock on my door. Stupidly, I opened it. It was them. They were drunk. I don't know how they found my room number, but they did. They pushed their way in and asked if I had anything to drink. I said I didn't and told them to get out. It was one of those rooms that had a lounge area and a separate bedroom. One of them went into my bedroom, so I ran after him to get him out. By that time, I was getting scared. I tried to pull him out of the room and he started getting nasty. He pushed me down on the bed and started tearing at my nightdress. His friend came in and I heard him say: "She giving you some trouble, mate?" The other one said: "Yeah, hold her down for me, will you?" That's when I saw red. I just thought how dare they come bursting into my room and think they can treat me like this. So, I brought my knee up hard between the legs of the one that was on top of me. You should have heard him scream."

"Good for you," I said, impressed. "What happened next?"

She grinned. "I turned to the other one and asked if he wanted more of the same. They were smaller than me and I think I must have scared him, because he said: 'No, don't touch me' in a pathetic voice. I told them to get out before I called the manager and report them for attempted rape."

"Did they go?"

"Oh, yes. As soon as they'd gone, I locked the door to my room and called Reception. But d'you know what the worst thing was?"

"What?"

"No-one believed me. The Night Porter said I'd have to wait until morning. When I reported it the next day, the manager said there was no way an incident like that could have happened in their hotel. He said I must have invited them in. When I showed him my torn nightie, he said it wasn't evidence. After it happened, I was shaking. I couldn't stop crying. I was really frightened and not one person believed me."

"They obviously thought you'd asked for it. Was it a good hotel?"

"Yes. I paid a lot of money for that room. It was my treat to myself."

"There you go. They didn't want any scandal. Bad for business. And they only had your word it happened. What did you do?"

"Checked out the next day. I was scared they might come back. I wanted to get as far away as possible." She paused for a moment. "I felt awful. There was no one I could talk to and the fact nobody believed me made me feel grubby. I'd never felt so alone."

I thought about what she'd told me and it struck me that she'd done a brave thing coming out here on her own. No one had helped her. She'd found work, established a life for herself and made friends. The last few years must have been tough. I wished with all my heart she could walk away from her affair and be with Stuart. He'd take care of her and give her security. Why is it we always go for excitement over safety I wondered?

The next day, Stuart's driver arrived in a smart black saloon and drove us back to Melbourne. He dropped us off at Acacia Avenue and I was back to my shed room. It seemed pokier than ever. I was alarmed to see around twenty missed calls from Jake on my cell phone. I read his text messages, each more urgent than the last.

Monday 25th April 20.57
Abigail, where r u? Why don't you answer yr fone? Need to speak to you.
J xx

Monday 25th April 21.30
Abs, please CALL ME! Need to speak to you.
J xx
Love you.

Tuesday 26th April 11.00
Abigail, I'm getting worried. R u alright. Please tell me you haven't met someone else.
CALL ME!
J xxx

I smiled in delight. He was desperate to speak to me. That meant one thing. He'd told Tiffany. At last, we were going to be together. I dialled his number and he answered immediately.

"Abigail, where've you been? I've been so worried. Have you met someone?"

"Of course not. We went up the coast for a few days and I couldn't get a signal. Now we're back in Melbourne. You sounded desperate to speak to me. Have you told Tiffany?"

"Thank goodness. I thought you'd met someone else."

"Jake, have you told Tiffany? I thought you had something to tell me."

"It's been difficult, Abs, you know, to find the right time."

"You haven't told her, have you?"

"Not yet, but I will. Now I know you're still there for me."

"How can you think I'd go off with someone else? Is that why you were panicking?"

"Yes. Sorry. I should have trusted you."

"Jake, I've spent the last few days thinking how wonderful it would have been if you'd been with me. That's never going to happen if you don't make the break from Tiffany."

"I know." His tone changed. "Okay. Great. Thanks for calling. I'll put a quote in the post. Goodbye."

The line went dead.

Tiffany had obviously walked into the room. I threw the phone down on the bed in frustration. There was one word to describe my relationship with Jake. Shabby. The whole thing was shabby. I was living in a world of half-baked promises that were coming to nothing. I'd thought I held it all in my hand, but when I opened my fingers, my palm was empty.

The reality was Jake at home with Tiffany, his son and the growing bump that would soon become another child. In place of hope and expectation there was only bitterness and broken dreams.

Sure, it had been exhilarating at the start, those knowing looks and hidden moments. But its intensity had soon possessed my every thought, and pity for Tiffany had rapidly turned to hatred and envy. I thought of the long weekends and evenings waiting by the phone, willing it to ring, and going to bed disappointed. How could someone profess to love you so much, but hurt you so badly?

There was nothing good about my liaison with Jake. It was underhand and ugly. I felt the hopelessness of my situation more keenly than ever.

Holding back the tears, I walked into the kitchen and found Miranda and Ken sitting at the breakfast table, drinking coffee and laughing.

"Hi Abigail, how was Port Fairy?" Miranda started to ask, then saw my face, "What's happened?"

"Nothing," I said, bitterly. "Absolutely nothing. That's the problem. Jake was supposed to leave Tiffany and guess what? He's still there. He's said nothing and I don't think he will."

"Men! Who'd get involved with them?" said Ken, rolling his eyes.

"I'd have more respect for him if he told me it was over," I said, making myself a coffee. "To keep me dangling like this is just cruel. Never let anyone tell you an affair is an exciting, wonderful thing. It's not. It's destructive and negative and puts lines on your face." I stirred my cup vigorously.

"The guy sounds a dick," said Ken. "He's messing you around, Abigail. You need to get rid of him."

"I know. It's just so difficult. Where's Rosalyn? Have you seen her?"

"Had a mystery phone call and went rushing out," said Miranda. "Something about her aerobics friend needing help with a routine. But we know what that means." She looked at me archly.

I looked into my coffee cup, aware I'd promised Rosalyn I wouldn't say anything.

"Possibly. We don't know for sure. She never mentioned anything while we were away." I changed the subject quickly. "Actually, I was wondering if you could recommend any more trips, Miranda. I feel a need to do some sight-seeing."

"Yeah, sure," said Miranda, looking momentarily puzzled. " How about the Dandenong Mountains. It's not one of mine, but it's a great trip. I can book you a place, if you like."

She took out her phone.

"By the way," she added. "I solved the mystery of the empty biscuit tin. It was Ken. Caught in the act. So, we kind of owe Rosalyn an apology."

"Yeah. I guess we do." I wished I hadn't told her about Rosalyn's eating issues. I hoped I could trust her not to say anything.

My judgment wasn't too good at the moment.

CHAPTER 15

I sat on board Puffing Billy, its green body gleaming, chrome shining and steam billowing out in great white clouds.

The old train seemed impatient for the passengers to board, huffing and puffing, ready for its regular trip into the Dandenong Mountains. It was Melbourne's only restored miniature steam train, my guide book informed me, warning it would be packed with tourists. It was. Mostly Japanese. Along with a few Europeans and Australians. I'd got one of the last seats on the tour and now I sat in my compartment, soothed by the rhythmic clickety-clack of the wheels and occasional 'whoo- whoo' as the train chugged its way up in to the mountains.

At the end of the line, we left Puffing Billy and continued our trip by coach, in the capable hands of our driver, Bill, who gave us a running commentary. After twenty minutes of driving through cool eucalyptus glades, he stopped the coach in a car park on the side of the road and began to unload various implements.

"I'm making you some billy tea," he explained, lighting a small stove and filling a billy-can with water, "using tea and eucalyptus leaves."

To prove his point, he went over to the nearest eucalyptus tree and pulled off a handful of leaves, which he thrust into the bubbling water. As the water boiled, he swung it round his head in a huge arc.

"This is how the old bushmen used to do it," he informed us.

I had to hand it to him, he was quite the showman. I guessed he was in his early 40s, an attractive man, but too full of himself for my liking. When he'd finished, he poured out the dark liquid into plastic cups for each of us to try. It was unexpectedly pleasant and thirst quenching. Even more pleasant were the small jam sponge cakes, rolled in chocolate and coconut, called Lamington cakes, which he handed out.

"You're now standing in the middle of the Blue Dandenong Mountains," he told us, as we drank and ate. "So called because of the blue vapour that comes off the eucalyptus trees. If you look around, you'll also notice a number of gum trees. You can identify them by their peeling bark. Gum trees don't shed their leaves, they shed their bark. See?" He pulled a piece of bark off a nearby tree, "It hangs off in shreds, ready for the new growth underneath. If you're lucky, folks, you may see a kookaburra."

We looked around expectantly, but the kookaburras were obviously busy elsewhere. Bill continued his educational chat.

"The eucalyptus vapour is a major hazard in times of bush fire. It hangs in the air and is highly inflammable, causing huge fireballs to erupt. That's why you must never drop a lighted match or a lit cigarette. See how dry it is at the moment?" He picked up some kindling on the ground. "That's because we haven't had much rain recently. We're coming out of the hot season, which means there's plenty of dry brushwood and dead grass around. Drop a lighted match and the whole area will be a mass of flames within a few minutes. If the wind's against you, there's nothing you can do. Except pray." He grinned at us.

The Japanese exclaimed vociferously at this information, as did a party of old ladies, and I began to wonder whether I'd done the right thing. I was the youngest person there by miles. Still, Miranda had said it was a good trip, so I had to give it time. Our tour guide was certainly entertaining.

"Okay folks," continued Bill, "if anyone needs the toilet, you'll find the facilities just over to the right of the car park."

Most of the coach party immediately walked across the car park in herd-like fashion. I decided to investigate the stripping gum trees. Taking hold of a piece of bark, I gave it a quick tug. Immediately, the bark came away in my fingers and a small red spider lurking beneath leapt onto my hand. I jumped back, screaming. Bill, who'd been busy packing up his equipment, looked up.

"What's the problem?" he called.

"A redback spider just jumped onto my hand."

"A redback, eh? You know about redbacks?" he asked in a serious voice, walking over to me.

"I've heard about them," I admitted. "I haven't actually seen one. I know they bite and they're poisonous. I think I had one on my hand."

"Quite probably," he said in his laconic way. "Still, it didn't bite you, did it?"

"No."

"So, there's no harm done?"

"No."

He started to walk back towards the coach, then called out over his shoulder.

"I wouldn't hang around under the trees, if I were you. We've got some big brutes called Huntsman spiders. Great long-legged things that drop on you from above. Nasty." He looked up to the spreading branches above, then walked back to the coach. I glanced up, then sprinted back to the coach as fast as I could.

"Where are you from?" he asked, glancing in my direction, as he packed up. "England?"

"Yes," I replied. "The Midlands."

"Anywhere near London? I went there once, many years ago."

"Not too far. A train ride away."

"So you can get to the city lights when you want to?"

"Something like that," I said with a smile.

Most of the tourists had returned and he began ushering people on to the coach, helping old ladies up the steps, chatting and answering questions.

I watched him, trying to work out whether I fancied

him or not. He'd obviously spent a lot of time outdoors, judging by his weathered skin, and was slightly overweight in a cuddly kind of way, with greying hair, regular features and twinkly blue eyes. He was around five foot eleven and dressed in his coach driver's uniform of white short-sleeved shirt, blue shorts and white socks, displaying his tanned arms and legs to perfection. He wasn't particularly good looking, but he had a certain charm. Probably because of his take it or leave it attitude. I felt he was secretly laughing at us. Me in particular.

I was the last one on to the coach and as I climbed up the steps, I was suddenly aware of my short skirt. When I reached the top step, I turned round. He was still standing on the ground, looking up. He winked as I caught his eye and I felt myself blushing horribly. I stumbled to my seat, feeling like an adolescent.

We carried on, passing through beautiful woodland settings, resplendent with ferns, eucalyptus trees and stripping gum trees. The sun streamed through the branches, reminding me of Jake's woodland fantasy.

Once, when we'd been out walking, we'd found a beautiful woodland glade. Tall trees formed a canopy overhead, thick green moss a lush carpet beneath. Occasionally, the sun shone through, dappling the dark interior. Under the trees, it was cool and peaceful, the velvet moss soft and yielding. Jake told me it was his fantasy to make love in such a place, hidden from view, miles from anywhere.

I let my thoughts drift on, remembering the tenderness between us, the longing and the intimacy of knowing each other's bodies so completely. We both knew exactly where to touch, what to do, how to sustain the pleasure. The fresh air and proximity of nature created a primal need that heightened and intensified the experience.

That day our lovemaking reached a metaphysical level and I truly believe our souls touched, rising out of our bodies in a spiritual consummation. No one could ever come close to what I had with Jake. We were meant to be, two parts of the same whole, sharing a destiny whatever the obstacles in our way.

Bill's voice interrupted my thoughts with the announcement that we were approaching the summit of Mount Dandenong, the highest point in the mountains.

"There's a fantastic view here, folks," he announced. "If you want to take photos, now's the time."

He stopped the coach and stood lazily propped against the driver's door, watching with amusement as we clicked away with phones and cameras. Next stop was lunch at a funny little place called Gumnut Village, home to the Australflora Gardens, craft shop and tearoom, Bill informed us. I bought a sandwich and sat by myself on the terrace, enjoying the sunshine and the solitude, feeling quite content.

Rosalyn's absence had a lot to do with it. I was finding her volatile, unpredictable and totally preoccupied with her physique and looks. Her secret affair was doing nothing for her self-esteem and she obviously felt threatened by my friendship with Miranda. She seemed to exist on a diet of next to nothing and I had no idea how she managed to sustain her grueling routine of jogging and aerobics.

I finished my lunch and got up from the table, deciding I might as well take a look around. I took out my phone to check for messages from Jake and totally failed to see the steps in front of me.

Next thing I knew I was sprawled unceremoniously across the pathway, blood pouring from my leg. I sat there, feeling like a prize idiot, too shocked to move. Unfortunately, my fall didn't go unnoticed and a crowd of old ladies assembled around me. Next thing, Bill was crouched over me, examining my leg.

"Nothing fatal, I'm afraid," he said, opening a small first aid bag and cleaning the wound with an antiseptic wipe.

"Thanks, Bill, I'll be okay," I said, feeling stupid. "I only tripped on the steps."

"Sit there while I clean the wound," he instructed.

I let him tend the wound, rather enjoying the touch of his hands. I noticed his fingers were long and slender, and his nails were well manicured. He wasn't as rough and ready as he made out.

"There. All done," he said, applying antiseptic cream and a dressing. He quickly packed up his medical bag. "Show's over, folks. If you'd like to make your way back to the coach, we'll continue the tour." He turned to me. "Are you okay to walk?"

"I'm fine, thanks."

I winced as I stood up. It might only be a graze, but it hurt and the antiseptic cream made it sting.

"Here, hold on to me." He offered his arm and I gratefully hung on to him. Slowly we walked back towards the coach.

"Enjoying your stay?" he asked, making conversation.

"Yes thanks."

"Are you here on your own? No boyfriend or husband?"

"I'm visiting an old friend. I used to know her in England."

"And where is she today?"

"She's busy. I preferred to come on my own."

I glanced up at him, holding his gaze for a fraction too long. There was definitely something attractive about him.

"What's your name?" he asked.

"Abigail. And you're Bill, obviously."

"That's right. Bill McGregor."

"Sounds Scottish."

He smiled. "It is. My father came from Perth. He came over to Oz after the war and married my mother."

"I see," I said, enjoying his attention, "Been doing this job long?"

"About three years," he answered. "I like it. It's a good job. You meet a lot of people."

"And get asked a lot of questions," I pointed out.

"Yeah. Par for the course. 'Bill, when will the sun shine?' 'Bill, when will it rain?' 'Bill, why is so hot today?' I don't bloody know. I'm not the bloody weatherman. But it's good fun and they usually tip well. I can't complain. So, have you got a boyfriend back home?"

His change of direction caught me unawares. "No. Yes. I mean, yes I have."

"You don't sound too sure. Why isn't he here with you?"

"He couldn't make it. Work commitments." I sounded like I was making excuses.

"Ever been married?" asked Bill.

"No."

"Bet you've had lots of offers though, an attractive girl like you." His eyes looked me up and down and I felt quite naked.

"A few."

"What I like about you English girls is your nice soft skin."

His familiarity took me aback. "Really?" I said in a voice somewhat higher than my own.

"Yeah, you've got lovely skin."

He slowly ran his finger down my arm and I felt goose-bumps rise on the back of my neck. If I wasn't mistaken, he was coming on to me.

"How much longer are you staying here?" he asked

"Another three weeks. Then back to England."

"And back to the boyfriend," he said, looking into my eyes.

"Yes," I said, feeling out of my depth.

"D'you want to sit down for a moment?" he asked, pointing to a bench by the side of the pathway. "Rest your leg for a second?"

"Okay."

The bench was set back amongst the trees, out of view from the coach. We sat down and I realised my hand was still hooked around his arm. This was too close for comfort. He turned to me and suddenly his lips were on mine in a surprisingly soft, caring kiss. I broke away in confusion.

"I don't think…" I began to say.

"Don't think, Abigail. It's better not to think," he murmured and his mouth was on mine once again.

He pulled my body close to his in a powerful bear hug and I was powerless to do anything but close my eyes and yield. It felt divine. I willed him not to stop but all too soon he pulled away and looked at me, his gorgeous blue eyes hungry with desire.

"Shame on me taking advantage of an injured woman," he said. "Mind you, I've been wanting to do that all day. You don't disappoint, Abigail."

"Oh, thank you," I said primly. "Neither do you."

Now I felt stupid.

"Come on, I've a coachful of tourists waiting for me," he said, standing up and helping me to my feet. "Much as I'd love to stay here all day kissing you, I have work to do."

He led the way back to the coach.

En route, Bill gave us a brief commentary about our next destination, the Healesville Sanctuary.

"It's one of best places in the country to see Australian wildlife, folks," he informed us.

"They do a fantastic job rescuing sick and injured wildlife, and many of the animals are allowed to roam free in compounds that resemble their natural habitat. If you're lucky you'll see kangaroos, koala bears, possums, platypus, dingoes, wombats and crocodiles. If you're not, they'll be asleep. Don't forget to check out the 'Animals of the Night' Nocturnal House. But remember, it closes at 4.30pm."

"Some other delights to look out for," he continued, "include the Spinitex Hopping Mouse and the brown Antechinus. The male dies after mating, so if you see a dead one at the bottom of the cage, you'll know what he's been up to!"

I blushed uncontrollably when he said this and hoped he wasn't looking at me in the mirror.

"You'll also see the Mountain Pygmy Possum. Apparently, where they come from, the males lived on one side of a busy road and the females on the other. When it came to mating season, you can guess what happened. Lots of squashed Pygmy Possums. To solve the problem, they built a tunnel under the road. D'you know what they called it? The Love Tunnel."

I began to think Bill had a one-track mind. Before he could come out with any more animal mating stories, we arrived at the entrance to the Sanctuary.

"Enjoy yourselves folks," he instructed us. "See the animals, take a walk in the woods, sample some local wine or afternoon tea in the cafes, but make sure you're back here by five o'clock."

We left the coach. I didn't get a chance to speak to Bill as once again he was surrounded by old ladies asking questions. 'Just as well,' I thought to myself, 'I wouldn't want him to follow me into the woods. Anything could happen.'

For the next hour and a half, I wandered around, desperately searching for animals. Because of the heat, most seemed to be flaked out in the recesses of their large compounds. I saw some brown blobs in the distance that could have been kangaroos or possibly dingoes. The wombats were nowhere to be seen, the platypus had done a disappearing trick and the koalas were small furry bundles at the top of the trees. I saw some crocodiles, but they just lay in the sun with their mouths wide open and could have been stuffed for all I knew. At least the budgies and parrots were livelier in the Land of Parrots.

At four o'clock, I realised I hadn't yet seen the nocturnal house. After a couple of wrong turns, I eventually found the entrance to 'Animals of the Night'. I looked at my watch. Nearly four fifteen. I had just quarter of an hour to look around.

I entered its dark, cool interior with a sigh of relief. It felt wonderful to get out of the sun. A UV light enabled spectators to see, giving the whole place an eerie glow. As my eyes adjusted to the semi-darkness, I made out glass displays in which small animals scurried around. I watched, transfixed by a small mouse-like creature hurriedly building its nest. Suddenly, without warning, a hand grasped my waist and I felt lips kissing my neck. I gasped and tried to pull away.

"I wondered where you'd got to," said Bill's voice. "Perhaps we can continue what we started."

"What, in here?" I turned to face him.

I could see him smiling in the dim light. "Why not?"

"What if we get disturbed?"

"Don't worry about that. The nocturnal house is closed."

"I don't understand."

"Anyone wanting to come in will find the 'Closed' sign up. We won't be disturbed."

"You mean we're locked in?" I said in dismay.

"Only until we want to get out."

"Oh, I see."

I wasn't sure if I wanted this or not. My desire had cooled from its earlier ardour and I felt tired from walking around in the heat. Bill pulled me to him and gently started kissing me.

One touch of his lips on mine was enough to re-ignite my desire and I felt my body starting to respond.

"You are so gorgeous," Bill murmured and started kissing me deeper.

I felt his tongue probing my mouth and opened my lips further. I wanted this so badly. All the frustration of my situation with Jake, the disagreements with Rosalyn and the strangeness of my holiday came together and I knew this was one thing that would make me feel better.

Bill put his hand round the back of my head and drew me closer to him.

"D'you want me?" he asked in a low voice.

Although the voice of common sense in my head screamed 'no', the wanton devil on my shoulder took control and I whispered 'yes' into his ear. He responded by pushing me up against the wall and pulling up my T-shirt. This man knew what he was doing. His fingers found all the right places, sending delicious sensations through my body. There was no going back now even if I wanted to.

"Does that feel good?" he asked in a low, deep voice.

"Yes," I murmured. "It feels fantastic.

"D'you want me?" he asked again.

My conscience screamed no, but my body said yes. I was out of control and incapable of rational thought, giving myself totally to the enjoyment of the moment. No one would ever know, I reasoned. Why not enjoy it and be damned?

"Yes, do it now," I whispered urgently into his ear.

His hands moved down to my shorts and with one deft movement he'd pulled them down, his fingers exploring my body. This was pure, unadulterated lust and I savoured every second, giving myself to a man who was obviously an experienced lover and knew exactly what to do. I felt all the tensions of the past few days disappear.

Maybe it was the strange ultra violet light or the fact that Bill was a stranger, or maybe it was the thrill that we could be discovered, I don't know, but this was unlike any other experience I'd ever had. The sex was amazing. I was living totally in the moment, a slave to my body's needs. If I'd thought it couldn't get any better I was wrong, because Bill suddenly pulled away.

"Turn around," he said urgently.

"What?" I said, not understanding.

"Turn round. I want to take you from behind."

He gently turned me around so I was facing the wall and the fact I could no longer see his face seemed to intensify the experience. I felt his hand brush across my buttocks. It felt divine. Wicked and exquisite.

You are beautiful, Abigail," he whispered in my ear. "Soft and beautiful."

Then it was all happening again, he thrust deep inside me and I knew I couldn't hold on any longer. We came together, both lost in the moment, waves of pleasure rippling through our bodies. Then it was over. I felt weak, spent, drained and fantastic. Bill leaned into me, breathing deeply and pinning me to the wall so I was unable to move.

Out of the corner of my eye, I saw the small mouse moving in the UV light. It stood up on its hind legs, with its tiny pink paws curved up in front of its body and put its nose in the air, its fine whiskers bristling. Slowly, Bill released me and took a step backwards. I heard him pulling up his shorts.

"That was something else, Abigail. You know how to turn a man on. Are you okay?" He tenderly turned me round to face him and kissed me gently.

I smiled up at him. "Yes I'm fine," I said, suddenly feeling very naked. "Apart from feeling like a wanton hussy. I can't believe I just did that."

"It was pretty unbelievable," he agreed.

"No, I mean, I can't believe what I've done. I don't even know you."

He put his hand on my shoulder and pulled me towards him. "Did you enjoy it? Was it good?" He looked into my eyes.

"Yes."

"So, no problem. This is what life's all about. Grasping the opportunity, enjoying the moment, living for the day. Or, in our case, the night."

He looked around and laughed.

"No one's got hurt. Your boyfriend doesn't know. So, no worries. Now, get yourself together because I've got a coach to drive back to Melbourne. I'll go first and see you back on the coach, okay?"

"Okay," I said doubtfully, still shocked at my loose behaviour.

He kissed my forehead and quickly walked out of the Nocturnal House. I spent a few more minutes fixing my hair and smoothing my clothes, then emerged, blinking blindly in the bright sunlight. Outside, a park ranger sat on the grassy bank, chewing a piece of grass.

"All right?" he asked, tilting his khaki hat towards me and grinning.

I flushed bright red.

"Yes, thank you," I muttered, wondering if he knew what had just happened.

I didn't stop to think about it. I hurried along the pathway back to the coach. Bill was sitting in the driver's seat, chatting to one of the old ladies. He turned to look at me as I climbed on to the coach and I caught his eye briefly. He winked and I flushed again, hurriedly walking down the aisle to find my seat.

I thought of Jake and a guilty feeling flashed through my mind.

What was I doing? How could I be unfaithful to Jake? If I truly loved him, how could I behave like this? I sat and thought things through. I wasn't really being unfaithful. It was just a momentary loss of control. It didn't mean I loved Jake any less, and besides, who would ever know?

We set off back for Melbourne, Bill speaking into the microphone.

"I hope you've all had a memorable day, folks. I look forward to being of service to you in the future and sincerely hope you decide to come with me again."

I stared at his face in the driving mirror. That last sentence was for my benefit, I knew. The man was incorrigible.

We approached Melbourne and I began to recognise familiar landmarks. Soon, we were close to Acacia Avenue and it was time for me to go. I made my way down the central aisle, lurching with the movement of the coach.

"The next corner will be great," I said to Bill.

"Righto."

He swung the coach towards the pavement and brought it to a halt. The automatic door hissed open and I climbed down the steps. When I reached the pavement, I turned and looked up at him.

"Bye, then."

He smiled down at me. "Hope you enjoyed yourself, Abigail."

"Oh, yes," I replied. "Unbelievable."

He winked. Then with a hissing sound, the door closed and he was gone. I watched the coach pull away, exhaling smoke as it accelerated.

'Probably going back to his wife,' I thought, looking at my watch.

Seven o'clock.

I had a wedding to think about and nothing to wear.

CHAPTER 16

We crept into the back of the gazebo, Miranda, Rosalyn, Ken and I, giggling like naughty school children, the stifled laughter masking our embarrassment at nearly missing the event. It was 11.35am. The wedding was supposed to start at 11.30am.

It had all begun so well. We'd got up in good time, showered, breakfasted and put on our glad rags and make-up. Miranda looked stupendous in her little black number. She hadn't managed to lose any more weight, and had possibly even gained a couple of pounds with pre-wedding stress, as she put it. Her dress couldn't be any tighter. Ken looked like a rock star, with his pink spiky hair, shades, black silk shirt and tight black jeans.

"You can never have enough black," he said with a wink. "As I said to Leroy in the Jamaican gay bar last week."

"Ken, stop it, I'm warning you," said Miranda. "Best behaviour please. No lewd behaviour, innuendoes or disgusting jokes. This is my family you're meeting."

Rosalyn, naturally, was breath taking. She walked out of her bedroom wearing a long, white, tight-fitting halter-neck dress that showed off her tan perfectly. Her blonde hair was piled high, with small tendrils escaping here and there, and she wore a fabulous white gold pendant round her neck. High platform shoes made her even taller than normal, and she looked down on us lesser mortals like a goddess.

I'd done my best with a figure-hugging little red number I'd borrowed from Rosalyn. It was a halter neck too, but the comparison with Rosalyn's stunning white number finished there. I couldn't compete in the tan stakes or with her physique. Let's face it, I couldn't compete in any stakes with Rosalyn. She outshone us all. The jewel in the crown.

We piled into Miranda's VW Beetle and set off, with over an hour to spare. But twenty minutes into the journey, the car began to cough and splutter, eventually dying at red traffic lights on a major junction.

"Belinda, don't do this to me," shrieked Miranda, frantically turning the engine over.

"Belinda?" said Ken. "Oh, pur-lease. How twee can you get?

"Shut the fuck up, Ken. I think she's in trouble," said Miranda. "You're going to have to get out and push."

"Who me?" he asked indignantly.

"Well, we're sure as hell not going to push, all dressed up in our finery. At least you're wearing black. Any dirt won't show."

Exhaling loudly, Ken climbed out and started to push the car.

"Not now," shrieked Miranda. "Wait till the lights are on green. You're going to get us all killed."

She pulled up the handbrake forcefully to anchor us to the spot.

An hour later, we'd abandoned Belinda on the side of the road and hailed a passing taxi. It delivered us with seconds to spare at the pretty boutique hotel on the outskirts of Melbourne where the wedding was being held.

"This is so fucking 'Four Weddings and A Funeral'," said Ken in delight, as we leapt from the cab and ran into the hotel foyer.

"It'll be your fucking funeral if you don't shut up," hissed Miranda. "Come on, the wedding's somewhere in the hotel grounds."

We followed her along a carpeted corridor through to the rear of the hotel and on to a stone terrace.

"There!" shouted Miranda, pointing across a central lawn to a white gazebo. She unbuckled her stilettos. "Take your heels off, girls."

"Come on, follow me!" said Ken, taking the lead.

Shoes in hand, we ran after him over the grass. The

white gazebo was decked out like a grotto, with small white and yellow flowers and twinkling fairy lights. Inside, wedding guests sat on chairs covered in white silk and decorated with large ornate bows. Thankfully, the back row was empty and we crept in, giggling and out of breath, trying to ignore the turned heads, as people looked around to see who was causing the commotion. Two minutes later, the bride walked in, a massive smile on her face.

"Typical Paula. She's so laid back, she's in yesterday," whispered Miranda. "Doesn't she look gorgeous?"

Paula was reed thin and tall, dressed in a simple, flowing pale blue dress. Her feet were bare and she had a flower garland in her long blonde hair. 'Perfect Day' by Lou Reed was playing and she walked up the central aisle, on the arm of an older, white-haired man.

"She looks like a fucking hippy," whispered Ken.

"That's because she is a fucking hippy," Miranda hissed back. "She'd have had the wedding in a field if it was up to her. The only reason it's in a hotel is to please her Mum and Dad."

The bridegroom, waiting at the front, turned to watch her walking towards him, an equally big smile on his face. It was so romantic I felt like crying.

He, too, had gone for the hippy look, with a matching pale blue shirt open at the neck, white jeans and open toed sandals. His unruly blonde dreadlocks were tied back in a ponytail and he wore a leather thong around his neck.

"Er, hello, are we back in the 1960s?" asked Ken facetiously.

"Shut the fuck up, Ken," said Rosalyn. "She looks amazing. Look at that figure."

"I prefer his," said Ken. "Now that is something I could go for. Shame he's getting married."

I looked around the room. There were about fifty or sixty guests, in varying levels of dress. Some, mainly the younger ones, had gone for a casual festival look to match the bridge and groom, with the guys wearing jeans and t-shirts, and girls in flowing, patterned dresses. Others, generally the older ones, had gone for more formal wedding attire, the women favouring tailored outfits and big hats, and the men in suits. On the whole, it looked tasteful and low key, with none of the usual wedding fashion disasters.

It was a short, civil ceremony, taken by a lady registrar, and was over in less than twenty minutes. The bride and groom made their vows, promising to love, honour and obey each other, which seemed a little old fashioned. We sang a jolly hymn, 'One More Step Along the Road I Take', then they placed their rings on each others' fingers and the registrar declared them husband and wife.

"Before we conclude," she said, addressing the wedding guests, "the best man, Melvyn, would like to read out an Apache Wedding Blessing."

The name hit me like a bolt out of the blue. Melvyn. Where had I heard that name recently?

"Oh my god," I whispered to Miranda. "Melvyn's the son of the couple I met on the plane, Daphne and Reggie. It has to be him. How many Melvyns can there be attending a wedding round about now?"

"It's the sun," said Ken, raising his eyes. "It's affected her head. She's fucking lost it."

"Ssh," I said, crossly. "Let me listen."

A large man, in his early thirties, stood at the front and faced the guests. I'd recognise that moon face anywhere. I'd looked at enough photos of him. It was Melvyn, which meant somewhere among the guests were Daphne and Reggie.

"Apache Wedding Blessing," said Melvyn, reading from a sheet of paper.

> *"Now you will feel no rain, for each of you will be shelter for the other.*
> *Now you will feel no cold, for each of you will be warmth to the other.*

Now there will be no loneliness, for each of you will be companion to the other.
Now you are two persons, but there is only one life before you.
May beauty surround you both in the journey ahead and through all the years.
May happiness be your companion and your days together be good and long upon the earth."

"That's so beautiful," said Miranda, going all misty eyed.

"Would you believe it?" I whispered to Rosalyn. "That's Melvyn. I met his Mum and Dad on the plane. They said they were coming to a wedding. They were lining me up as his future wife."

"Looks like a real catch," she whispered back.

"Rather you than me," said Ken.

Melvyn paused and looked at the happy couple. "I think you can kiss the bride now, Archie," he said with a smile.

Everyone cheered as Archie and Paula kissed, and I stared, feeling like a voyeur. A stab of jealousy went through me and I wondered whether Jake and I would ever walk down the aisle. At this point, it seemed very unlikely, not least because he already had a wife.

"Don't they look lovely?" said Rosalyn. "I love her dress."

"It'll be Abigail and Melvyn next," said Miranda.

"Fuck off, Miranda," I said, then felt guilty, remembering Daphne and Reggie. "I'm sure he has a nice personality. Just not my type."

"Plug ugly, you mean," said Ken waspishly.

The bride and groom walked out arm in arm to the operatic sounds of the Flower Duet. Gradually the guests followed, talking excitedly, heading for the champagne reception on the terrace. I watched as they walked past, and there they were, Daphne and Reggie. She wore a lemon yellow suit with a matching fascinator that bobbed alarmingly as she walked, he was in a beige suit with a

Abigail's Affair

matching lemon tie.

"Hello, Daphne. Hello, Reggie," I said in a loud voice as they approached. They started, then stared, Reggie's magnified eyes peering scarily through his milk bottle bottom glasses.

"It's Abigail," I explained. "From the plane."

"Abigail!" exclaimed Daphne. "Reggie, look! It's Abigail from the plane. D'you remember?"

"Of course I do," he said. "Abigail. Sat next to us on the plane. Followed us round Singapore Airport."

"What are you doing here, dear?" asked Daphne. "You never said you knew Archie or Paula."

"I don't know them, " I said. "And I didn't know I'd be coming to the wedding. Paula is the cousin of the flatmate of the friend I'm visiting, if you follow. I was only invited last week."

Daphne looked confused. "Well, it's lovely to see you, dear. Isn't it Reggie?"

"Yes, very nice to see you again."

Daphne and Reggie traded looks and I knew what was coming next.

"We must introduce you to Melvyn. He'd love to meet you. We told him all about you, dear. He was hoping you'd phone."

"Er, yes, I was going to. I've been a bit busy since I got here. Are you going to the champagne reception? I can introduce you to my friends."

"That would be very nice, dear. And we'll introduce you to Melvyn."

The champagne reception was in full swing. Uniformed waiters drifted around carrying trays of champagne and delicious canapés, and a string quartet played classical music on one side of the terrace, the gentle sounds wafting on the breeze. The sun shone, the champagne flowed and the guests mingled. It was all very tasteful. I quickly downed a glass of champagne in anticipation of meeting the dreaded Melvyn.

"Abigail," said Daphne, proudly. "This is our son, Melvyn."

I looked up into the most amazing blue eyes.

"Pleased to meet you, Abigail. I've heard all about you," said Melvyn with a big smile. "Visiting a friend, I believe?"

"Yes, that's her over there…" I stammered, momentarily knocked off kilter, simply because he was so nice. "That's Rosalyn. She lives with Miranda, who's over there, who's Paula's cousin, which is how I came to be here."

"I think I follow that," he glanced at Daphne. "Mother, can you get me a glass of champagne?"

"Yes, of course, dear. Back in a second. Come on Reggie."

They drifted away in search of a waiter.

"So, how are you enjoying Melbourne?" asked Melvyn.

"I love it," I said warmly. "I hadn't realised it was so European. The architecture is fabulous, the food is amazing and the people are lovely. How long have you been here?"

"Two years. My company sent me over to set up an IT department in their Melbourne office, which I've just completed."

"So what happens now? Do you go back to the UK?"

"No. It's Sydney next. I've got a massive data migration project to oversee. I'm flying up there straight after the wedding. I start work next week."

"Wow, you must be good at what you do," I commented, genuinely impressed.

"Well, IT's always been my thing. A bit boring, I know, but somebody's got to do it. And what could be better than getting paid lots of money to do a job you love in a great part of the world? Sometimes, I can't believe how lucky I am."

This sounded a little different to the picture Daphne and Reggie had painted of a geeky, misfit son desperate to find a wife. Melvyn seemed capable, confident and totally happy with his lot. My face must have reflected my thoughts, because he suddenly laughed.

"Don't tell me. Mum and Dad have been giving you the old hard luck story. Poor Melvyn, on his own, can't find a girlfriend?"

"Well, yes," I admitted. "They wanted me to look you up. I got the distinct impression I could be a prospective daughter-in-law."

He laughed again.

"They don't change, bless 'em. They're always trying to fix me up. The truth is this job has been pretty demanding. I've been on-call 24/7 and there have been a lot of hiccups setting up the system. It hasn't been conducive to having a love life. Believe me, I'm not as desperate as they'd have you think. And don't worry. You're safe. I'm not looking for a wife just yet."

"Oh, right," I said, feeling relief I wasn't being set up and liking him immensely for his down to earth approach.

"You two seem to be getting on very well," commented Daphne, returning with a glass of champagne, Reggie in tow. She looked at us hopefully.

"Mother, stop matchmaking," said Melvyn. "You'll make Abigail run a mile."

"No I won't," she said, indignantly. "I was just thinking perhaps you could take Abigail out for a drink. Show her round a bit."

"That would be difficult, seeing as I'm flying to Sydney tomorrow," he pointed out.

"Actually, I'm going to Sydney as well," I said. "One of my Mum's old friends lives in The Rocks area, and I'm going to visit her. Day after tomorrow."

"There you go, Melvyn," said Daphne triumphantly. "You can show Abigail around Sydney."

"I'll be happy to," said Melvyn, looking at me. "The

only trouble is I'm starting a new job and won't have a lot of spare time. But if you'd like to meet for a drink one evening, I'm sure we can arrange something. Here, take my card and give me a call."

"Okay, thanks. I will." Somehow the tables had been turned. Instead of me taking pity on a lonely IT geek, he was fitting me into his busy schedule.

My mobile rang suddenly, taking me by surprise. I glanced at the number. It was Jake and I felt a brief flash of annoyance.

"Sorry, Melvyn. I need to take this. Can I catch up with you later?"

"Sure," he smiled. "I ought to mingle. I am the best man after all."

I moved off the terrace and into a quiet part of the garden.

"Hello?"

"Hi, Abigail, it's me. What are you doing?"

"I'm at a wedding, Jake. It's a bit difficult to talk."

"Sorry, I was just missing you, that's all. Who's getting married?"

"Miranda's cousin, Paula."

"Who's Miranda?"

"Rosalyn's flat mate. I told you, remember?"

"Yeah, I think so."

"Is everything all right, Jake?"

"Yeah, just feeling a bit overwhelmed with everything. Tiffany had a false alarm last night. I thought the baby was on its way. Made me realise how difficult it's going to be to leave."

This was not what I wanted to hear.

"So what are you saying?"

"I'm not saying anything. I was just missing you."

"But no nearer to telling Tiffany. In fact, further away than ever from telling her."

"Abigail, why are you being like this?"

"Because I'm facing reality, that's why. I've just

witnessed two people who are deeply in love getting married. And it's made me realise that no matter how much we love each other, there's no chance we'll ever get married."

There was silence on the other end of the line. I paused, wondering if I'd said too much. Then Jake spoke.

"Abigail, that's what I want more than anything."

"What?" I demanded.

"To marry you. I want you to be my wife."

"Are you proposing, Jake?"

"I suppose I am. I can't imagine anything better than marrying you."

I suddenly felt dizzy.

"D'you mean it?"

"Of course I do. As soon as I've sorted things out with Tiffany, that's what we'll do. We'll get married."

"And will that spur you on to talk to Tiffany?"

"Yes. Knowing that I have a future with you will make it easier to sort things out with her."

"Oh, Jake, you don't know how long I've waited to hear these words."

"Listen, I've got to go. Sorry. I love you. Bye."

The phone went dead and I stood, biting my lip, my mind in turmoil. Jake had proposed. All my life I'd waited for this and now it had happened. But did it really mean anything? Was this yet another fantasy on Jake's part? Could I really believe him? He hadn't phoned to propose, he'd reacted to what I said. But still. Jake's wife. It sounded good.

I walked back to the champagne reception and looked for Melvyn, hoping to pick up our conversation. I needed to speak with someone who was solid and dependable to bring me back down to earth.

Everything with Jake was smoke and mirrors. I didn't know where I was with him, whether his proposal was genuine or just another way of stringing me along and keeping me involved.

I saw Melvyn deep in conversation with a pretty blonde girl and felt irritated she was monopolising him, but I could hardly go and barge in.

I accepted another glass of champagne from a nearby waiter and located Miranda and Rosalyn.

"Hi you two. Where's Ken?"

"Wouldn't you know it?" asked Miranda. "He's found a waiter he knows from a gay bar in town. That boy is unbelievable."

"Looks like we're being summoned for the sit down meal," said Rosalyn. "Let's hope we have some interesting people on our table. I couldn't face sitting next to some crusty old relative."

We were ushered into a light airy dining area with a glass roof, known as The Atrium. Luckily the four of us were seated together, along with two other couples of a similar age. I could see Melvyn sitting between the groom and his mother, and was pleased to see the blonde girl was nowhere nearby. Lunch was served: smooth chicken liver parfait with Cumberland sauce & brioche, followed by chicken stuffed with sundried tomato and Morel mushrooms, carrot & cumin puree & chive mash. Hungry once again, I savoured every mouthful.

"This is divine," said Miranda, summoning the waiter to fill her wine glass. "I only wish this dress wasn't so tight. I feel like I'm going to explode."

Food conscious as ever, Rosalyn ate the bare minimum and drank bottled water. "Perhaps you should have got a size bigger," she pointed out, to which Miranda responded by giving her the finger and Ken could be heard making a loud 'meow' sound.

Fortunately, the couple on Rosalyn's right engaged her in conversation and the gay waiter appeared miraculously at Ken's shoulder, so further confrontation was avoided.

"Jake's asked me to marry him," I whispered to Miranda.

"How can he do that? He's already married," she whispered back.

"He says it's given him another reason to leave Tiffany."

"Or another little fantasy to indulge in."

I stared at her. "You don't think he's going to leave, do you?"

"I don't want you to get messed around, Abigail. Especially now Melvyn's on the scene." She grinned at me.

"Melvyn's a very nice man. But I can assure you he's not on the scene."

"He keeps looking this way," Miranda said. "From where I'm sitting, I'm looking straight at him, and let me tell you, he keeps looking over."

"He's offered to take me out for a drink when I'm in Sydney," I admitted. "He's flying up tomorrow and I go the day after."

Dessert arrived: sticky toffee pudding, toffee sauce and vanilla bean ice cream.

"Oh, Christ," said Miranda. "How am I going to fit this in? This is torture." She turned to her right and noticed the empty chair.

"Where's Ken gone? And more to the point, where's the waiter?"

The wedding lunch bowled along, helped by numerous glasses of Sauvignon Blanc.

Thankfully there were no speeches to sit through. Archie and Paula did the rounds, stopping to speak to the guests at each table.

"Miranda, you look amazing," said Paula, arriving at our table and embracing her cousin.

"So do you, darling. Exquisite. I can't believe you're married. Let me see the ring."

It was a tasteful band of white and yellow gold, setting off a small diamond engagement ring.

"Nothing showy, " said Paula. "You know me, I like to keep things simple."

"That's why she married me," quipped Archie, grinning at us.

"Sorry, let me do the introductions," said Miranda. "Archie and Paula, this is my housemate, Rosalyn, and her friend, Abigail, visiting from England."

"Pleased to meet you both," beamed Archie. "I hear you met Aunty Daphne and Uncle Reggie on the plane coming over, Abigail."

"Yes, that's right."

"No doubt trying to fix you up with Melvyn?"

"Well, yes, they were."

"I don't know why they bother. He's not interested. He's either a confirmed bachelor or gay, we haven't worked out which." They both laughed.

"Well, he's taking me out for a drink when I go to Sydney next week," I informed them.

They exchanged a glance and I had the distinct impression this was big news.

"How long are you staying for?" Paula asked, sitting down in the empty chair next to me.

"Another couple of weeks." I said. "I'm going to Sydney for a week to see one of my Mum's old friends, then I'll come back to Melbourne for the final week."

"Sounds good," she said then leant forward conspiratorially. "How do you think Miranda is?" she asked.

"Fine," I answered. "Why?"

"I feel so guilty. I've been so busy planning the wedding, I haven't seen much of her in the last six weeks. She was so down after she split up with that scumbag coach driver."

"Coach driver?" I asked suspiciously, an alarm bell ringing.

"Yeah, Bill. The guy she met when she first came to Melbourne. She was devastated when she found out he was cheating on her."

My mind was reeling. "Bill? He was called Bill?

"Yes. Why?"

"No reason." I fought to keep my emotions in check. "She told me she'd split up with someone. I didn't know his name was Bill."

"They worked for the same company," explained Paula. "That's how she met him."

I felt hot then cold as things fell into place. Miranda had set me up. She'd suggested I go on the Dandenong Mountains trip, knowing Bill would be the driver. I remembered how she'd questioned me when I got back. "How was the tour guide?" "Was he good looking?" "Did he flirt with the ladies?" I felt sick when I thought how nearly I'd confided in her. For some reason, instinct had kicked in, not to mention embarrassment, and I'd kept silent. Thank goodness. She'd never have forgiven me if I'd told her the truth. I looked over at Miranda and bitterly regretted what I'd done. I turned to Paula.

"Miranda's fine," I said. "She's over him. Believe me, he's ancient history."

I only wished it was true. She was obviously very far from over him.

Three hours and six bottles of wine later, Miranda, Rosalyn, Ken and I were giving it some on the dance floor, throwing caution to the wind. Ken had arranged a date later in the week with the hunky waiter and was in an excellent mood. Rosalyn was doing what she did best, showing everyone what a great body she had. And Miranda was just happy that her lovely cousin was married. She beamed with bonhomie, all thoughts of Bill out of her mind.

I'd been such a mess of conflicting emotions, euphoric at my proposal of marriage yet aghast at my tryst with Bill, that I'd done what anyone would do under the circumstances. I'd anaesthetised myself with alcohol and it seemed to be doing the trick. I'd even had a couple of dances with Melvyn, who'd unexpectedly turned out to be a really good dancer. All was going well, until the evening spun out of control and reality hit me squarely in the face.

We were sitting at our table, having a breather, while a slow dance played. The couple on the next table, who'd introduced themselves as friends of Paula, decided to dance and asked us to keep an eye on their sleeping baby. Personally, I would have thought a disco was the last place to bring a baby, but I suppose it was a family wedding. Amazingly, the baby slept most of the evening, tucked cosily in a pink fluffy blanket inside its baby carrier. As Rosalyn was closest, the couple asked her and, smiling, she readily agreed. As soon as they were on the dance floor, she quickly changed her tune.

"Yuk, look at it. Who'd want to have a baby? You lose your shape for nine months, go through the agony of giving birth, then your life changes beyond all recognition. You're forever changing nappies, up all hours and have to pay for a babysitter if you want to go out. Where's the fun in that? Can't see me ever having a baby. I detest them. Here, Abigail, you watch it."

She pushed the carrier closer to me and I looked at the baby, soft and plump, fast asleep, oblivious to all that was going on. It had the dearest little face, with tightly closed eyes and a pink rosebud mouth. One of its tiny hands clutched its pink blanket and I ran my finger along its tiny, perfectly formed nails. Suddenly its fist opened and closed around my finger, squeezing tightly.

"Oh, how sweet," said Miranda, peering into the carrier. "It's holding Abigail's finger. Look at that weeny little hand."

I stared at the small creature and swallowed. This was what Jake and Tiffany would soon be bringing into the world. A tiny, innocent baby, who'd never done anyone any wrong, and who was about to be abandoned by its father. How could Jake even think of leaving? What kind of man walks away from his new-born child? And how could he propose to me on the same day that Tiffany had a false alarm. A massive alarm bell started ringing in my head.

"He's not going to do it, is he?" I said to Miranda.

"Do what? What are you talking about?"

"Jake. The bastard proposed to me to keep me hanging on, knowing that Tiffany's about to bring another baby into the world. How can he think of leaving? And if does leave, what kind of man does that make him? Plus, if he's done it to her, he could do it to me. How can I trust him?"

"Okay," said Miranda, seeing the desperation on my face and taking control of the situation. "Ken, watch this baby. Abigail, come to the bar. You need a stiff drink."

She thrust the baby towards Ken, who recoiled in disgust.

"What do I do with it? I need a stiff drink more than Abigail. A stiff something, anyway."

"Ken, shut up," said Miranda firmly. "Stop being an arse for once in your life and look after the fucking baby. Its parents will be back any minute. Look, it's waving its hand at you. It likes you."

"Does it?" he asked, peering into the baby carrier, then looking up in panic. "What do I do if it starts crying?"

"Try breastfeeding," said Miranda drily. "Come on, Abigail, let's go to the bar."

She seized my hand and led the way

"Did you see his face?" she murmured. "Priceless. He's not going to let me forget this."

I followed Miranda to the bar, where she ordered me a double whisky. I sat on a bar stool, holding the glass tightly to calm my trembling hands, relishing the warm, burning sensation as the double malt hit my throat.

"What have I got myself into, Miranda?" I asked her forlornly. "There's no way out. Either he's a complete bastard and leaves his family..."

"… or he's a complete shit and lets you down." Miranda finished my sentence.

"Oh God," I said, signalling to the barman to refill my glass. "I wish I'd never met him. I wish I could rewrite the last three years. It started when I lost my sister. Did you know about that?"

"Yes," said Miranda, gently. "Rosalyn told me. A car accident."

"She was only taking a local trip. It should have taken her ten minutes. Instead of which, a lorry's brakes failed and she never came back. I miss her so much, Miranda. I turned to Rosalyn when it happened, but she couldn't handle it. She's not good with emotions. So she left and came to Australia and I was on my own. That's when I met Jake. He was kind. He understood, made me feel better. He listened. And I couldn't help it. I fell in love with him. I knew he had a wife and a baby, but I let myself fall for him. Then it got serious. I gave him an ultimatum. Tiffany or me. But not both. He said he'd leave her."

I stared into my whisky glass. "D'you know what, Miranda? I didn't realise what I was doing until I saw that baby tonight. I always saw Tiffany as the enemy, a pathetic woman hanging on to her man, who got pregnant to make him stay, whether he wanted to or not. But a baby is a living thing. And Jake will be its dad. How can I make him do this?"

"You can't make him do anything," said Miranda. "It's his decision. But he is stuck between a rock and a hard place. Damned if he does and damned if he doesn't. Poor bastard. I wouldn't like to be in his shoes. He's in an impossible situation."

"I've got to get out of this, Miranda?" I said, beginning to slur my words, as the effects of the whiskey mixed with the wine. "By the way, I'm sorry about Bill."

She looked at me sharply.

"How do you know about Bill?"

"You told me."

"I didn't tell you his name."

"No, Paula told me. I just wanted to say I'm sorry it

didn't work out."

She shrugged. "That's life, isn't it? You have to deal with it and move on."

"You do," I agreed. "You have to move on."

I sat and thought for a moment, then stood up, swaying slightly.

There's something I must do, Miranda. Back soon."

"Don't you think we ought to get a taxi home?"

"Yeah, good idea. You order the taxi and I'll be back shortly. Don't forget the baby," I said as an afterthought.

The room tilted dangerously, but I realigned myself, forced my eyes to focus and set off on my quest, vaguely aware Miranda was following at a distance.

I went back into the disco room, where Chris De Burgh was singing 'The Lady in Red'. Perfect. This was my song. I was wearing a red dress and it had been written for me.

Unsteadily, I made my way around the room, searching until I saw him. There was Melvyn, sitting with his mother and father. I went up to them and put my hand on his shoulder.

"Melvyn," I slurred. "Would you like to dance? This is my record."

He looked up in surprise, then smiled.

"Hi Abigail. Yes, of course."

I was vaguely aware of Daphne grinning widely, as Melvyn took my hand and led me on to the dance floor. He placed one hand in the small of my back and the other round my shoulders and chastely, we began a slow dance. I pushed my body closer to his.

"Melvyn," I began.

"Don't speak, let's just enjoy the music."

It was no good. I had to say my piece.

"Melvyn, I just want you to know, that you are a really nice man, and I really like you. If you'd like to get together with me, I think it'd be a great idea."

I was hanging on to his shoulders now, as my legs

seemed unable to support my weight.

"Abigail, you've drunk too much. Perhaps we should sit down?"

"No, keep dancing," I insisted. "You're a very sexy man, has anyone ever told you that? You have beautiful eyes and I would really like to have sex with you. Would you like to have sex?"

"Abigail," he said, more firmly, "flattered though I am, I think you need to sober up. You're going to regret this in the morning."

It was the last thing I heard him say. Suddenly, the room was spinning, the lights were flashing and I was on the floor, people's legs all around me. I was vaguely aware of Melvyn looking down at me, but I couldn't work out his expression.

Then I passed out.

CHAPTER 17

I stared miserably out of the window of the small plane heading for Sydney. Melbourne Airport was a rapidly disappearing dot far beneath us and the second part of my adventure was about to start. I should have been excited, but I didn't know what I felt about anything.

I'd spoken to Edna Corvaggio on the phone and she seemed very pleasant.

"I'd love you to come and stay, darling," she'd enthused, when I told her my plan. "It's years since I've seen your mother. We used to be so close. I'm intrigued to see you."

I'd arranged to meet her at the airport.

"How will I recognise you?" I'd asked and she'd laughed.

"You can't miss me, darling. I'll be the one in bright colours with pink hair."

So, here I was, about to stay with a mad artist and possibly hook up with Melvyn, although given my drunken behaviour at the wedding that was doubtful. My future with Jake looked equally doubtful, given his ridiculous proposal. All I wanted to do was snuggle up in my duvet, escape from the world and hibernate.

Just before I'd left for the airport, Jake had sent me a long email and I took my phone out for the tenth time, re-reading his message.

> *Hi Abby, my future wife.*
> *God, that sounds good. Can't tell you how much I'm missing you. You were right. Your absence is really making me focus on what I want. I just long to touch you, be with you, lie next to you. I'm so miserable without you. I've got nothing to say to Tiffany. Life at home is awful, just long silences and no physical contact.*
> *I drove past your flat the other day and it made me cry*

when I thought of our last time together. I'm sorry I accused you of meeting someone else. I know that would never happen, I know you'd never be unfaithful to me. It's just my insecurity. I wouldn't blame you if you did go off with someone else. It must be awful waiting around for me to sort things out, but the thought of you with anyone else makes me feel so jealous.

I know I should trust you, and I do. You have no idea how you've turned my life upside down. I watched a film about Nelson and Lady Hamilton last night, about how a man's love life can dictate the rest of his life, and it made me think of us. I miss you so much Abby, I can't wait for you to come home, so I can hold you again.

All my love, forever.
Jake xx

I think my heart had already begun to harden towards him because I felt angry and cynical rather than sad and upset. He'd clearly done nothing about his situation and was feeling sorry for himself. His proposal was nothing but a platitude. And I didn't feel guilty about my fling with Bill, not where Jake was concerned anyway. After all, he'd got Tiffany pregnant, twice. And I had to live with that.

It was a different matter where Miranda was concerned. Out of all the men in Australia, why did I have to have a fling with her ex?

All in all, I was glad to be getting away, even though a mad 75-year old artist wasn't my ideal choice of companion.

Until I saw her, that is.

As I emerged from the Arrivals gate, I recognised her immediately. She was a tall woman of large proportions wearing a long gown in blue, pink and purple. A purple beret was positioned jauntily on her bright pink, bobbed hair, and she wore big, celebrity-style shades.

She was a cross between Dame Edna Everage and

Zandra Rhodes.

I stood still, my jaw all but hitting the ground. Even as I approached her, a man stopped by and asked for her autograph. She obliged, signing her name in big scrawling letters on the piece of paper he offered. I approached her tentatively.

"Edna?" I asked, timidly.

"Abigail, darling!" she exclaimed in a deep, loud voice. "My God, you're the spitting image of your mother. How are you darling?"

She kissed me on both cheeks and I was enveloped in a cloud of musky perfume. She was so warm and colourful and loud, I couldn't help but like her. A press photographer appeared from nowhere and I was aware of a flash going off, capturing Edna kissing me on the cheek.

"Who's the visitor, Edna?" asked the young photographer.

"This is my friend, Abigail Aske, that's A-S-K-E, visiting from England," she declared proudly, pulling me alongside her. "Come on dear, have your picture taken." We both smiled at the camera, and she whispered in my ear: "Keep the paps happy, darling, makes life so much easier."

The flash popped again and the photographer disappeared.

"Got your luggage, dear?" asked my new famous friend. "Let's get a cab back to my place."

Edna's place turned out to be a vast warehouse apartment in The Rocks area of Sydney. With its historical buildings, cobbled streets and vast assortment of pubs, cafes, shops and art galleries, The Rocks was quaint and quirky and I couldn't wait to explore it. The cab turned down a narrow cobbled street into a hidden courtyard, and pulled up outside a small art gallery with the name 'Corvaggio' above it.

"Here we are," said Edna, paying the cab fare. "Go

into the gallery, dear. It leads up to my apartment."

She held open the door and I walked in, pulling my case behind me. Inside, gnarled oak beams stretched above, running the length of the gallery, and the dark oak floor looked as if it had come straight from a pirate's ship. The light was dim, giving the place a mysterious feel, but each of the large canvases on the walls was subtly illuminated, displaying the pictures to best effect. I looked at them as I walked past. Edna had a vibrant, almost child-like style, using bright colours in a semi-abstract way to depict scenes from Sydney and across Australia.

"Whaddya think?" she demanded, standing back and watching my reaction.

"I think they're great," I said. "I love the energy and the colour. They're fab."

"Happy pictures, that's what I create," said Edna. "Pictures that make you think of sunshine and happy times. Anyway, you've plenty of time to look round the gallery later. Let's go up and have a cup of tea. Or something stronger. It's not too early for a tipple, is it?"

"Er, no. Midday's good for me.'

I followed her to the back of the gallery, where a young man wearing earphones sat reading a book, with his feet on a desk.

"Anthony!" shouted Edna, pushing his feet off the desk. He looked up startled, dropping his book and pulling the earphones out.

"Oh, hi, Edna. Didn't hear you come in," he muttered sheepishly.

"Obviously. I hardly dare ask if we had any sales this morning. Unlikely, by the look of it."

"No sales, but an enquiry about an exhibition next year, and a request for a radio interview…"

"Okay, sounds good. Give me the details later. This is my friend's daughter, Abigail."

"Hi, Anthony," I said, waving.

"Hi, Abigail, pleased to meet you," he said, flicking

his long blond fringe out of his eyes and revealing a spotty forehead.

"Now, be a darling and carry her case upstairs," instructed Edna.

Anthony did as he was asked and we followed him up a metal flight of steps leading from the gallery up to the first floor. He opened the door to a massive studio, where light flooded in from enormous floor-to-ceiling windows. Various canvasses, in different stages of progress, stood propped against the walls and on easels, and a profusion of palettes, tubes of paint, brushes and rags adorned every surface.

"Sorry dear. Looks like a bomb's exploded in a paint factory," said Edna. "It's just the way I work. I've always got a least half a dozen pictures going at any one time. And, as you can see, I don't do clean and tidy. Put the case at the back there, Anthony, then get back down to the gallery and see if you can get me some sales."

Anthony pulled my case through the obstacle course, navigating between the easels and paintings, before disappearing back down the stairs.

"Nice boy," said Edna. "A bit clueless, but he's reliable and, more to the point, he's a brilliant sculptor. I'll be displaying some of his work soon. He's got a bright future, especially with me as his mentor. Now, sit down, dear, while I fix us a drink."

Edna, I realised, liked telling people what to do.

I sat on a huge old sofa in what appeared to be the living area, to one side of the studio. A small open plan kitchen lay to one side and it was here that Edna prepared our drinks. She handed me a large gin and tonic, more gin than tonic, with a slice of lemon floating on top.

An old record player stood on an old mahogany sideboard, with a collection of vinyl nearby. Edna carefully selected an album and the strains of Iggy Pop and 'Lust for Life' filled the air.

I looked at her impressed. This was unexpected.

"Gin and tonic and Iggy Pop," said Edna, sitting back on the sofa alongside me. "What could be better? Cheers!"

"Cheers," I said, raising my glass and grinning at her.

"Love your studio, Edna," I said looking round, "and your gallery is fantastic. How long have you been here?"

"Years, darling, too many to count. I came here in the 70s, before The Rocks was fashionable.

"It looks pretty old. What did it used to be?"

"This was Sydney's first settlement, back in the 1880s," she explained. "Not that I was around then, contrary to what you might think." She grinned at me. "It was a squalid place, full of robbers and thieves, with open sewers and ladies of the night. Then bubonic plague struck and they had to raze many of the old streets to get rid of it. Some years later, they built the Harbour Bridge and that took away another chunk of the area. Then in the 1970s, just after I'd arrived, they decided to make it the trendy area of Sydney. They converted the old buildings and warehouses into apartments and shops, and, voila, it took off.'

She sipped her drink and looked at me conspiratorially. "These days, the real estate is worth a fortune."

"Which means….?" I asked.

"I'd be rich if I sold up. Not that I ever will. I love it here. Best place in the world. Now, tell me about your mother. How is Louisa? We used to be such good friends and now it's just the occasional Christmas card."

"She's fine," I answered. "Sends her love. I suppose you heard about my sister?"

"I did, dear. Sorry to hear about that. Your mother mentioned it in her card. Car accident wasn't it?"

"Yes. It's been hard for my Mum and Dad."

"Hard for you all, I imagine."

I smiled at her sadly. "Yes. But we're coping. Life goes on. Did you know my dad?"

"Not really, dear. I knew your mother in the late 60s,

before he was on the scene. That was when I lived in the UK. She and I met at Art College in London. Both went to St Martins. Boy, did we party. Those were the days. Mary Quant, Biba, Kings Road, Twiggy, mini-skirts, free love... Your mother was a talented sculptor. Shame she never did anything with it. But she met your dad and we went our separate ways. She got married and discovered suburbia. I stayed single and embraced bohemia. The rest is history, as they say."

I was starting to see my mother in a new light. I'd never thought about her having a life before she met my dad. Particularly not a life of free love in London's swinging 60's.

"You never married then, Edna?"

"No. What was it Mae West said? Marriage is a great institution, but I'm not ready for an institution yet. Just about sums it up. I did have a son, though."

I looked at her surprise. That was unexpected.

"That's him in the photo, there."

She pointed to the sideboard and I looked over to the framed photo holding pride of place. A thick-set man with small piercing eyes and a shock of dark hair looked back at me. I looked more closely. There was something about him that was not quite right. He was grinning manically, revealing buck teeth.

"He, er, looks very nice," I said embarrassed.

"That's Frank," said Edna. "He's a wonderful boy. He was 40 last week. We had a big celebration."

"Where does he live?" I asked.

"He lives here, darling, with me. He could never live on his own."

Edna laughed in a knowing way.

"Why's that?" I ask lightly.

"Starved of oxygen at birth, dear. It's given him a few problems. Don't worry. He's quite harmless. He's a lovely boy and he can't wait to meet you."

"Where is he?" I asked, looking around, imagining a

lunatic son kept under lock and key.

Edna looked at her watch.

"Should have left work about ten minutes ago, which means he'll be back for lunch any time now."

Right on cue, I heard heavy footsteps pounding up the metal stairway and seconds later the large man from the photograph burst into the studio.

"Is she here?" he demanded excitedly.

"She's here, darling," said Edna, nodding in my direction.

For a horrible moment the thought flashed through my head that I'd been procured for his evil pleasure in a real life Hammer horror. I fixed a smile on my face.

"Hey, Frank, good to meet you. I'm Abigail." I held out my hand.

To my amazement, he became ill at ease and looked down at the carpet, unable to speak.

"Come on, Frank, don't be shy. Say hello," chided his mother.

"Hello, Abigail," he said in a small, awkward voice and continued staring at the carpet.

"Your Mum says you've just come from work. Where's that?" I asked kindly.

"By Circular Quay," he mumbled, still not looking up.

"Come on, Frank, tell Abigail what you do," encouraged his mother.

"Pick up rubbish," he said quickly.

"He's a public hygiene operative," explained Edna, "which basically means he picks up litter."

"I keep Circular Quay clean," he said, looking at me for the first time and I was struck by the child-like quality of his face. His eyes were small and bewildered, and my heart went out to him. The problem was, once he'd dared to look me in the eye, he couldn't stop. He stared at me with an intensity that was quite unnerving, taking in every part of my body.

"Nice," he said, bringing his gaze to my bare legs. I

nervously pulled my dress over my knees and he watched fascinated, his mouth open and his tongue showing.

"All right, Frank, that's enough," said Edna. "Why don't you go and make yourself a sandwich?"

"I've eaten already," he answered. "I got a sandwich from the kiosk." He looked at my face once again.

"You're very pretty, Abigail. But you're sad."

I laughed nervously. "I'm not sad, Frank. I'm excited to be here and I'm really looking forward to discovering The Rocks."

He smiled at me, his face lighting up. "I can show you round, Abigail. I know everywhere. I can show you where to go."

I smiled back. "That would be great, Frank. Thank you."

"Now, Frank, why don't you go and have a rest in your room before you go back to work?" suggested Edna.

"Okay, I will. See you later Abigail." He grinned at me, looking me up and down. Then he trundled to the back of the studio and disappeared through a door.

"Don't be put off by him," said Edna, leaning forward and topping up my glass with a large amount of gin. "He's a good boy, just not used to having women around him, apart from me. He was so excited to hear we were having a visitor."

"It's fine, Edna," I said, hoping my bedroom had a lock on it. The last thing I wanted was an adolescent man-boy prowling round at night. "Has it always been just you and Frank?"

"You mean, where's his dad?" asked Edna.

"I suppose so."

"The answer is I don't know, dear. He left when Frank was born. Couldn't face the prospect of having a brain-damaged child. He was an artist, like me, but very volatile, very unstable. It was for the best. He wouldn't have coped."

"So, you were left on your own with a baby?" I asked.

"Was it difficult?"

"The early years were tough," admitted Edna, "trying to get commissions and look after a baby. I couldn't afford childcare. But I got through somehow and everything was okay. In fact, looking back I wouldn't change a thing. Without a partner in the way, it meant I could concentrate on Frank, give him the attention he needed. He came on in leaps and bounds. Did far more than the doctors ever said he would. And I've learned to see the world through his eyes, which has given my paintings a completely different perspective. It's as if my eyes were opened for the first time when I started to understand Frank. I saw life as it was, not as the carefully wrapped package most people see. I tell you dear, I have a lot to thank Frank for. He's made me the person and the artist I am today. The day his father decided to leave was the best thing that could have happened."

She topped up my glass, adding: "Don't get me wrong, dear. I'm no saint. I've had my fair share of flings. It's just that Frank always comes first."

I sat on the sofa, my mind bamboozled by gin and Edna's words. This put a whole new slant on things. Perhaps it wasn't always such a good thing for a father to stick around, especially if things weren't good. Perhaps Jake was doing the right thing by leaving. I wondered what Edna would think of my situation. Dare I ask her? Would she take my side or would she tell my mother? I was plucking up the courage to find the words, when steps sounded again on the metal stairs and a wild haired man rushed into the studio.

"Stanley!" exclaimed Edna in delight, rushing over to embrace the dreadlocked, flamboyant creature that stood before us.

He wore a green velvet jacket, turquoise ruffed shirt and baggy blue and purple trousers, with a multi-coloured knitted scarf thrown carelessly over his shoulder. His face was tanned, leathery and lined, and I guessed he was mid

70s. He beamed at Edna and his face broke into a million tiny lines, criss-crossing his features. I stared mesmerised at this exotic vision, my gaze drawn to his flashing brown eyes. I don't think I've ever seen more energy come from a person. It surrounded him like a force field and one thing was sure. Stanley was made for fun.

"Come on, Eddie," he laughed. "What are doing sitting around here when The Hooch Club is open? Grab your coat and let's party."

"Sounds good to me," said Edna, looking like a schoolgirl with a crush. "Are you up for it, Abigail?"

"Yes, Abigail, how about it? Pleased to meet you by the way," echoed Stanley, fixing me with his gaze.

"Sure," I answered, not having the slightest idea what I was letting myself in for.

I was about to find out.

CHAPTER 18

I sat on an old, red velvet seat that had seen better days and gazed through the smoky air of The Hooch Club, soaking up the atmosphere. The lights were low, giving the place a dim, eerie feel, and the air was heavy with the sweet smell of marijuana. A jazz band played slowly and soulfully on the stage, the musicians so old and laid-back, it seemed the instruments were playing themselves. Looking around, I reckoned the average age to be well over 70. Other than me, there were no young people. Edna and Stanley sat cross-legged on a pile of ancient, embroidered cushions, carelessly strewn across the floor. A hubble-bubble pipe stood between them, and they occasionally passed it to one another.

"It's quite harmless, dear, only herbal," said Edna, offering me the pipe.

I refused, not willing to chance it, even if it was only herbal. When we'd arrived, I'd partaken of the joint they'd passed round, skilfully rolled by Stanley with one hand while he drank his pint of 'brew' with the other. I wasn't sure what 'brew' was, but it looked cloudy and strong, and I certainly wasn't willing to give it a go, as Edna encouraged.

I stuck with gin and tonic, although I guessed by now I must have consumed at least half a bottle of gin. The room seemed to be moving strangely and I'd never felt so mellow in my life.

"Are you an artist, too, Stanley?" I asked, when we first sat down.

"Piss artist, more like," laughed Edna.

Stanley gave her the finger.

"I have been known to paint," he informed me, "although nothing on the scale of Edna."

She gave him the finger back.

"Stanley's an impressionist," explained Edna. "A bit

like Turner only more so. In the sense no one has a fucking clue what's going on. Looking at Stanley's paintings is like peering into an opium den wearing sunglasses. Or gazing into a sea mist when you're very shortsighted. Everything's ethereal and faint, a mass of hazy colour and dim shapes. Who knows if there's anything there? Stanley sure as hell doesn't."

"Who wants to live their life in tangibles?" asked Stanley, passing me the spliff and exhaling a cloud of smoke. "Abstract is so much more liberating. My paintings are open to interpretation. They're whatever you want them to be."

"Here's to a world of whatever, not what is," said Edna, raising her glass. "To abstract!"

"To abstract and myopia," said Stanley, raising his glass. "May they be forever entwined. Cheers!"

I realised we were descending into a world of substance-induced bollocks-talk and that this was a regular thing. I also realised I was assuming the role of gooseberry, which felt odd. I felt more like an adult chaperone, with two teenagers, rather than the daughter of my mother's elderly friend. How had this happened? I tried to get the conversation on to more solid ground.

"D'you live nearby, Stanley?" I asked.

"I live at the rainbow's end," he answered.

"Yeah, and I'm a leprechaun," I said in a scathing voice.

"No, he really does, dear," said Edna. "He runs a gift shop called Rainbow's End in the courtyard next to mine. It's got the most fantastic coffee bar at the back. I'll get Frank to take you there tomorrow when I'm working."

"Great idea," said Stanley. "You haven't lived if you haven't had one of my cinnamon cappuccinos."

"Okay, sounds good. Shouldn't you be there now?"

"Wednesday afternoon is half-day closing, which means it's playtime." He winked at me.

A ripple of applause sounded amongst the audience

as an older black woman, dressed in a scarlet dress, made her way on to the stage.

"Wait for this, dear," said Edna. "This girl is fantastic. Knocks spots off Ella Fitzgerald."

She was right. As the woman began to sing, everyone fell silent. Her voice was low, husky and pure gravel, and she held the audience in the palm of her hand. I felt the hair rising on the back of my arms and watched her, spellbound. She sang four songs, all smoochy jazz numbers and finished with a jazz interpretation of La Vie En Rose.

As she reached the final few bars, the audience gave her a standing ovation and she bowed low.

"I can see why you come here," I said to Edna. "Who'd have believed this was going on behind such an unassuming green door?"

I was referring to the clandestine nature of the club. After we'd left Edna's, we'd turned out of her courtyard and gone down a couple of cobbled streets, eventually coming to a halt outside an innocuous-looking door with peeling green paint, set in an old brick wall. Stanley had knocked three times, obviously giving some kind of hidden signal, and it had opened immediately. A wizened old gnome of a man, with a large hooked nose and deep frown, peered out as if he was guarding the entrance to a hidden world. As soon as he saw Stanley, his face relaxed.

"Stanley, y'old gizzard, how the divil ar'ya? Come on in. And Edna, too. Whadda treat! And who's this?"

"This is Abigail Aske from the United Kingdom," said Edna, in an imperious voice.

I felt somewhat ridiculous, as if I were being announced as a titled personage, hailing from an overseas kingdom. The gnome stared at me.

"Bit young, isn't she? You know the rules…"

"For Pete's sake, let us in Horatio," said Stanley.

Horatio? This was getting more bizarre by the second.

"All right. As long as she's with you," said the gnome, standing back.

We squeezed past him into a small, dark vestibule. There was nowhere to go but down a narrow flight of stairs. Horatio closed the door behind us, and we filed down into a gloomy Hobbitesque underworld.

The faint sound of music came from below, getting louder as we descended, and I watched, intrigued as Stanley rapped on another door at the bottom of the steps. It opened and another wizened old man let us in, revealing the smoky, underground cellar-world, inhabited by stooped, aged people.

Now, I sat, feeling mellower by the minute, watching Stanley and Edna share their hubble-bubble pipe, giggling like lovesick teenagers.

Eventually, Stanley wandered off to see some other wizened goblins and Edna came to sit with me.

"This is great, Edna," I said. "D'you come here a lot?"

"Most Wednesday afternoons, dear, when Stanley shuts up shop."

"Is he, like, your boyfriend?"

"Boyfriend?" Edna threw back her head and laughed. "No, dear. Boyfriend is far too conventional. And far too exclusive. Let's just say we're good friends."

"Does he have any family?" I asked.

Edna wrinkled her nose.

"Stanley's not the settling down kind. He tried the whole wife and kids thing but it wasn't for him. He's a free spirit. Like me." She grinned at me. "Why settle for one chocolate when you can have the box? That's my motto."

"Too right," I said, wondering if I should tell her about Jake.

I was just trying to find the right words when the lights were suddenly switched on, revealing The Hooch Club in all its sleazy glory, and Horatio burst in through the door, shouting: "Raid! Make yourself scarce."

In two seconds, everything changed. It was like a well-oiled machine. A door to the side of the bar opened quickly and everyone filed out as fast as possible. Well, as fast as their old legs would let them. Perhaps that's why there was no panic.

Edna grabbed my hand.

"Come on, dear. It doesn't do to get caught up in a raid. Especially when you're an overseas visitor and you've been taking illegal substances."

Her words sobered me instantly. She led the way up a flight of steps leading to the rear of the club and I followed, my heart beating rapidly. Behind us, I heard shouting and the sounds of furniture crashing. We soon reached ground level, where a door at ground level opened on to a car park at the rear of the building. My eyes blinked in the sudden bright sunshine. All around us, old age pensioners were making a quick getaway, or as quick as they were able.

"This way," said Edna, taking my hand. "The police can't follow us up here."

She darted into a alleyway, too narrow for a car to drive along, pulling me with her. At the end was a brick wall about three metres high. It was a dead end. Already I could hear shouts coming from the car park.

"What are we going to do, Edna?" I asked panicking. Visions of being thrown into an Australian jail on drugs charges filled my head. "There's nowhere to go."

"Follow me," she said heading straight for the brick wall. "See, Stanley's made steps for us."

She indicated a number of bricks that had been pulled out from the wall, creating a series of steps, leading up to the top.

"Up we go."

In less than a minute, I'd climbed the wall and dropped down into a rubbish skip on the other side. Edna followed, kicking the brick steps back into the wall as she climbed, leaving no trace of our escape. She dropped into the skip alongside me. There was a movement to my left and Stanley's face appeared through the rubbish.

"Jesus, Abigail. I thought you were gonna land on top of me. You found the steps then?"

"Cheers Stanley," said Edna, removing a piece of orange peel from his shoulder. "That's another fine mess you got me out of."

They both started giggling and I stared at them, horrified.

"We were nearly busted."

"Relax, dear. We've never been caught yet."

"The fuzz only do it when they have a quiet afternoon," added Stanley.

"I could have been thrown in jail and deported," I protested

"But you weren't dear," said Edna, pulling something grungy off her jacket.

"Chill, Abigail," said Stanley. "Life's all about pushing back the boundaries and taking risks."

"He's right," said Edna. "You've gotta live dangerously."

I stared at them both, sprawled inside the skip in their brightly coloured clothing, covered in rubbish, and I couldn't help it. I started laughing too.

Then we were all laughing, doubled over and clinging on to each other, until the tears were rolling down our cheeks.

All in all, it had been a very strange day.

CHAPTER 19

Lying in bed that night, I thought about The Hooch Club incident. Edna and Stanley were right. Life was all about pushing back the boundaries. It reminded me of the time Jake and I had tried living dangerously. What an eye-opener that turned out to be.

I'd just finished reading The Dice Man, the 1960s classic book by Luke Rhinehart about a man who decides to live his life by the throw of the dice. It was all about living on the edge, giving yourself options but letting a random throw of the dice decide for you. In the book it all goes horribly and hilariously wrong as the Dice Man falls into a downward spiral of depravity and murder. But we liked the idea.

We decided to have a go at dice living and see how liberated we really were. It proved to be great fun. Roll the dice and if it's a three or a six, make love in the open air. If it's a two or a four, have a cup of tea. If it's a one or a five, go out without any underwear. It was hardly death defying stuff, just silly options that gave us the illusion we were throwing caution to the wind and being wild.

Then my friend Dan called with an invitation.

"Would you like to go to a sex party?"

"What d'you mean, a sex party?"

"I don't know exactly. The man in the local sex shop asked me. I'd gone in to buy some stuff as a joke," he explained quickly. "Apparently it's in a bar somewhere outside Stratford and it's by invitation only. D'you want to come?"

We threw the dice. It said yes.

On the appointed evening, we met Dan and his girlfriend, Wendy, at the bar. I was disappointed. It all looked very ordinary. No glamorous young nubiles in thongs and G-strings. No muscular young men with large penile posing pouches. Just a collection of frumpy, middle-aged women in floral frocks accompanied by their pot-bellied, florid-faced spouses.

Some women, I noticed, wore tight rubber dresses, stretched tautly over voluminous curves, but it wasn't what you'd call decadent or outrageous. It was just sad. Gradually, it got busier and after an hour, the DJ announced that a groping session would begin on the dance-floor. We looked at one another expectantly. Maybe now we'd see some action. As the music slowed down, people moved onto the dance floor and we watched with interest.

"Come on, Jake," I said. "We might as well have a dance while we're here."

We moved onto the dance floor and began swaying our bodies slowly to the music. Suddenly, I stared at him. "Jake, where are your hands?"

"Round your shoulders."

"If your hands are round my shoulders, whose hands are on my backside?"

He manoeuvred us in a different direction and the hands disappeared.

"You shouldn't have done that," I joked. "I was quite enjoying it."

Jake said nothing, but he looked uncomfortable. After a few more seconds, he said: "Let's sit down. I need a drink."

We joined Dan and Wendy at our table and I told them what had happened.

"It was great," I enthused. "Very sensual."

The DJ announced that the first groping session was over and now we saw that many of the floral frocks had disappeared, replaced with suspenders, stockings, basques, peep hole bras and other lacy items. I looked at Wendy.

"What have you got on underneath?" I asked her.

"A white basque and suspenders," she answered. "What about you?"

"Black bra and suspenders. D'you feel a bit overdressed?"

"I suppose so."

"You know what they say? If you can't beat 'em, join 'em."

Giggling, we went to the Ladies. It was one huge dressing room. Fat, fleshy bodies struggled out of dresses, blouses and skirts, revealing an array of provocative lacy underwear. Huge bosoms spilled over brief underwired bras. Waists were nipped in by tight-fitting basques, and milky white thighs strained beneath suspenders and stockings.

It was a sea of heaving flesh, constantly moving as one lingerie-clad body left and another entered.

"This your first time?" asked a woman in a loud Birmingham accent, painting thick red lipstick onto her lips.

"Yes," we smiled nervously.

"You'll get used to it. We're a friendly bunch. Just get stuck in. It's the best way." She snapped shut her handbag and left the room, her enormous chest leading the way.

Once we'd stripped down to our underwear, we felt a little less conspicuous, and went back to join Jake and Dan. Two other couples now sat opposite.

A totally naked woman with long dark hair walked passed and we all turned to stare.

"Did you see that?" asked Dan. "Bloody hell."

"First time, is it?" asked the ruddy-faced man opposite.

We grinned at him sheepishly.

"Thought so. You can always tell. It's a bit of fun, you know."

What shocked me more than anything was how normal these people looked. They were all Mr and Mrs Average, the sort of people you passed every day in the street. Who'd have thought they were secret sex maniacs and rubber fetishists?

"He could be my Bank Manager," I whispered to Jake. "Makes you think, doesn't it?"

"Just what I've always said," he answered. "There's no such thing as normal. This is the tip of the iceberg. There's a whole underworld of kinky sex going on, right in front of our eyes, if we only but knew it."

"Wow, I'll never look at my Bank Manager the same way again."

The DJ announced a second groping session and I took Jake's hand.

"Come on, we've got to join in now we're here."

Reluctantly, he followed me onto the dance floor. Dan and Wendy came too. We all started dancing slowly and again, after a few minutes, I felt a hand stroking my backside. This time I didn't say anything. It was quite nice being lost amongst a sea of dancers, all undulating gently, held tightly in the arms of the man I loved, with an anonymous hand softly stroking my bottom. I closed my eyes and let myself slide into the experience. It was lovely. The soft, slow music, the closeness of Jake, the intimacy of the other dancers and this persistent, unknown hand gently fondling me. I realised how easy it would be to get carried away at an event like this. Thank goodness Jake was with me. I opened my eyes and saw him looking over my shoulder with a stony glare in his eyes.

"Come on, let's go," he said through gritted teeth, without looking at me.

"What's the matter?" I asked stupidly.

"I said let's go." He pushed me ahead of him.

"What is it?" I asked when we were back at our table.

"The other guy. That was the problem," he said angrily. "Have you any idea what it's like dancing with your girlfriend and staring over her shoulder into the eyes of another man who's feeling her up?"

"It was quite harmless," I started to say, but he cut me short.

"I'm leaving," he announced, his face red and

blotchy. "If you want to stay, fine. But I'm going."

He jumped up and started elbowing his way through the crowds.

"Jake, wait, I'll come with you, just let me say goodbye."

I pushed my way on to the dance floor and found Dan and Wendy.

"Jake's upset and he's left. I have to go after him. I'll talk to you tomorrow."

As I left the dance-floor, I saw the naked girl surrounded by a group of men, all fully clothed. She was dancing in the middle of them and their hands were all over her, pressing, prying, probing every part of her. Thank goodness Jake hadn't seen that. I hurried after him, noticing on the way out a large noticeboard covered in hand-written advertisements. I stopped for a second and read a few:

> *Experimental couple looking to meet AC/DC girl for fun and games. Call Phil and Fiona.*
>
> *Rubber fetishist, large, buxom figure, looking to meet similar minded man. Please call Ruby.*
>
> *Slave looking for mistress. I need to be humiliated. I need to serve. I need to be beaten. Please help. Call Jim.*

Pulling on my clothes, I left the wine bar and ran to Jake's car.

He sat inside with the engine running, his face grim. I opened the passenger door and got in.

"What's wrong with you?" I demanded. "Why did you leave me on my own?"

"I thought you were enjoying it," he said spitefully.

"For heaven's sake. A man had his hand on my bottom. He wasn't doing anything. You're over-reacting."

Jake hit the accelerator and the car shot off at speed.

"Jake, what's the matter?"

"Did you see which man had his hand on your bottom?" he shouted. "Remember that idiot in the black leather trousers when we first came in?"

"The one with the large girlfriend in the purple rubber dress?"

"That's the one. Well, it was him. And you were enjoying it."

"Ugh. Are you sure? He was revolting."

"How d'you think I felt, looking over your shoulder into his eyes?"

"Not very good, I suppose." I sighed. "Bit of a disastrous evening, really."

"Well, it's made me realise something," said Jake.

"What's that?"

"I thought I was broadminded. But I'm not. And what made it worse, you were enjoying it."

"Only because you were there to look after me. Now I know who was touching me up, I feel sick."

"I guess it proves one thing," said Jake. "Fantasies are okay as long as they don't become reality. One of my fantasies was to see you with another man, but now I've seen it, I hate it. The last thing I feel is horny."

"Let's just put it down to experience shall we?" I suggested. "Next time, we'll stick to fantasies. Forget about turning them into reality."

For the next few weeks, our fantasies were very tame. The party remained a sad witness to Jake's lack of bottle. What previously had been unfulfilled potential was now a permanent reminder of Jake's inhibitions, no matter how wild the fantasies in his mind.

The story had an interesting ending, though. The sex party was held on a regular basis and a month later it was exposed in the tabloids.

Dan brought a copy of the newspaper round to show me. He opened up a double page spread with the headline 'Bondage Bar', showing photos of women in various states of undress, cavorting around with groups of men. It all looked incredibly seedy. Thank goodness we hadn't gone a month later or we could have been looking at images of ourselves.

Try explaining that away.

"I know I'm in my underwear, mum, but honestly, I only went for a laugh."

And Jake would have been in big trouble. It would have been a double exposure for him!

CHAPTER 20

Next morning I awoke feeling curiously alive. I felt better than I had in weeks and attributed it to being away from Rosalyn and with Edna. I'd never met anyone quite like her and had fallen totally under her spell. She'd given me a strange little box room at the rear of her studio and although there wasn't much space, the bed was immensely comfortable. I checked my phone. Three text messages from Jake. I decided to ignore them. I still felt angry with him. There was another from Edith, asking about Rosalyn. That was also territory I didn't want to visit, so I didn't reply to that either.

Putting on my dressing gown, I walked in to the studio and found Edna and Frank enjoying breakfast in the kitchen area.

"Morning, dear. Come and help yourself," instructed Edna, indicating fresh juice, fruit, coffee and rye bread. I sat down next to Frank at the kitchen table.

"Morning, Abigail," he said, keeping his head down, but giving me sly glances when he thought I wasn't looking.

I helped myself to coffee and a bread roll.

"I have to work this morning, dear," said Edna.

"I have a commission and I need to do some preliminary sketches. Heaven knows why they can't choose one from the gallery, but there you go. They want a purple picture for a purple room and they're prepared to pay for an Edna Corvaggio original, so who I am to argue? As Frank's doing the late shift today, he thought he'd show you round The Rocks this morning. What d'you think?"

"Sounds great," I said.

Frank went bright red.

"This afternoon, I'll take you to Bondi Beach if you like, Abigail, " said Edna.

If I liked? Images of muscle-bound surfers filled my

head and I readily acquiesced. What's not to like? Roll on Bondi!

I told Frank about Stanley's invitation to go to his coffee shop and he happily agreed to accompany me. But first he had to introduce me to his hobby.

"I think you'll find this very interesting, Abigail," he said, putting a CD into the portable player that stood on the breakfast table.

"What is it, Frank?" I asked curiously.

"It's the Flying Scotsman travelling across Australia," he said proudly.

I looked at him in disbelief. "What, the whole CD is a recording of the train?"

Edna beamed at him.

"It's his favourite thing," she said. "He loves trains. He knows the history of all Sydney's tram and railway system. And he knows the history of British trains, too. Get Frank talking train numbers and he can't stop. He knows them off by heart."

I made a mental note never to mention the subject of train numbers. Or that I'd been on Puffing Billy. But for now, I was a captive audience, and for the next half hour, I had no option but to listen to the Flying Scotsman chug, chug, chugging its way across the countryside. Every so often it would let out a 'whoo, whoo', at which point Frank would get very excited and join in. All the while, Edna sat sketching at her desk, occasionally looking over in our direction and bestowing a loving gaze on Frank. Finally, when the Flying Scotsman had chugged its last, my ordeal was over.

I stared at Frank, realising I had no control over the twists and turns my holiday was taking. It was if a pebble had been thrown into a pond, creating ripples, and I was caught up in their outward motion, carried along whether I liked it or not. I felt strangely passive and fatalistic.

By 11 o' clock, we were ready to explore The Rocks. Frank dressed sartorially in my honour, wearing a fetching cream safari suit with matching fedora hat and cream bag that made him look like a foppish, turn-of-the-century gentleman-explorer.

"Nice suit, Frank," I complimented him, resisting the urge to say 'Dr Livingstone, I presume'.

He beamed all over his pudgy face, his little eyes sparkling with pleasure. Frank, I decided, could easily become your favourite pet. As long as you treated him right, he would give you undying loyalty, and it was so lovely to see him happy.

He led the way out of Edna's art gallery, nodding in Anthony's direction, who once more sat with his earphones in and feet up. For the next hour we had a wonderful time soaking up the atmosphere of The Rocks and exploring the many art and craft shops that nestled in the cobbled streets. They were full of aboriginal art, colourful clothing and indigenous crafts. I loved it all.

In one shop, Frank bought me an abalone shell necklace and earrings, carefully selecting them, then nervously pushing them into my hand, muttering: "This is for you, Abigail".

I was genuinely touched. He'd obviously developed a major crush on me. I planted a kiss on his cheek as a thank you, and he looked as though he was going to burst with pride. For the next ten minutes, he kept rubbing the place on his cheek where I'd kissed him, a strange little smile playing on his lips. He might be odd, but he was also a man of surprises, as I found out when we arrived at Stanley's coffee shop.

"This is The Rainbow's End, Abigail," he said, as we approached an interesting little shop, its windows crammed with all kinds of art and crafts.

"So, this is Stanley's place," I said, peering through the doorway. "Come on, let's go and have one of his famous cinnamon cappuccinos."

We walked in and found Stanley standing behind the counter, colourfully attired in a purple, pink and turquoise caftan, matching beads threaded through his dreadlocks, red sandals on his feet. His crinkled face lit up when he saw us.

"Abigail! Frank! My two favourite people. After Edna, of course. Great to see you."

With an agility beyond the capabilities of most younger men, he leapt over the counter and embraced us, planting a kiss on my cheek and shaking hands with Frank.

"It smells wonderful in here, Stanley," I said, inhaling the pungent aroma of coffee beans.

"The best coffee shop in Sydney," said Stanley proudly. "People come from all over just to drink my coffee. I had someone from the Northern Territories last week. Said he'd come to Sydney just for my coffee."

"Really?" I said, impressed.

"No, not really," admitted Stanley. "Sounds goods though." He winked at me, then called out: " Stella, fix these good people up with a couple of 'chinos will ya?"

A waif-like girl dressed in a punk outfit with more piercings than I would have thought humanly possible and a purple Mohican hairstyle appeared from the back of the shop.

"Sure thing, Stan. D'you guys wanna sit down?"

"Go find a table," instructed Stanley "I'll see you in mo. I have customers to serve."

He indicated a Japanese couple trying to work out how to play a large didgeridoo at one side of the shop. Frank and I went into the small coffee lounge at the rear of the shop. It was exactly as I imagined it. Retro, with low lighting, old wooden tables and chairs, and walls covered with pictures, postcards and messages. Jazz music played in the background and in no time Stella placed two steaming cappuccinos on the table, laced with cinnamon. I sipped mine slowly. It tasted heavenly. I could well believe someone would come from the Northern Territories just for Stanley's coffee.

I realised just how much I'd enjoyed myself looking

round The Rocks with Frank.

Jake would love it here, I mused. I'd definitely bring him here when we visited Australia. The thought had entered my head without warning and I felt the pain of our separation sear through me. Who was I kidding to think it was over? I'd been angry with him but now my heart was speaking again. I remembered our last coffee in the Frith Street coffee house in Soho and felt suddenly empty. I shouldn't be visiting Sydney on my own. I should be with Jake. Beautiful, soulful, sexy Jake. The man I loved, who could turn me on just by looking at me. I sighed involuntarily.

"You're sad," said Frank, looking concerned. "Are you not enjoying yourself?"

I snapped back into the present. "Sorry, Frank, I was thinking of something, that's all. Good God, what's that?"

A deep, guttural sound filled the air.

"It's a didgeridoo, Abigail," said Frank. "Stanley's showing the people how to do it."

He laughed and I couldn't help laughing, too.

"You look pretty when you smile," said Frank. "Can I draw your picture?"

He pulled out a small drawing pad and pencil.

"Yes, of course," I said surprised. "I didn't know you could draw."

"I draw everything," he said simply and started to sketch.

In a few minutes, he'd finished and held it up for me to see.

"What do you think, Abigail?"

I was astounded.

It was the most stunning pencil sketch I'd ever seen. He'd captured my likeness perfectly, even the sad expression in my eyes.

"Frank, this is amazing," I exclaimed. "Where did you learn to draw like this?"

"I didn't learn," he said, looking at me as if I was

some kind of idiot. "I just do it. I've always been able to draw. I see things and I remember them. Sometimes I draw them later."

"Can I see your sketch pad?" I asked.

He handed it over and I turned the pages, finding the most incredible sketches imaginable. There were people, animals, street scenes, boats and more, all sketched with perfect perspective and, I had no doubt, complete accuracy.

"I see you've discovered Frank's hidden talent," said Stanley, joining us at our table and pulling up a chair.

He's good, isn't he?"

"He's fantastic. He says he remembers things and draws them later on."

"Yep, a perfect photographic memory," said Stanley. "I don't think there's anything he can't draw. See that picture hanging over there?"

He pointed at a large impressionistic view of Sydney harbour, finished in inks and wash. "That's one of Frank's."

"Oh my God. He's really talented."

"What do you expect?" said Stanley. "His dad was an artist and his mother's one of the best. He's genetically programmed to draw."

I looked at Frank, with his close-set eyes, buck teeth and wild dark hair. Who would have thought it? Living proof that you should never judge a book by the cover. And I'd thought he was a simpleton.

I was beginning to find out that nothing was quite as it seemed on this holiday.

CHAPTER 21

The waves crashed on to Bondi Beach. Muscle-clad surfers in coloured shorts rode them with abandon, and Edna and I sat on the sand ogling them shamelessly.

"Look at that one, dear. Over there in the blue. Look at the six-pack on that."

"Never mind him, Edna, what about that blonde guy over there. He's gorgeous."

"What about that life-guard over there?"

"Ooh yes. He is hot."

"What I wouldn't give to be twenty-one again. I'd certainly give him one."

Edna laughed raucously and lay back on the beach, soaking up the sunshine. Today, she was wearing a pink silk onesie, with a large purple sash belt, and a matching bandana around her head. Huge shades were perched on her nose and her mouth was a vermillion slash. The bronzed surfers may be attracting our attention, but it was Edna who was creating the biggest splash. Out of nowhere, a photographer appeared and took her photograph.

"Sydney bloody Morning Herald," she muttered under her breath. "Gets everywhere." Raising her voice, she called out: "Darren, how are ya, mate?"

"I'm good Edna, who's the friend?"

"She's my new lesbian lover."

"Really?"

"No, of course bloody not, and if you print that you're dead. This is Abigail Aske, a famous writer from the United States of England, got that?"

"Great. Thanks. How are you spelling Aske?"

"Ask with an 'e'. Now bugger off."

"Cheers, Edna."

I tried to look international and enigmatic as he took one more photograph, before disappearing up the beach.

"Would you really like to be twenty-one again?" I asked Edna, as we settled back down to sunbathe.

"Hmm, would I want to be twenty-one again? Would I do anything differently if I were? What a question!"

"Would you?"

"Well, you know dear, my life is pretty darn perfect. There's nothing I would change. I have financial freedom. I make money out of doing what I love. I have a wonderful son who inspires me, amazing friends, and the best place on earth to live. Why would I want to go back and change anything?"

"You wouldn't want to go back and try the more conventional route of marriage and kids? Have a proper relationship? Share your life with someone?"

She grimaced. "No thank you, dear. I'm too much of a handful for any man to take on. I can't tell you how relieved I was when Frank's father went walkabout. He was stifling me. Far too needy. I couldn't breathe. It was difficult financially, but we got through. And once my paintings started selling, it was plain sailing. Bit different to the pathway your mother chose."

I thought about my mother. Middle-class and precise. Women's Institute on Tuesday, Bridge Club on Wednesday, lunch with friends on Thursday, hairdressers on Friday. Every week the same. Boring and predictable. There was no hint of the artist she'd once been.

"You said you and my mother had a wild time in the 60s?" I prompted.

Edna laughed. "Wild doesn't come into it, dear. We lived bohemia to the full. Drugs, lovers, psychedelia. And that was just an average day. We worked hard and played hard. You should have seen the works of art your mother produced. She was a big thinker. Great big canvasses. Wonderful abstracts."

"I thought you said she was a sculptor."

"Did I? Well, she did a bit of everything. Sculpting, painting, performance art."

"Performance art? What did she do?"

"She once shaved herself, painted her body green and planted herself, completely naked, in some earth in Piccadilly Circus. Some kind of deforestation protest."

"My mother? Are you sure?" By now I was beginning to doubt everything Edna said.

"She was great fun. She might have sold out to suburbia, but underneath I'm sure the creative spirit's still there."

Having seen the twin set and pearls and regularly permed hair, I wasn't so sure. But it was an interesting insight into my mother's past, even if it was mostly fiction.

"How about you, dear? Is there anything you'd do differently?"

"Choose men more wisely," I said before I could stop myself.

"Aha! Do I detect a love life that's not going to plan? Do tell. Only give me the edited version, dear. I have the attention span of a gnat when it comes to emotional matters."

I sighed. I'd decided not to tell Edna about Jake, but suddenly it all came spilling out. "I've made a bad choice, Edna. I've got involved with the wrong person. He was my boss. I met him at work. He and his wife had a baby but it drove a wedge between them and we ended up having an affair. I was getting over my sister's death and my best friend had left for Australia. I was on my own. He was kind and he understood. It started out as fun, then it got serious. When I found his wife was pregnant again, I told him he had to choose. Her or me. And he chose me. But guess what? He's still with her and the baby's due. That's why I came to Australia. To force his hand, make him see what life would be like if I wasn't there."

"Ugh, tricky!" said Edna, frowning. "Forcing someone's hand's never a good strategy, dear. In my limited experience, relationships need to come from the heart. They need to be spontaneous. They're not something you can manipulate."

I carried on. "He even proposed a couple of days ago, even though he's still married. I don't know what to think. One minute, I think he's a spineless waste of space, the next I miss him and want to be with him. I don't know what to do."

Edna gave the only advice she could think of.

"I think this calls for a drink, dear. Why don't we go and find a bar? I'm having withdrawal symptoms. Sorry, dear, I can't think clearly without a gin."

We sat in a bar overlooking Bondi Beach, each sipping a large gin and tonic. Edna was right. Gin made the world a far more manageable place.

"Do you have any advice, Edna?" I asked.

She sat back in her seat and looked into the distance, thinking deeply.

"Not really, dear. Being an agony aunt's not my thing."

"No moral judgement, then?" I asked.

"Moral judgement? Moi? I don't think so. I do know you can't stay in a relationship that's not right just because a baby comes along. I'm living proof of that. There again, can you handle the guilt of taking a man away from his family? Oh my God. What's happening to me? I'm turning into an agony aunt."

She pushed my drink towards me.

"Drink your gin, dear. It's getting cold." Her glass was empty and she gestured to the barman to bring another.

"It all sounds horribly complicated, dear. If I was you, I'd draw a line under it and start again. There are loads of gorgeous guys in Australia."

On cue, a voice sounded to my right.

"Abigail? What are you doing here?"

I turned around to find Melvyn standing at the bar. Solid, reliable, smiling Melvyn.

"OMG," I squeaked, flushing deep red. "Melvyn. What are you doing here?"

The world had suddenly become a very small place and I found myself babbling in a high-pitched voice. "Edna, this is Melvyn. I met him in Melbourne last week. Melvyn, this is Edna. I'm staying with her."

"Edna Corvaggio, if I'm not mistaken," said Melvyn. "I'm a big fan. I love your work."

"Well, thank you," said Edna, looking please. "Your friend has taste, Abigail. Would you like to join us, Melvyn?" She indicated an empty chair at our table.

"Unfortunately, I can't," he replied. " I'm taking my team out for lunch." He indicated a group of men and women, casually dressed, standing by the door. "There's a great fish restaurant here." He grinned. "This is the motivational lunch to soften them up before the hard work begins."

"You have a team?" I said, impressed.

"Yes. These are the Techie guys," he said, "hence the casual dress. There's a sales team as well."

"Wow. Sounds impressive."

Melvyn shrugged. "Not really. Just your standard set up." He frowned at me. "I thought you were going to call, Abigail?"

"I only got here yesterday," I explained. "Besides, I didn't think you'd want to see me again. Not after last time." I looked down, feeling my face go red.

He laughed. "Don't worry. All forgotten as far as I'm concerned."

"Sounds intriguing, dear. What did you do?" asked Edna.

I glanced at her and grimaced. "Got drunk and behaved badly."

"Ha!" exclaimed Edna. "A woman after my own heart!"

"It's not as bad as it sounds," said Melvyn kindly. He glanced at his watch. "Sorry, ladies, I have to go. We have a reservation in the restaurant. How about tomorrow evening, Abigail? Are you free?"

I looked at Edna, who shrugged. "Nothing planned, dear."

"I've been invited to a dinner party in Mosman, over on the North shore," explained Melvyn. "Old ex-pat friends of mine I haven't seen for ages. I'm supposed to take a guest. Why don't you come along?"

"Okay, sounds cool."

"I could meet you at Circular Quay around 7 and we'll get the ferry over. Stay over, if you like, there's plenty of room."

"Fab. That sounds great."

"Give me your number and I'll text you."

He quickly keyed my details into his phone, then leaned forward and lightly kissed my cheek.

"See you tomorrow."

"Okay. Bye."

"You're a dark horse," said Edna, after he'd gone. "You have men coming out of the woodwork, dear."

"Don't get too excited. He's hardly husband material. Besides, I've got to sort things out with Jake."

"Ah yes, Jake the snake." She gave me an arch look. "I have an idea. Why don't we go to Manley Beach tomorrow afternoon? It's beautiful there and there's a lovely little cake shop. Afterwards, we can get the ferry back to Circular Quay and you can meet up with Melvyn. How about it?"

"Sounds perfect," I said

Sydney was beginning to shape up much better than Melbourne.

CHAPTER 22

Of course, nothing is ever as perfect as it promises to be.

Earlier in the afternoon, Edna and I walked over to the ferry terminal at Circular Quay. I had my first glimpse of the Opera House, with its famous white beaks glinting in the sun. Soon we were on the ferry, sitting on the top deck. As we sailed across the bay, I turned back and saw the Opera House, Harbour Bridge and Sydney Tower all framed in one incredible picture. I couldn't resist it. I took a selfie with this amazing scene in the background. Then I posted it on my Facebook page, with the comment:

> *Having the most fab time in Sydney. Bondi Beach yesterday, Manley Beach today, dinner date tonight. Life doesn't get much better.'*

Eat your heart out, Jake. Us single girls knew how to live. We didn't need a man to see the world. We could do it ourselves. And have more fun into the bargain. I had two replies immediately. Miranda posted: "Go for it, girl!" and Edith wrote: "So jealous. It's cold and raining here. Wish I was with you."

Soon, Manley's rows of spruce trees came into view and we disembarked.

"Let's walk over to the Pacific Beach, dear," Edna said. "It's beautiful there."

She was dressed in a flowing, bright yellow and orange silk tunic, with orange harem pants, a yellow bandana on her head and enormous yellow-framed sunglasses. It was like walking alongside a flamboyant fruit. People kept stopping to stare as we walked down the main street, a wide pedestrian mall called the Corso, lined with cafes, restaurants and shops. Half way down, we called in to Edna's favourite coffee shop and sat outside devouring

'Manly-sized' cakes and drinking delicious coffee frappé. I wondered when the first photographer would show up.

"Hi, Edna, take your photo?" said a sleazy-looking bald-headed man, wearing a battered leather jacket and brandishing an enormous camera.

"Hello, Clive. Make it snappy. I've got company," instructed Edna.

We both posed and Clive clicked away. I was getting used to being a temporary celebrity.

"Who's your friend?" asked Clive, scribbling in a small black notebook.

"This is Abigail Aske, visiting from the UK. She's my secret love-child, recovering from rehab. Now, piss off, Clive."

Clive mock-saluted and melted into the crowds.

"Bloody paps," said Edna, but I could tell she loved it.

We carried on to the ocean beach. She was right. It was stunning. Rows of tall spruce trees along the esplanade gave it an expensive, exclusive feel. This was the kind of place I could live. For the next couple of hours, we lay on the beach and sunbathed, Edna revealing a startling yellow swimsuit beneath her outfit and causing as big a stir on the beach as she had on the Corso. At least three more photographers took our picture. She was polite to everyone, stringing them along with increasingly tall tales.

"This is Princess Abigail from Buckingham Palace in England. She's the Queen of England's niece. This is Abby Aske, the famous pop star from London, England, taking a break between concerts. This is my nurse, Miss Aske, she makes sure I'm taking my regular medication."

At 5 o'clock, Edna decided it was time to leave.

"Frank will be home by 6 and I need to get back for him. Do you want to come with me or will you be okay on your own, dear?"

"I'll be okay. I'm meeting Melvyn at Circular Quay. How difficult can that be?"

"All right, dear. Have a lovely time. I'll see you some time tomorrow. Don't do anything I wouldn't do." She winked and made her way back up the beach.

No sooner had she gone than a text message from Melvyn pinged onto my phone.

> *'Hi Abigail,*
> *Really sorry. Going to be delayed. Problem with software. Can you make your way to the dinner party and I'll meet you there? Get the ferry over to Taronga Zoo, and take the Mosman bus. The address is 2a Salisbury Street. Ask for Finola. I'll be there as soon as I can. Sorry again.*
> *Melvyn x*

I stared at the message. Great. Not only was I going to have to get there on my own, but meet people with names like Finola. I thought about not going, but the thought of spending an evening with Frank, listening to the Flying Scotsman, wasn't a great alternative.

I caught the ferry back to Circular Quay, took another to Taronga Zoo and then a bus to Mosman, just like Melvyn told me to, feeling quite the international traveller. It was just finding 2a Salisbury Street that proved difficult.

I arrived in Mosman and searched in vain for number 2a Salisbury Street. The afternoon that had started so well was rapidly going downhill. I found numbers 1, 2 and 3 and rang the doorbells but nobody answered. 2a didn't appear to exist and there was no one to ask. It was like a ghost town. If only Melvyn had been with me.

After half an hour of searching, getting increasingly hot and bothered, I finally realised 2a was an apartment within one of the larger houses. Feeling tired, sun burnt and grubby, and more than a little stupid, I pressed the doorbell. I was beginning to think the whole thing was a bad idea. I'd had no time to freshen up and I was still wearing my shorts and vest from the beach. I had no make-up on, my hair was tied up in a ponytail and my scalp felt itchy with sand. What had I been thinking of?

A tall, elegant, blonde-haired girl dressed casually but expensively, answered the door.

"Sorry, we don't buy anything on the doorstep," she said in a cut-glass British accent and went to close the door.

"I'm not selling anything, I'm here for the dinner party," I informed her.

She looked me up and down. "Are you sure?" she asked, looking puzzled.

"Yes, I'm Melvyn's guest. He said to ask for Finola. Is that you?"

"Yes, it is," she answered. She looked me up and down again, a hint of disapproval passing over her perfect features. "You'd better come in, I suppose. Where's Melvyn?"

"He's delayed. He'll be here as soon as he can. Do you have somewhere I can change? I've come straight from the beach."

I felt like a twelve-year old who'd been playing out all day. Finola wrinkled her nose as if I was a bad smell.

"How quaint, getting changed when you arrive at a dinner party. That's a new one on me. You can use the cloakroom down at the end of the corridor. Don't make a mess. I don't want sand everywhere."

I hated her on sight. An evening with Frank seemed suddenly preferable.

I located the bathroom and opened my bag, realising with horror I'd forgotten to pack my washbag containing everything I needed to look halfway decent. My make-up, hairbrush, mini-straighteners, cleanser, toner, face-cream and toothbrush were all back at Edna's. I looked in the mirror and saw a sunburnt, dishevelled hobo gazing back at me, hair like straw going in all directions. At least I hadn't forgotten to pack my red shift dress. I pulled it out of the beach bag, and saw with alarm that I'd mistakenly packed a red T-shirt instead. There was nothing for it. I would have to spend the entire evening in shorts and T-shirt, with no make-up, looking like a scarecrow. I splashed cold water on my face trying to cool my sunburnt cheeks, but it was no good, they shone out boldly, eclipsed only by my beacon-like nose.

The doorbell sounded and I heard noisy voices in the hall, even more upper class than Finola, if that was possible.

"Darling, wonderful to see you."

"Darling, you look divine."

"It's been simply too long. You look fabulous."

That decided it. There was no way I was attending a dinner party full of posh people. I would sneak out as soon as the coast was clear. I waited until they'd moved into the lounge and cautiously opened the cloakroom door. The coast was clear. Tip-toing to the front door, I quietly opened it, noticing it was dark outside. Too late I realised someone was standing there, waiting to come in.

"Abigail, what are you doing?"

It was Melvyn.

I jumped back, my mind working overtime.

"Oh, Melvyn. Hi! I was just looking to see where you were. And here you are. What a coincidence. Come in."

He looked at me curiously.

"Are you all right?"

"No, I'm not," I said, miserably. "I've forgotten my make-up bag, my hairbrush, my dress, everything I needed for tonight. Sorry, Melvyn, I can't go to a dinner party looking like this, not with all those fabulous people. I think it would be better if I left."

"You look lovely," he said kindly, planting a kiss on my cheek. "A little sunburnt, maybe. But what's wrong with the beach babe look? I refuse to let you leave. Come on. You can come in with me."

"Okay," I said reluctantly, wondering if I was going to regret my decision. "You go first. I'll follow."

Melvyn led the way down the hallway and opened a

door to the right. There was a shriek as he entered the room.

"Melvyn, darling! I didn't hear the doorbell. How did you get in?"

"Abigail let me in," he explained, standing to one side, so the assembled party could see me. I waved nervously, feeling like a fraud.

The scene that met my eyes was exactly as I knew it would be. Finola stood centre stage, willowy and gorgeous, with straight blonde hair that fell instantly into place as she turned her head. Two other Finola-clones stood alongside her, also blonde, willowy and gorgeous. They were all dressed in pale, clingy outfits that emphasised their perfect figures. Three men completed the party, each with fleshy, pink, well-fed faces. Like pigs, I thought.

Finola stepped forward to embrace Melvyn, who looked pleased to see her I couldn't but help notice. I felt horribly self-conscious, standing there, sandy and sweaty, in my beach attire.

"Let me introduce you, Melvyn," said Finola, taking his arm and ignoring me. "This is Juliana, who I think you've met, and this is Fenella. And here we have Rupert, Rochfort and Julian."

They all shook hands and embraced. I hung back, feeling like the adolescent daughter who'd gate-crashed her parents' party.

Melvyn turned to me. "This is Abigail, folks. She's visiting from the UK."

"Hi, everyone," I said, trying to smile and wishing I could disappear.

"Interesting choice of clothes, Abigail," said Finola. "I thought you were going to change?"

"It's the beach grunge look, Finola," said Fenella, looking at me with half-lidded eyes. "They featured it in Vogue last week."

"Oh, yah, I saw it, too," said Juliana, barely moving her lips. "Not sure I'd go for it myself."

"Well, I like it," said Julian, fixing his eyes on my bare legs. "I'm a thigh man myself. Can't beat a bit of flesh."

They all laughed, like a bunch of braying donkeys, and I looked at them aghast. It was like being dumped in the middle of a posh horror movie.

"Where are you from, Abigail?" asked Rupert, coming to stand by me, also fixated by my thighs. "London?"

"No, the Midlands," I said apologetically.

"Someone's got to live there, I suppose," said Fenella rudely. "Never been north of Watford, personally. My parents have a country house in the Home Counties and an apartment in London," she informed me. "I tend to flit between the two when I'm in the UK."

"What brings you to Sydders?" asked Rochfort, coming to stand by Julian and Rupert. He also spoke to my thighs.

"I'm visiting a friend," I started to say, then realised none of them were actually listening.

The women were intent on blanking me or putting me down, and the men seemed content to ogle my sunburnt flesh, like I was some kind of serving wench, up for a quick roll in the hay.

"Come on, everyone, let's sit down," said Finola. "The food's just about ready. Go through, please."

She indicated an adjoining open plan dining area, where a large round table was set for dinner. It was all very 'Homes & Garden', with a shag pile white carpet, glass table with tubular steel legs, Bose sound system, cream walls and large abstract paintings.

"Oh, you have an Edna Corvaggio," I said, as we sat down, noticing a large, brightly coloured picture of the Harbour Bridge.

"Yah, I love her work. I have another in the bedroom," said Finola. "Have you been to her gallery in The Rocks? I simply love it there. Some friends of mine have just commissioned her to do a study in purple for their new beach house."

"Isn't that the Simperly-Smythes?" asked Finella. "They're friends of my parents. Fab new house."

"I know Edna's gallery well. I'm staying with her," I informed Finola. "She's a friend of mine."

A lack of comprehension passed cross her features.

"Edna Corvaggio?" she asked incredulously. "But she's famous. How would you know her? You must be mistaken."

"She's a family friend. She went to art college with my mother in the 60s. In London," I couldn't resist adding.

"Oh, how charming." Finola looked like she'd swallowed a frog.

"That's where I've seen you before," declared Rochfort, triumphantly. "Front page of this morning's Herald. I thought you looked familiar. Anybody got a copy?"

I was amazed he'd even noticed my face given his interest in my thighs.

"Yes, in my briefcase," said Melvyn.

He went into the drawing room and came back with the paper.

There, on the front cover, was a picture of Edna and me, sunbathing at Bondi Beach.

"Sydney's favourite artist, Edna Corvaggio, takes in the rays at Bondi Beach accompanied by English writer, Abigail Aske," he read with satisfaction.

"Golly, we have a celebrity in our midst," said Juliana. "You're a writer. How frightfully exciting."

Finola looked daggers at me.

"Today's news, tomorrow's fish and chip paper," she said dismissively. "Melvyn, will you help me serve?"

She grabbed his hand and pulled him into the kitchen.

"So, tell me what you write, Abigail," demanded Juliana.

"Oh, this and that," I said vaguely, mentally throttling Edna.

By the time we'd reached the dessert course, I was heartily sick of my dinner party acquaintances. The men were inbred, self-opinionated knobs, with the sex appeal of a piece of wood, and that was doing wood a disservice. The women were affected, self-centred stick insects, and that was doing stick insects a disservice.

The first course had been revolting.

"Jellied eels," declared Finola. "Specially for you, Rochfort, I know they're your favourite."

"Oh, golly gum drops," he declared. "What a treat."

What a disaster, I thought, pushing the horrible rubbery things around on my plate. I tried eating one and nearly gagged. How could people eat stuff like this? I'd rather poke pins in my eyes. Things went from bad to worse with the main course.

Finola sent Melvyn out of the kitchen carrying a large earthenware dish. She followed, carrying the vegetable platter. It all smelled delicious and I felt my taste buds watering.

Until Finola told us what we'd be eating.

"It's an old recipe my grandmother used to serve. Brings back memories of childhood when father and grandpops used to go hunting in the woods," she told us proudly.

"Pheasant?" asked Julian hopefully.

"Boar?" suggested Rochfort, possibly referring to himself.

"No, sillies," said Finola. "It's lapin builli. Or as granny used to call it, Boiled Bunny."

At the mention of the word 'bunny', I started to feel a little queasy. Finola took the lid off the serving dish and there it was, steaming and bubbling, looking quite disgusting.

"Marvellous," said Julian. "You can't beat a decent bit of bunny. Brings out the colonial in me."

"Oh my God, it reminds me of being back on the estate," said Fenella. "Our cook used to do a marvellous rabbit dish. You clever old thing, Finola."

"Come on, dish out," said Rupert, rubbing his hands.

Finola dolloped a generous helping on to my plate, which I rapidly passed to Melvyn.

"Not too much for me. I'm not very hungry," I pleaded.

"Nonsense, once you've tasted it, you'll love it. You Northern girls always have big appetites," she said, passing me an equally large portion.

Northern girls? Big appetites? Where did she think I was from? There was definitely a class thing going on here.

I stared down at the grey sauce and stringy meat on my plate and could barely stop myself from heaving. The vegetables followed. Dauphinoise potatoes, bronzed aubergines and fresh garden peas. Despite my nausea, I persevered, my lower class upbringing dictating that I must be polite and finish my meal. The girls, I noticed, barely ate a thing. Their enthusiasm was all show, and they were clearly determined not to put on an extra ounce of weight.

It was the peas that were my downfall. As I tussled with the stringy rabbit meat, trying in vain to cut it, my knife slid over my plate with an ear-splitting sound, causing everyone to wince, and sending peas flying in all directions. I couldn't have done it more spectacularly if I'd tried. Some landed on plates, some skidded on to the floor, at least three landed in Finola's wineglass and the rest littered the table top.

My humiliation was complete. I was a working class upstart, without manners or social graces, clearly out of my depth in polite society.

Never had I wanted the ground to open up and swallow me as much as I did then. Rochfort, Rupert and Julian all thought my faux pas was a complete a hoot and fell about laughing.

"Wow, spectacular, Abigail. You've scored a goal in Finola's wine glass."

"Top hole, old girl."

"Bet you couldn't do that again if you tried."

"Don't encourage her," said Finola frostily, fishing the peas out of her wineglass.

"Sorry. I'm so sorry," I mumbled, trying to gather up the errant peas and flushing an even brighter red than my sunburn, if possible.

"It's all right," said Melvyn kindly. "I did the exact same thing at an important dinner last year. Even managed to lodge a pea in the CEO's top jacket pocket. How embarrassing was that?"

He smiled around the table and Finola's frostiness immediately thawed. She reached across and touched his hand.

"You're so funny, Melvyn. It really is good to see you."

"What is it you do, old chap?" asked Rupert. "Finola said something about computers."

Before he could answer, Finola butted in.

"Melvyn's very clever. He's Operations Director of this whizzy automotive software firm that's tremendously cutting edge and I believe is about to float on the stock market?" She looked to Melvyn for clarification and he nodded slightly. "He'll soon be worth a fortune. I take it the directors all have share options, Melvyn?"

He nodded again, looking totally embarrassed. This was obviously not something he wanted bandying about at the dinner table. "Plus, rumour has it, he's the new Australian CEO designate."

"As you said, Finola, it's nothing more than a rumour," said Melvyn firmly. "Now, can we drop the subject? The last thing I want to discuss over dinner is work. This is my time to relax."

He smiled encouragingly at Finola, who flushed slightly at her outspokenness.

"Of course, Melvy, I'm sorry. I'm just so proud of you, that's all," she said obsequiously, touching his hand. "I was only repeating what Bro told me."

"Bro?" I asked. "Who's that?"

"My brother, Edmund," laughed Finola, affectedly. "He and Melvy studied Computer Science together at Cambridge. He sends his regards, by the way, Melvyn." She dropped her voice conspiratorially and said to me: "Melvyn got a first, you know. He's absolutely brilliant."

A first at Cambridge, CEO designate, share options that would make him wealthy… I began to look at Melvyn with new eyes. Perhaps he wasn't quite the moon-faced nerd I'd thought. He certainly had Finola's attention and I was starting to get irritated by her over-familiarity. After all, I was his dinner guest, not her.

"So, that's how you know Melvyn, is it, through your brother?" I asked, keen to have all the facts. At least now I understood their unlikely friendship. Having met his parents, I knew they were classes apart.

"Yah, Eddie used to bring Melvy back for weekends to the country estate and we got friendly then. I haven't seen him for absolutely ages, which is why I was so delighted to hear he was coming to Sydders. Gives us a chance to rekindle, doesn't it Melvyn?"

She bestowed her sickly smile on him and although he responded, I was pleased to notice his eyes remained cold.

"What's your connection with Melvyn, Abigail?" she asked pointedly.

Before I could respond, Melvyn spoke: "Abigail is a family friend. She was a guest at my cousin Archie's wedding in Melbourne last week and it was only natural to meet up in Sydney."

I mentally thanked him for bigging me up. So long Finola. Sling your hook.

"But you'll be leaving soon, Abigail?" she asked hopefully.

"Yes," I admitted reluctantly. "I have a couple more days in Sydney, then I'm heading back to Melbourne and after that, the UK."

Finola looked triumphant and I began to feel tired.

It was hard work swimming up stream against so many undercurrents. The conversation meandered along and I lost myself in my wine glass, welcoming its anaesthetising effects until I remembered my last encounter with Melvyn. I stopped myself from drinking any more. I couldn't risk an action replay.

Dessert followed and I hardly dared hope for something edible.

"It's Spotted Dick with a twist!" declared Finola, giving me an unwelcome mental image.

"What's the twist?" asked Rupert.

"Wait and see," she answered.

I hardly dared look as she carried out the pudding on a silver platter. As I feared, she'd made it in the shape of male genitalia, causing much mirth and merriment around the table.

"Ho ho ho," laughed Rupert, holding his sides.

"Talk about rude food," said Rochfort, his eyes watering with laughter.

"Who's for a gonad?" shrieked Finola, causing a fresh wave of guffaws.

I tried to join in, but I couldn't. This was a meal from my worst nightmare, and the juvenile company was no better. I tried a mouthful, but given my dislike of currants, I could barely swallow, and given its shape, I found myself gagging all over again.

"Melvyn, could you help me with the coffees?" asked Finola, when the dessert course was over. She got up from the table.

"Sure, of course."

They went into the kitchen, and I made my excuses to go to the cloakroom. I couldn't stand any more of the nauseating company or food. I hurriedly splashed cold water on my burning cheeks, willing the disastrous evening to come to an end. Walking back down the hallway, I passed by the kitchen and wondering if I could help, I pushed open the door.

To my great surprise, I found Melvyn and Finola in a clinch. She was looking into his eyes, and his hands were on her shoulders. They were either about to kiss or had just been kissing.

For a second I stared, rooted to the spot.

"Sorry," I exclaimed, red-faced. "Thought you might need a hand with the coffee. Obviously not."

Melvyn looked at me with a startled expression and immediately pulled away from Finola. She turned to face me with a satisfactory smirk.

"Abigail," she exclaimed sweetly. "How kind of you. We were just about to come through, weren't we, Melvyn?"

He looked embarrassed and without saying a word, picked up the cafetiere and walked passed me, out of the kitchen. Now I really was confused and the questions came quick and fast. If Melvyn was interested in Finola, why had he invited me? And why did I feel jealous?

I somehow got through the rest of the evening, Finola darting self-satisfied glances at me whenever she could.

At last, the hideous party was over and everyone was saying goodbye. Finola reluctantly bid Melvyn and me goodnight and went off to bed.

"You can have the guest bedroom," he said to me.

"And you'll sleep with Finola?" I asked scornfully. "Don't mind me, Melvyn. I've been thoroughly humiliated tonight, a little more won't make any difference."

"I didn't mean that," he answered. "I meant I'd sleep on the sofa."

"Oh, I thought you and Finola…"

"Me and Finola nothing," he said firmly. "What you saw in the kitchen wasn't how it looked. She threw herself at me just as you opened the door. Nothing happened and nothing was going to happen. She's not right for me. I can't think why she's interested in me."

Because you're kind and decent and successful and dependable, unlike those other pretentious prigs, I longed to say, but didn't.

"Believe me," he continued, "you're worth a hundred Finolas. She's all skin and bone and Botox. Give me a beach babe any day."

"Really?"

"Really. Now, why don't you go and find the spare room. And if you like, I'll show you round Sydney tomorrow. I don't need to be in the office until lunchtime."

"Cool! That'd be great. See you in the morning."

"Good night, Abigail."

'Night, Melvyn." I closed the lounge door behind me and leant against the doorframe for a second, grinning widely. It was only a small victory but it was sweet.

Life was looking up once again.

CHAPTER 23

We arrived back at Circular Quay around 9.30am, having got up early, breakfasted and caught the 9am bus from Mosman. The kitchen was full of dishes from the night before, and we'd loaded the dishwasher and tidied up before Finola emerged. She clearly wasn't a morning person.

"Thank you," she said faintly, falling on to the sofa. "I probably won't revive until lunchtime. It's been wonderful to see you Melvyn. I hope I'm going to see more of you now you're in Sydney."

Once again, she ignored me. I didn't care. It had been a horrible evening and I didn't like her. All I wanted to do was escape with Melvyn and begin my tour of Sydney. I couldn't think of a nicer way to spend the day. Unless it was with Jake. The thought went through my head before I could stop it. I sighed. What was wrong with me? One minute I wanted him, the next I never wanted to see him again. I couldn't seem to make up my mind.

At Circular Quay, we went our separate ways. I went back to Edna's and Melvyn to his hotel. We both needed to freshen up and get a change of clothes. Within half an hour, I was back, watching the ferries arrive and depart and the buskers entertain the waiting queues. Melvyn was late, so I sat on a bench, eating an ice cream and enjoying the view. It wasn't every day you could sit facing Sydney Opera House with the Harbour Bridge behind you. I took a couple of pictures with my phone and posted them on Facebook, with the caption:

> *"On a guided tour of Sydney with a hunky man. Life just gets better!"*

I didn't know if Jake looked at my Facebook page, but I hoped he would. Then I thought about Melvyn reading my comment and was just about to remove it when he arrived.

"Hi Abigail, you look great." He planted a kiss on my cheek.

"Hopefully better than last night," I grinned. "See? I can scrub up when I try."

"You look great, scrubbed up or otherwise," he said diplomatically. "Now, where shall we go first?"

He'd changed into jeans and a sweatshirt, and I realised it was the first time I'd seen him without a suit. He looked different somehow. More cuddly. More relaxed. And he wore sunglasses rather than his usual black-rimmed glasses, which made him look trendy.

"I'm in your hands," I said. "I don't mind where we go. I just want to soak up the atmosphere."

"How about we take a walk past the Opera House into the Botanical Gardens," he suggested. "Then we could visit Darling Harbour."

"Sounds great. When d'you have to be back at work?"

"Good news," he beamed at me. "We're waiting for a part that's being flown over from Hong Kong. So I have until lunchtime tomorrow." He paused. "If you like, we could go to the Blue Mountains this afternoon. I can take a company car and borrow a tent if you fancy camping overnight."

"Fantastic," I said, a huge grin on my face. "Let's do the overnight trip. Blue Mountains here we come!"

Melvyn held out his arm. I slipped mine through his and we set off, just like a regular couple.

Three hours later, we sat in a restaurant at the top of Sydney Tower, enjoying smoked mozzarella Ciabattas with champagne. It was perfect. All of Sydney lay before us, the streets no bigger than small white strips and the tops of skyscrapers reaching upwards like stalks. Darling Harbour shimmered like rippling silk, the Festival Marketplace was a sprawling green snake and the suburbs beyond stretched endlessly into the hazy skyline.

We'd had a lovely morning, taking in the Opera House, walking round the beautiful Botanical Gardens and visiting Darling Harbour, the massive waterfront leisure park, with its shops, museums, craft centres and crowds. We were just about to order lunch at a pavement café, when Melvyn had a better idea.

"Let's have lunch up Sydney Tower," he said. "It's a clear day and we'll be able to see for miles. That'll be something to remember when you get back, the day you had lunch looking out over Sydney."

He was right. The view was amazing, the company was great and a glass of champagne provided the perfect finishing touch.

"This is fantastic, Melvyn," I said. "I'm having such a nice time. Thank you. It's all been so weird in Melbourne."

I told him about Rosalyn and Miranda and Ken, about my strange shed-room, Rosalyn's Fun Run when I first arrived, the lack of waterless shower, the aerobics class, the arguments, our trip to Port Fairy … It all sounded amusing when I told Melvyn and he was soon laughing.

"I'm sorry, I know I shouldn't," he said, "but you have to admit, you couldn't make it up."

I half thought about mentioning Jake, but decided it wasn't appropriate. Why spoil a beautiful day with my complicated love life? Today was one day I wouldn't think about Jake. No sooner had the thought gone through my head when my phone pinged. It was a message from Jake and I read it quickly.

> *Abigail, what's going on? Why aren't you returning my calls?*
> *Getting frantic. I miss you. Please call or text.*
> *Jake xxx.*

I turned off my phone. I didn't want Jake getting in the way of my perfect day.

"Just a sales message," I said to Melvyn. "Now, are we going to the Blue Mountains?"

We drove along the Great Western Highway, the air conditioning keeping us cool, Bruce Springsteen blasting from the speakers. The scenery flew past and after an hour or so, the Blue Mountains were in sight, blue and mysterious, stretching into the distance.

"Wow, what an amazing sight," I said. "Have you been here before, Melvyn?"

"Once," he answered. "I went camping with a couple of guys from work last year. It's pretty awesome, that's why I wanted to bring you here."

Another kilometre along the road and I spied a 'Car park & Picnic' sign.

"Why don't we pull in and check out the view?" I suggested.

He turned the car off the road and we crunched along a rough track, leading through the forest to a small picnic area. We stood by the car, admiring the picture postcard view. It was amazing. You could see for miles.

"We could take a walk," said Melvyn. "There's a pathway over there."

We scrabbled down the narrow mountain pathway until it led to a rocky outcrop that provided a natural viewing platform. The valley sides stretched before us like faded velvet, shadows and light creating different textures, the eucalyptus vapour creating a misty blue haze. It was completely silent and we stood in awe, transfixed by the beauty before us.

"Let's sit on the edge," suggested Melvyn, walking to the lip of the rocky platform and sliding his legs over.

"Careful, Melvyn, that's a sheer drop below," I said alarmed.

"It's all right. I'm not going to fall. Come and sit by me."

Nervously, I sat beside him and we dangled our legs over the edge. Hundreds of metres below us a waterfall fell on to a mass of rocks and boulders. Once I'd got over my fear, I felt strangely liberated.

"When you sit here looking at all this, it feels like anything is possible," I said. "If I was a bird, I'd take off and fly over the valley."

"Forget being a bird, I'd like to get one of those jet packs on my back," said Melvyn. "Can you imagine what it would feel like jumping off the edge?"

"I'd only do it if you were there to catch me," I laughed. "I'd be scared my jet pack wasn't working."

"Perhaps we'll try it one day, if you ever come back to Sydney," said Melvyn.

His words made me sad when I thought about flying back to Melbourne. This was probably the last time I'd see him. Then it would be home to England and Jake and a whole host of problems.

"I'll come back," I said determinedly, although whether it would be with Jake or not, I didn't know.

"If you think this is spectacular, wait till you see what's coming next," said Melvyn jumping up.

"What is it? Tell me."

He shook his head. "Wait and see. You won't be disappointed."

He was right. When we got to our destination, I was bowled over. We arrived just as the sun was setting, creating the most perfect lighting conditions you could wish for. It was a photographer's dream. From our viewing platform at Echo Point, we looked across the Jamison Valley to the rocky peaks known as The Three Sisters. As they caught the setting sun, they shone and dazzled, their rocky crags illuminated with golden light, made all the more brilliant by the sombre colours surrounding them.

"What d'you think?" asked Melvyn.

"Awesome. The most beautiful scenery I've ever seen. The light is amazing."

As we watched, the colours changed. The sky became darker and the rocks brighter. Gradually, the picture changed from golden brilliance to dark eeriness as the sun disappeared behind the mountains and the shadows fell. Only a dim after-glow remained, silhouetting the gum trees in front of us. For a moment, we were silent, absorbing the sight before us. Then Melvyn spoke.

"Better make a move, I suppose. We have camp to set up."

It was getting cold and I shivered, not relishing the thought of spending a night under canvas.

"Yeah," I said unenthusiastically. "Where do you suggest we go?"

"Back to the picnic area? At least there are loos there."

"Okay. Let's go."

We found a secluded area beneath the trees and Melvyn unpacked the tent and sleeping bags. It was one of those tiny pop-up tents and took all of five minutes to put up. Melvyn pinned it down with small silver pegs. Inside, it was compact and cosy, and I wondered whether I was doing the right thing. I didn't really know Melvyn. What if he was a secret sex fiend? I looked at him busy checking the guy ropes and suppressed a smile. The thought was just too ridiculous. He was kind and cuddly and completely trustworthy. The complete opposite of Jake…

I pushed thoughts of Jake firmly from my mind. He wasn't here. He was back in England with his pregnant wife. He still hadn't sorted out his situation, so what did the future hold for us? It wasn't looking too good from where I stood. Melvyn might not be my dream man, but he was a good friend and I liked him. And he certainly wasn't the moon-faced geek his mother and father had made him out to be.

"Was that true about you being CEO designate?" I asked him, as he put the mallet back into the car boot.

"Do we have to talk about that now, Abigail? I want to forget the office for a while."

"No. I just wondered, that's all. Your Mum and Dad said you were a computer geek, but you're not, are you?"

He laughed. "A computer geek, eh? You can always rely on parents to bring you down to earth. I suppose I was a computer geek once. When I studied computer science at uni."

"At Cambridge," I prompted.

"Yes."

"And you got a first?"

"Yes."

"So, you're pretty clever?"

"In certain areas, yes."

"And what did you do after Cambridge?"

"What is this? A job interview? Why all the questions?"

"I just want to know who I'm spending the night with, that's all."

"Okay. To satisfy your curiosity, I did a PhD after my degree, then an MBA in Business Studies at the London Business School. I was a perpetual student till I was twenty-five."

"And then you joined your present company?"

"Yes. I started in the London headquarters, moved to the Midlands satellite office, and was seconded to Melbourne to set up an office. Now I'm doing the same in Sydney, which brings you right up to date."

"And you're about to become the Australian CEO," I persisted.

"It's a possibility. I don't know. I may go back to London at the end of the year. Now can we leave my career alone, please?"

"Okay."

"You do realise, I know hardly anything about you, either."

"There's not much to know. But ask me anything. I have nothing to hide."

Except Jake, said the voice in my head, and you really don't want to tell Melvyn about Jake. He will not be impressed.

"Tell you what," I said, pulling on my jacket. "Let's go and find a beer and a bite to eat. Then you can ask me anything you like."

"Okay, deal."

We drove into Katoomba, the main town in the Blue Mountains, and found a quaint little café on the main street.

Soon we were enjoying a beer and eating a delicious meal of Dover sole, spring vegetables and new potatoes. I had to admit, everything with Melvyn seemed so easy.

"Ask away," I instructed him. "What would you like to know?"

"Okay. How about brothers and sisters?"

I fell silent for a moment. This was a tricky area.

"I had a sister," I said slowly. "Gracie. She died a couple of years ago. She was two years older than me. I miss her terribly."

"I'm sorry, I didn't realise. If it's any consolation, I do know what it feels like. I lost my younger brother."

"You did?" I asked, surprised. "What happened?"

"We went swimming in the sea at Padstow on a family holiday. He got into difficulty and I couldn't save him. He died of hyperthermia in the rescue helicopter on the way to hospital. He was ten and I was twelve. I've beat myself up about it ever since, wondering if there was anything I could have done differently. How about you?"

"My sister was two years older than me. She was my closest friend. She drove on to the M6 motorway to visit a friend in Birmingham and never arrived. A truck ploughed into her. She was killed instantly. The driver had twice the legal limit of alcohol in his blood. But he came from Turkey, so prosecution was difficult." I smiled at Melvyn sadly. "Life sucks sometimes, doesn't it?"

He put his hand over mine.

"Yep, it does. But we can't turn back the clock. You have to keep living your life, Abigail. I'm sure that's what Gracie would have wanted."

"I feel so angry," I admitted. "How could one lorry driver inflict so much pain and get away scot-free? That man will never know the lives he's devastated. It seems all wrong."

"I know," said Melvyn softly. "That anger you speak of, I directed it at myself. How could I let my little brother get into difficulties? Why couldn't I save him? What kind of a person did that make me? You have to learn to live with it. There are no answers, not satisfactory ones anyway. Life is cruel and unkind, and some people are unlucky. You have to focus on what you have, while never forgetting what you don't have."

I smiled and raised my glass: "Here's to focusing on what we have. Cheers, Melvyn."

He raised his glass: "To what we have. Now, tell me, why are you visiting Australia on your own? Isn't there a boyfriend in the background?"

"Sort of," I replied. "I was seeing someone, but I don't know if it's going anywhere. I thought a break would do us good."

"And is it?"

"I don't know, Melvyn. I don't know how I feel. D'you know what? I don't want to think about him right now. I just want to enjoy the evening."

"Okay, sounds good." He raised his glass. "Here's to spending the night in a small tent, freezing our asses off."

I raised my glass. "I hope those sleeping bags are warm."

They weren't. After an hour of lying in the tent, I was freezing. I'd kept all my clothes on, with extra socks, a jumper I'd borrowed from Melvyn, plus my coat and two blankets thrown over the sleeping bag and I still couldn't get warm.

"Melvyn," I whispered. "Are you awake?"

"Yes,' he whispered back.

"I'm freezing."

"So am I? Whose great idea was it to camp overnight?"

"Yours."

"Oh, yes. Move closer to me and I'll try to keep you warm."

I wriggled my sleeping bag closer to his and he put his arm round me.

"Is that any better?"

"Yes, but isn't your arm getting cold?"

"I'm made of strong stuff."

"You're a real cave man."

"Thank you."

Gradually, I began to get warm and was just dozing off, when I heard a snuffling, snorting noise outside the tent.

"What's that?" I said in alarm.

"I don't know. Maybe it's wild pig."

"Do they get wild pigs round here?"

"I don't know."

Whatever it was moved round the tent and began sniffing and scrabbling at the entrance.

"Oh my God, it's trying to get in."

"Don't worry, it's all zipped up."

"What if it's got claws and teeth? You read stories about mountain lions and bears slashing open tents and eating the occupants. What if it's a Razorback?"

"Then we're buggered."

There was silence for a moment.

"I think it's gone," I said nervously, but I spoke too soon. There was a scurrying and rustling right by my head.

I screamed and squeezed myself as close to Melvyn as I could.

"D'you want me to go outside and have a look?" he asked, tightening his arm around me.

"No. Stay here."

"Good, I was hoping you'd say that."

"If it eats you, I'll be left on my own."

"Oh, I see. It's not my safety you're concerned about."

"Sorry. It's every man for himself when you're under attack from a wild animal."

Whatever it was outside snorted and Melvyn pulled me even closer.

"If we die, we die together. Okay?"

"Okay," I started to say, and then his lips were upon mine and we were kissing.

Whether it was the fact we were in a tent in the wilderness and nothing seemed quite real, or whether it was because we were in danger of imminent death, Melvyn's kiss was intense and electrifying. And I couldn't help but respond. It was like no other kiss I'd ever experienced. I surrendered to the moment, vaguely thinking if this was the end, at least I'd go out on a high. But nothing happened and it was silent outside. Unable to find food, the animal seemed to have gone. Melvyn broke away.

"Sorry, Abigail, I don't know what came over me. That's not the way I usually behave."

I smiled to myself in the darkness.

"It's okay. I enjoyed it. We were making the most out of our last few seconds on earth."

"Except they weren't…"

"No, but we didn't know that."

"No."

"Shall we go to sleep now?"

"Okay."

And then I did sleep, curled up in Melvyn's arms, feeling warm and alive and wonderful.

We awoke in the morning to a glorious sunrise. I peered out of the tent, inhaling the fresh dewy smell of the forest. Melvyn rubbed his eyes.

"What time is?"

I looked at my watch. "6.30."

"Jesus. No chance of a lie in."

"No chance. Come out here and smell the air. It makes you feel glad to be alive."

"I'm already glad to be alive. Especially after last night," he paused. "About last night, Abigail…."

"Last night was great, Melvyn. Please don't apologise."

"I wasn't going to. I was going to say, if it doesn't work out with your boyfriend, I'm first in the queue, okay?"

I laughed. "Oh, okay. Can I think about it?"

"Be my guest. D'you need a reminder of how good it was?"

I threw a shoe at him.

"Melvyn! You're incorrigible. No, I don't. Morning breath and all that. It might not be as good as it was last night."

"So, it was good?"

"Yes, you know it was. Can we leave it at that for now?"

"You can't blame a bloke for trying…"

"No, I can't. But you know what? I'm starving. I need some breakfast. If I don't eat, I'll be like a bear with a sore head. And you don't want another wild animal round here."

"Oh, I don't know," he said and grinned.

We packed up camp and drove until we found a roadside diner. Melvyn bought us both a full cooked breakfast and we ate with relish. All that mountain air had given us a hearty appetite.

"When d'you fly back to Melbourne?" he asked.

"In two days time," I answered. "Then it's back to the mad house."

"Do you want to meet up again before you go?"

"Sure."

"How about dinner tomorrow night? There's a

fabulous seafood restaurant overlooking the harbour. Michelin starred. How about it?"

"Michelin starred, eh? How can a girl refuse? But don't you need to book months in advance?"

"Let's just say, our company has an arrangement. It won't be a problem."

"Melvyn, you are a man of surprises. There was me thinking you were this real computer geek and you're about as far removed from that as you could be."

"Which all goes to show…"

"What?"

"Don't believe everything you hear when you meet an elderly couple on a plane."

"No, you're not quite as desperate as they made out."

He groaned. "Daphne and Reggie strike again. Instead of focusing on what I've achieved, all they can see is my failure to get married."

"You and me both, Melvyn. I get exactly the same from my parents."

"So, what's stopping you, Abigail? Why don't you get married to your boyfriend? I don't mean to be rude, but your biological clock is ticking away."

"Melvyn!" I said, indignantly. "You don't pull any punches, do you?"

"Sorry, but it's true, isn't it?"

"I suppose so. Look, it's difficult with Jake. I don't want to go into details."

"Jake."

"Yes, that's his name. I won't know what's going on till I get back home."

"It sounds mysterious."

"Melvyn, can we drop the subject? I don't want to talk about it."

"Okay, but I really like you, Abigail. I know you have somebody else, and I know we'll soon be continents apart, but who knows? I may be back in London some day."

I smiled and put my hand over his.

"I really like you too, Melvyn, but at the moment I can't offer much except friendship. I couldn't be unfaithful to Jake."

He smiled ruefully. "Oh, the old friendship card. I should have seen that coming."

"Let's not get heavy. I hope I haven't led you on. I never meant to."

"You can't blame me for asking, can you?"

"No."

"And it's not over till the fat lady sings. Or in my case, the fat man."

"Melvyn…."

"So, we'll just stay friends for now?"

"Okay. Does this mean dinner is still on?"

He grinned. "You betcha. It's not every day I can walk into the company restaurant with Sydney's best looking woman on my arm. I have my street cred to think about."

I got back to Edna's around 11am. She greeted me with a big hug and an anxious look.

"How was camping?"

"Great. Apart from freezing our asses off and being attacked by a wild animal."

"That's no way to speak of Melvyn."

"Ha ha."

"Have you checked your messages?"

"No, I had no signal. Why?"

"I think you might find a few messages from Jake."

"How do you know?"

"He's been on the phone. Lord knows how he got this number." She paused, "I might as well tell you. He's left Tiffany. And he's catching the next plane to Melbourne."

CHAPTER 24

I stared at Edna, gawping like an idiot.

"What?"

"You heard. Jake said to tell you he's left Tiffany and he's catching the next plane to Melbourne. Apparently, he's been trying to contact you but you weren't responding. So, hoorah! Party time, eh?" she beamed at me. "It's what you wanted, isn't it?"

I didn't feel much like partying.

"Oh, Edna, what have I done?" I stared at her in horror. "I don't know what I want. I'd half convinced myself it was a terrible thing he was about to do, abandoning his family and all that. I thought nothing would have changed when I got back. And now he's on his way here."

"But I thought that's why you came to Oz in the first place?" asked Edna. "To force his hand. Or am I missing something? Something called Melvyn, for example?"

"I don't know. I like Melvyn, but I don't think I'm interested in him. Anyway, it's academic now. I have to get back to Melbourne. When's he arriving?"

Edna shrugged her shoulders. "I don't know. Why don't you check your cell phone? Or better still, give him a call?"

When I checked, I found a dozen messages from Jake, each more anxious than the last.

Abby, why don't you return my messages? What's going on?

Abby, have you met someone else? Is that why you're not responding? I need to know.

Getting worried now. Please text or call me, any time of day or night. I don't mind.

Saw your post on Facebook. What's going on?

OK. I've told tiffany I'm leaving. I know you're spending the last few days in Melbourne. I'll fly out to join you there.'

Still no response? Please text or call. Arriving in Melbourne Friday. ETA 2pm. See you then.

"What day is it?" I asked Edna.

"Thursday. Why?"

"Oh, my God, he's arriving tomorrow. I have to call the airport. Get a flight back to Melbourne. And cancel dinner with Melvyn."

Within half an hour, I'd booked flight to Melbourne that afternoon, texted Rosalyn and Miranda to let them know my plans and spoken to Melvyn. The last bit had been the hardest.

"Hi Melvyn, it's Abigail."

"Hi, how are you doing?" He sounded pleased to hear from me.

"I'm fine. Something's come up. I can't make dinner tomorrow night."

"Okay, no problem. How about tonight? Or the day after? I could juggle things around."

"I can't. Sorry. I'm flying back to Melbourne this afternoon."

"I see. Is everything all right?"

"No. Yes. Yes, everything's fine. I just need to get back to Melbourne."

"Is the prospect of dinner with me so terrible?"

"Yes. No. Sorry, Melvyn, I just need to go."

"So this is goodbye?"

"I'm afraid it is. Sorry."

"I'm sorry, too, Abigail. I don't know what's changed."

"Nothing's changed. I'll message you when I get

back."

"Okay, you do that. Look, I have to go. I'm in a meeting. Goodbye, Abigail."

I couldn't but help notice the frosty tone in his voice, but there was nothing I could do. Melvyn was the least of my problems. I had a newly available Jake to contend with.

I tried calling him, but his phone went to voice mail, so I texted him:

> *Got your message. Can't believe you've actually done it. Hope Tiffany is okay. Will meet you Friday 2pm at airport. Abby xxx.*

I said a fond farewell to Frank, who came back from work just I was packing.

"Sorry, I've got to go, Frank."

He looked at me with sad, puppy dog eyes.

I'm going to miss you, Abigail. I really like you. I've done some pictures for you."

He presented me with two pictures. The first showed me sitting in Stanley's café looking sad. The second showed me arm in arm with Melvyn at Circular Quay. I looked happy.

"Frank, were you watching me at Circular Quay?"

He went pink and looked at the floor. "I was picking up rubbish and I saw you. I saw that man, too. You looked happy with him, Abigail."

I smiled at him wryly, not sure what to think.

That's Melvyn," I said. "You're right. He does make me happy. Thank you, Frank. I'll treasure them."

I kissed him on the cheek and he went even brighter pink. "I won't forget you, Frank, you're a very special man."

"I've ordered a cab for you, dear," said Edna. "Sorry I can't come. I have a radio interview this afternoon. But here's a little something to remember us by."

It was a small, rolled up canvas. I opened it to find an abstract version, in various shades of purple and pink, of

Edna and Frank staring back at me."

"Wow, an Edna Corvaggio original. It'll be worth a fortune on eBay."

She laughed.

"Touché, Abigail. We'll make an Aussie out of you yet. Now, why don't you bugger off back to Melbourne and get your love life sorted out."

CHAPTER 25

I caught a plane later that afternoon and arrived back at Acacia Avenue early evening.

"Darling, how are you?" exclaimed Miranda as I walked in to the kitchen, pulling my suitcase behind me.

"All the better for seeing you," I replied, giving her a hug. "What's new?"

She wrinkled her face.

"Rosalyn is behaving very weirdly, rushing in and out, taking phone calls, being very secretive. She won't tell me anything, but she's more wired than an H-bomb, if that's possible. I bet you haven't heard from her, have you?"

"Not a word. Where is she?"

"Double aerobics class, won't be back for another hour."

"And Ken?"

Miranda looked at me conspiratorially. "Ken is another story. He's met someone. You're not going to believe this."

"Go on…"

"It's only the gay bloke from across the street. All this time, he's been playing the field and what happens? He finds love over the road."

"So, what happened? Tell me."

"Well, the guy comes across looking for his cat. Apparently, it's some kind of rare breed and it got out. Then, I'm telling you, it was like the movies. Ken goes to answer the front door, their eyes meet and bob's your uncle. They've been inseparable ever since. It's been three days now. He's practically moved in. We've hardly seen him. And what's even more amazing, this guy is a botanist. Works at the Royal Botanical Gardens. I mean, Ken doesn't know a buttercup from a daisy, so heaven knows what they talk about."

"I don't suppose there's a lot of talking going on at

the moment," I said.

"Well, that's what's so odd," said Miranda. "I was invited over for afternoon tea yesterday afternoon. I couldn't believe it. They're like an old married couple. Ken serving tea and cake. And then Stacey - I mean, Stacey - what a name, asks me if I'd like to see his orchid collection. Takes me into the back garden where he's got all these mini hothouses, and shows me the most fabulous collection of rare orchids I've ever seen. Well, the only collection of rare orchids I've seen. Calls them his babies. I tell you, Ken is absolutely smitten."

I stared at her speechless. "Wow. How amazing."

"Why don't we go over later? They're having a housewarming party, which I think means that Ken's moving in. You have to see it, Abigail. I can't believe he's turned his life around in just three days." She paused. "Anyway, more to the point, what's going on with you? What happened in Sydney? And why are you back early?"

When I told her the news about Jake, Miranda whooped.

"Wow! Whaddaya know? You mean he's actually gone and done it? He's told the witch he's leaving?"

"The thing is, I don't regard her as the witch anymore," I admitted. "I don't know if it's what I want."

"No way." Miranda looked at me incredulously. "I thought the whole reason you came over here was to force his hand."

"It was. But now I don't know. I mean, making a man leave his children is bad enough, but leaving a new baby, well, one that's not even born yet, it just doesn't seem right."

"You've changed your tune. What's happened? Oh, wait a minute. Something's occurred in Sydney. Tell!"

"There's nothing to tell. It was ever since I held that baby at your cousin's wedding, I've been feeling bad about things. I didn't know what to say to him, especially after he made that ridiculous proposal of marriage, so I didn't respond to his messages or phone calls. Next thing I know, he says he's left Tiffany. And he's on his way here."

"Whoa! Run that last bit by me again."

"Jake's on his way to Melbourne. His plane lands at 2pm tomorrow."

"Oh my God. Jake's coming here? This guy is serious. Abigail, he must really love you. Not only does he leave his pregnant wife for you, but he flies to the other side of the world for you. How romantic is that?"

I looked at her. "Very. I suppose."

"You don't look too excited. Please don't tell me you've changed your mind."

"I don't know. This is all so unexpected. I was supposed to be having dinner with Melvyn tomorrow night and I was really looking forward to it. And now Jake's arriving imminently and I've had to come back."

"Sorry…..? Rewind again. You were supposed to be having dinner with Melvyn. That's the fat guy from my cousin's wedding, right?"

"Yes. And he's not fat. He's cuddly. We went camping in the Blue Mountains and it was really nice. Made me realise how different life could be with an uncomplicated guy. Mind you, I told him I could only offer him friendship."

Miranda raised her eyebrows.

I grimaced. "Oh Miranda, I don't know what I want. Jake is the hottest guy I know, but it's so complicated with him. Nothing is easy and he's got all this baggage. Melvyn is smart and successful and easy to be with, and we get on really well."

I sighed. "I have until 2pm tomorrow to work out what I'm going to say to Jake. And at the moment, I haven't a clue."

"Probably not a good idea to bring him here, not with Miss Goody Two Shoes being all weird and all," said Miranda.

"No, I guess he'll check into a hotel. But what am I

going to say to him and what I am going to do with him?"

"You really want me to answer that? Hey, why don't you take him on my city tour of Melbourne? Buy yourself some time."

"Hm, I could do. There again, it would just be putting off the inevitable. I'll see how I feel."

"I have a tour leaving Flinders Street at 3.30. It's just a thought."

Later on that evening, when Rosalyn was back from her aerobics class, we went over the road to Ken and Stacey's party. Rosalyn seemed distant. She'd greeted me with a cursory "Hi, Abigail, how was Sydney?" as if I'd just popped out for a couple of hours, and had barely listened to my reply. She clearly wasn't interested, and when I'd followed her into her bedroom to ask if everything was okay, she'd been very short with me.

"Of course everything's okay. Why wouldn't it be? The guy I like won't commit to me, my modelling career has died a death, I have an apartment I can't afford to live in and I haven't heard from Stuart in over a week. Life's never been better."

She'd looked so miserable, I didn't have the heart to tell her about Jake. That would have been like rubbing salt in the wound.

"Why don't you come over the road to Ken and Stacey's housewarming party?" I'd suggested. "Miranda and I are going. It might be a laugh."

She'd reluctantly agreed to come along, and so at 10pm the three of us stood on the doorstep of 28 Acacia Avenue, ringing the doorbell.

Ken greeted us with a shriek.

"Girlies! Great to see you! Air kisses all round…mwaw, mwaw, mwaw… Abigail, you're back! How are you? How was Sydney? You won't believe what's been happening to me since you've been gone…. I've only gone and met the love of my life…. Would you believe it?

Come and meet Stacey, Abigail…"

We followed him into the house, where high-energy music was blasting from the speakers. Everywhere I looked, there were dancing bodies, smooching couples and people engaged in earnest conversation. Mostly all men, I noticed, although here and there I saw the odd heterosexual couple.

"Relax, don't do it, when you wanna go to it…" sang Ken, dancing ahead of us and pushing through the gyrating bodies.

"He's as high as a kite," said Miranda. "I bet he's been on poppers. Quite the party animal when he gets going is our Ken."

"There's Stacey in the kitchen," he shouted over the music. "Come and meet him."

I looked into the kitchen, where a tall, muscle-bound man with spikey blond hair, wearing a white vest and tight jeans, was drinking a beer.

"I might have guessed he'd go for a blonde god," I whispered in Miranda's ear. "He's hot. Shame he's gay."

"That's not Stacey," laughed Miranda. "That's Mark, a complete tart by all accounts. That's Stacey behind him."

I looked in surprise at the small, dark-haired, bespectacled man she indicated.

"Abigail, meet Stacey," shrieked Ken, pulling me forward. "Stacey, this is Abigail. You've already met Miranda and Rosalyn…"

"Pleased to meet you, Abigail," said Stacey, stepping forward and kissing my cheek. "Miranda…. Rosalyn…. great to see you."

I stared in amazement. This was not what I'd expected. Stacey looked staid and bookish, not at all the blonde bombshell I'd assumed was Ken's type.

"Pleased to meet you, too," I said, shaking his hand.

"Are you ladies okay for drinks?" asked Stacey. "Ken, why don't you do the honours? I hear you've just been up to Sydney, Abigail. That's my neck of the woods. How did you find it?"

"I loved it," I admitted. "I saw all the sights… Bondi, Manley, the Blue Mountains, Sydney Tower, The Rocks. It's a fabulous city. But I love Melbourne as well," I added diplomatically. "They're just so different. I couldn't choose between them."

"Go on admit it, Stace, your heart's in Melbourne now you've met me," said Ken, putting his arm round Stacey's shoulder.

"Of course it is," said Stacey, shyly, giving Ken a peck on the cheek.

"Yuk, save the canoodling for later, please," said Rosalyn in a prim voice. "There are certain things we don't want to see."

"Just 'cos your own love life's a mess, Rozzie-Wozzie," said Ken, in a camp voice, "doesn't mean other people can't be happy."

"Okay, children, break it up," said Miranda. "Come on, Ken, get us some wine. And Stacey, I wondered if Abigail could see your amazing blooms?"

"I take it you mean the orchids?" asked Stacey. "You haven't told them about the cannabis plants, have you Ken?"

I wasn't sure whether he was being serious, or if this was another Aussie wind up. Ken just smirked.

"I meant the orchids," said Miranda. "I'll pretend I didn't hear about the cannabis, although next time I need some blow, I'll know where to come."

"Depends what kind of blow you're talking about," returned Ken, in his best camp voice.

"Let's not go there, Ken, please," said Miranda.

"He's terrible, isn't he?" said Stacey grinning, like the cat that's got the cream.

"So, can I see the orchids?" I asked.

"Follow me," said Stacey.

He led the way out of the kitchen into the back garden. In the darkness I could just make out shrubs, plants and flowers growing in abundance. We followed Stacey to a greenhouse that stood to one side. He opened the door and flicked on a light switch, flooding the darkness with bright fluorescent light.

"In here," he said. "Once you're in, shut the door behind you. I don't like to disturb the temperature too much."

Miranda, Rosalyn and I crowded in behind Stacey and I gasped in amazement. The entire greenhouse was full of exotic purple and white flowers.

"These are my orchids," said Stacey proudly, as if introducing his offspring.

"They're beautiful," I said.

"Incredible," echoed Miranda.

"Amazing," said Rosalyn.

We stood, mesmerised by the abundance of exotic flowers that sprung from every shelf, flowerbed and pot. There must have been over a hundred, nestling mysteriously and silently in the white glow of the light.

"How long have you been growing them?" I asked Stacey.

"About five years," he said.

"If it's not a silly question," asked Rosalyn, "what do you do with them?"

"I display them at flower shows, I supply a couple of florists in Melbourne, and sometimes I do displays for theatres or art centres. Other than that, I just enjoy them."

"They are stunning," I said. "I've never seen anything like it. Just think Miranda, all this has been over the road and you never knew it."

"Ken's words exactly," she said, grinning. "He can't believe his luck."

We spent the next couple of hours dancing, drinking and having fun. The music, the energy and the atmosphere were fantastic, and for a short time I forgot my dilemma. Then it was 2 o'clock in the morning and we were staggering across the road, back to number 25.

I fell into my uncomfortable bed, glad to rest my bones, suddenly feeling very tired and thinking with dread about Jake's impending arrival. I checked my phone and sure enough there was a message from him:

> *Abs, can't wait to see you and hold you in my arms. My future.*
> *Not long now. I love you.*
> *Jake. xxx*

I didn't reply, just turned off my phone and stared into the darkness, thinking back to the evening when it had all become serious, when I'd stood at the crossroads and taken a wrong turn.

CHAPTER 26

It was a cold November evening, clear and frosty, and Jake had come round to my apartment after work for a little early evening relaxation. I tried to pull him towards me, longing to feel the warmth of his body against mine but he drew away.

"What's the matter?" I asked.

"There's something I have to tell you." He took a deep breath, paused, went a funny colour and exhaled loudly. "Tiffany's pregnant again."

The room turned upside down then righted itself.

I looked down at my knees. "I think you'd better go," I said in a tight voice.

"Are you okay?" he asked stupidly.

"What do you think?" I spat at him. "Just get out. I never want to see you again."

Tears filled his big brown eyes and he sat with his head in his hands, looking like a collapsed string puppet, folded up and lifeless.

"I can't go. Not just like that. I can't leave you."

"I thought you said you didn't have sex with Tiffany any more."

"It only happened once. The night we went on holiday. We both got drunk and it just sort of happened."

"And now she's just sort of pregnant."

"It's not like that."

"What do you mean 'it's not like that'? What is it like? There's only one way of getting pregnant to my knowledge. Do I have to spell it out? For heaven's sake, you've already been through it once. You told me you weren't going to have any more kids. How far gone is she?"

"Three months," he said miserably.

"Three months! Oh my God, it was three months ago when Helen in Accounts said she'd heard you talking about having another one. I told her she was wrong."

"I may have mentioned it. I didn't mean it."

"You planned it all, didn't you? At least have the decency to face up to it. You were probably at it the whole time on holiday. I feel sick."

"If you're going to be like that then there's no point talking," he retorted defensively.

"Three months," I repeated. "Three months. You've known for three months and yet you let us carry on, getting in deeper and deeper, knowing what you did."

"I didn't know three months ago. I didn't know until later."

"When did you know?"

"About a month and a half ago."

"That's just as bad. You knew mid September. You knew then and you didn't tell me. You let me carry on believing everything was wonderful, yet all the time you knew she was pregnant. She planned it, of course. You realise that. It's the one way she has of making sure you stay with her. My God, you must be stupid. She knows exactly what she's doing. Well, I hope it makes you totally miserable."

"I didn't think it would matter," Jake muttered.

His face looked grey, as if he'd been cast in concrete. I wished he had.

"You didn't think it would matter?" I said incredulously. "What are you talking about?"

"Well, you know, I have a child already. I didn't think another one would make any difference."

"Jake, what kind of person do you think I am? I thought the physical side was all over between you and Tiffany. You said there was very little left between you. I even remember you saying 'What's the point of going home? There's fuck all for me there.' Well, soon there's going to be another baby waiting for you at home - that's what'll be there for you. A baby. I can't believe how stupid I've been. Just get out."

"What? Just go?"

"Yes, get out. Leave me alone. I think you've done enough damage for one evening."

"I don't want to go. I don't want to leave you." Jake choked back the tears. He was very good at crying.

"Jake, you've hurt me more than you'll ever know. I think you'd better leave."

I led the way to the front door and opened it. He walked out without looking at me, emitting misery waves of seismic proportion.

"D'you know, Jake, in all this time, you've never once told me what you feel for me," I had to get the last word in. "I really don't know."

"D'you want to know?" he stared at me, wiping away his tears with a grubby handkerchief. "D'you really want to know?" He paused, then said in a half-choked voice: "I love you."

It was the grand gesture, with all the hallmarks of a classic B movie reaching its finale. The orchestra played, Jake disappeared into the night and the credits rolled.

I closed the door and went back into the flat feeling empty and angry. I couldn't believe what he'd just told me. If I'd had any sense I would have got out there and then. I should have walked away and never seen him again. But, when you're in love and when someone has just said those long awaited words, your judgment is impaired.

That particular night, the shock waves were hitting me with such force my judgment was in tatters. And so I made a bad decision. I let it carry on, getting deeper in to a relationship that could never go anywhere.

Now, I felt the blinkers lift and, for the first time in months, I could see clearly what a fool I'd been, how badly Jake had behaved and what a mess I'd created. Soon, he'd be here, expecting me to greet him with arms open wide, looking forward to a future that could never be.

What kind of a person did that make me?

CHAPTER 27

2pm came all too soon and I still didn't know what I was going to say to Jake.

How could I say I'd changed my mind after all he'd given up for me? Had I really changed my mind or was I just getting cold feet?

Perhaps when I saw him all the pieces would fall into place. Part of me was thrilled to be seeing him at last, to have him all to myself and be able to plan a future together. But another part of me knew it was a fraud. Someone was getting hurt so we could be happy. And it wasn't just one person. It was two small children, one not yet born. How could I do this to them? And could our relationship survive the guilt?

Perhaps I was only with Jake because he was unavailable. Our relationship had been built on sex and excitement, not on reality and everyday life. Did I really even know him?

I stood in 'Arrivals' at Melbourne Airport, waiting for Jake with more doubt in my heart than I ever thought possible. It was the moment I'd anticipated for so long, yet now it was within grasp, it felt empty. All I could feel was sadness and regret.

And there he was walking out, temporarily blinded by the sea of people, searching through the crowds for a glimpse of me. I stepped forward and called his name.

"Jake, over here."

He turned and the biggest smile lit up his face. If anything, he'd got better looking since I'd last seen him. He'd lost weight, giving his face a more angular look.

"Abigail…." He dropped his bags and ran to me, wrapping his arms around me and kissing me hungrily on the lips.

He broke away and held me at arms' length, looking at my face.

"My God, Abigail, I'd forgotten how beautiful you are, how soft your lips are… I've missed you so much."

I smiled weakly, feeling a familiar stirring within. He still had power over me. He could still affect me like no other man. The pull was irresistible. And yet I had to be strong, there was too much at stake to do the wrong thing now. I had to think beyond my pheromones. It was obvious that Jake couldn't.

"We have to get to my hotel room," he said in a low growl. "I want you so badly, Abigail, you have no idea."

I looked into his deep brown eyes and saw such pain and love and longing that it took my breath away.

"Which hotel are you booked into?"

"The Holiday Inn. Apparently it's not far."

His room was plush and comfortable, like any other room in any other Holiday Inn. He pulled me on to the bed, undoing my clothes.

"Jake," I muttered, trying to think clearly, but unable to control my lust. I'd been too long without his touch and my body took over. I couldn't help myself. We made love furiously and passionately, making up for lost time, devouring each other and losing ourselves in the moment. It was all over in a matter of minutes and we lay side by side, spent, letting the passion ebb away. The time for talking was approaching and I wasn't looking forward to it. Any delay was welcome.

"I thought we could maybe go on a tour of Melbourne," I suggested. "It won't be too taxing, you know, just sitting on a coach, listening to a commentary."

"I'd prefer to stay in the room with you," said Jake, hanging over me and starting to kiss me all over again. "We have so much to talk about."

"I know," I said, summoning what little will power remained, "but we can talk tomorrow. I thought it would be nice to see the sights this afternoon, if you're not too tired, that is?"

"I'm not tired. It makes me feel alive just being with you. Okay, let's take the city tour."

We took a cab into the centre of Melbourne to Flinders Street where the tour began. We found Miranda checking customers onto the coach.

"Hi everyone, this is the Melbourne Gardens Tour, starting in about 15 minutes. Make your way up the coach, please. My name is Miranda and I am going to be your guide for the afternoon."

"Gardens Tour?" I said in a loud voice, making everyone stop and stare. "What happened to the City Tour?"

"And good afternoon to you, madam. Would you like to take a seat?" She indicated a seat just behind her own, at the front of the coach.

"Sorry," she whispered. "I got it wrong. It's the Gardens Tour."

Her eyes went suddenly to Jake, standing behind me. "Hi, you must be Jake." She went to shake his hand and he looked somewhat bemused.

"This is Miranda," I explained. "She's one of my housemates. I'd probably have come home a lot earlier if it weren't for her. She's been brilliant."

"Hi, Miranda. Pleased to meet you," said Jake, shaking her hand. "How are you?"

"All the better for seeing you," she said, unable to take her eyes off him. "Abigail's told me all about you."

I let Jake sit by the window, aware of Miranda mouthing 'hot' to me, and giving me the thumbs up. I sat next to him and he took my hand in his.

"She's a bit full on," he said.

"I know, but she's great fun. I really like her. I'd have been miserable if she wasn't here. Rosalyn hasn't exactly been great company. Sorry it's gardens, by the way. I thought it was going to be the City Tour."

"It doesn't matter," said Jake. "I'm happy just to be with you."

He leant across to kiss me just as I heard someone say: "Abigail? What are you doing here?"

I pulled myself away from Jake and came face to face with Melvyn. Crimson was not the word. I turned puce and stared at him in shock. He seemed to have a habit of turning up just when I least expected it.

"Melvyn," I stuttered. "I thought you were in Sydney. Are you stalking me?"

"No, of course not. I flew in this morning to say goodbye to Mum and Dad. They're leaving tomorrow. They wanted to do the Gardens Tour before they left."

He looked at Jake. "So, this is why you came back to Melbourne so quickly. Sorry, I don't have the pleasure…"

"Hi, I'm Jake…"

Jake held out his hand.

"Hi," said Melvyn, shaking his hand. "Abigail mentioned you. I'm Melvyn."

I wished the earth would swallow me up.

"Who is it, Melvyn?" said a familiar voice behind him. It was Daphne, followed by Reggie.

"It's Abigail," said Melvyn. "You remember, the girl from the wedding, who you met on the plane?"

"Oh, yes, look Reggie, it's Abigail."

The familiar magnified eyes stared at me through milk bottle bottom glasses.

"Hello, Abigail. How are you? And who's this?"

"This is her boyfriend, Jake," said Melvyn pointedly.

"Oh, I thought you were here on your own, dear," said Daphne.

"She was," said Melvyn curtly. "Looks like Jake's come out to join her."

"Can you move along, please?" asked Miranda. "Sorry, folks, but there are more people trying to get on."

"Of course," said Melvyn, looking at me coldly. I felt my heart sink. He and his parents moved further down the coach. Thankfully, they didn't sit too close to us.

Miranda looked at me puzzled. "Isn't that Melvyn?" she mouthed at me.

"Yes," I mouthed back. "I thought he was in Sydney."

"So that's the mysterious Melvyn," said Jake. "The man you went away with. I spoke to your friend, Edna, remember. She told me you were with Melvyn. I assumed that's why you weren't returning my messages."

It seemed Edna had been putting in her two pennyworth.

"I didn't return your messages because I didn't receive them," I said sharply. "We were in the Blue Mountains and I couldn't get a signal."

He looked at me angrily. "But you were still with him, weren't you? Why else d'you think I came running out to Australia? If I'd known it was him, I might not have bothered."

"What d'you mean?" I demanded.

"Well, he's hardly competition, is he? I mean look at him."

"Melvyn's a really nice man."

"Nice!" scoffed Jake. "I rest my case."

This was not going well.

"So, that's why you came out? Because you were jealous?"

Jake looked at me with his big brown puppy dog eyes. "I thought I was losing you, Abby. I didn't know what was going on." He laughed. "If I'd known it was the Pillsbury Dough Boy, I wouldn't have been so worried."

"That is not funny, Jake. He's a better man than you'll ever be."

"What d'you mean?"

"At least he doesn't screw around behind his pregnant wife's back."

"Below the belt, Abigail. I've given up my wife and kids for you. I've walked out on Tiffany just as she's about to give birth."

"Yes, and what kind of man does that make you?" I demanded. "Not a very nice one."

"But it's what you wanted," said Jake heatedly. "It's what you've always wanted me to do."

"Okay, folks, perhaps you could cool it slightly," said Miranda, raising her head over the seat. "This is the Garden Tour not the Domestic Dispute Tour. Fascinating though it is, I don't want to frighten the customers away."

"Sorry," I said, realising the coach had gone very quiet.

Jake looked out of the window, refusing to meet my gaze.

"Right, folks, let's get going," said Miranda, speaking into her microphone. "Okay, here in Melbourne, we're very proud of our parks and gardens, and there are many to see. On this side of the river, we have the Treasury, Fitzroy and Flagstaff Gardens, then going south over the river, there's the Queen Victoria and Alexandra Gardens, and the wonderful Botanical Gardens."

I looked at Jake gazing out of the window, his lips a tight line of misery and frustration.

"Jake, I'm sorry," I reached over and took his hand. "This has all been a bit of a shock. I wasn't expecting you to come to Australia. I wasn't expecting you to leave Tiffany, if I'm honest."

"I thought it's what you wanted," he repeated in a small voice. "Have I just ripped my life apart for nothing? All because you just happen to have met Fat Boy?"

I ignored the insult. He was angry and tired and needed to lash out. Now was not the time for this conversation.

"I'm not with Melvyn," I said quietly. "Nothing happened in Sydney. He was just showing me round. We went camping in the Blue Mountains, but we had separate sleeping bags. When I got the message you were on your way, I came straight back to Melbourne. You have to believe me. I truly didn't receive your messages. That's why I never replied. Please stop being paranoid. I had no idea Melvyn would be on the coach today."

He smiled at me weakly. "Sorry, Abs. It's been fraught these last few days. I'm not thinking straight. If I found out you'd been unfaithful to me, I don't know what I'd do."

He put his hand over mine and I felt the familiar fluttering inside me.

"Okay, folks, we've just crossed the Yarra River." Miranda's voice sounded loud and clear across the speaker system. "To your left are the Queen Victoria Gardens, established as a memorial to the UK's longest reigning monarch. Coming up on your right, you'll see The Shrine of Remembrance, built as a memorial to World War One. The only problem was, it took so long to build, World War Two was under way by the time it was completed."

"I'm not sure I'm going to last the course," said Jake. "It's been a long journey and I'm shattered. What I'd like more than anything is to go back to the hotel and snuggle up in bed. What d'you say?"

I knew what my body wanted to do, but my head was saying something different. And my heart was just plain confused. I squeezed his hand and didn't reply.

"Across from The Shrine is Governor La Trobe's Cottage," continued Miranda, "and alongside it the Old Observatory where you can view the stars, and also The National Herbarium. Hang on a moment, stop the coach will you, Dave," she suddenly instructed the driver. The coach braked to a halt.

"Sorry, folks, won't be a second. Open the door, Dave."

The coach door hissed open and Miranda disappeared down the steps. We heard voices at the front of the coach and strained our necks, trying to see what was going on. After a couple of minutes, she reappeared up, followed by none other than Ken and Stacey.

"Sorry, for the delay, folks, these are good friends of mine. They'll be joining us on the tour. Stacey just happens to work in the hot houses at The Botanical Gardens. So if you have any questions, he's the person to ask."

Ken and Stacey walked up the aisle, looking for seats.

"Ken!" I said, as he walked past me. "What are you doing here?"

"Would you believe it?" he flounced. "I was meeting Stacey from work. Next thing you know a damn great coach pulls up and a mad woman tells us to get on board. Honestly! You can't do anything these days. Sit here, Stace."

They sat on the seat opposite us. Stacey waved at me and Ken noticed Jake.

"Ooh, who's this?"

"This is Jake," I said. "Jake, meet Ken and his partner, Stacey."

"Jake from England?" asked Ken, looking impressed and giving me a secret thumbs up sign.

"Yes, he flew in this afternoon."

"Good to meet you, Jake," said Ken, giving him the eye. "Need anyone to show you round?"

"No, I'm fine thanks," said Jake, looking at Ken suspiciously.

"Come to keep an eye on Abigail, have you? Don't blame you. She's wild."

"Don't believe a word he says, Jake," I told him. "Ken is the original wind up merchant. He's only trying to stir things up."

"Okay folks, let's crack on," said Miranda, in her best tour guide voice. "That imposing looking building you can see over there is Government House. That's where the Governor of Victoria resides, and up towards the city, you can see the Sydney Myer Music Bowl, where they hold outdoor concerts."

We continued the tour, Jake holding my hand and sleepily running his fingertips across the palm of my hand.

I wasn't aware there was an erogenous zone there, but it was certainly doing the trick. My resolve to tell him we didn't have a future began to crumble. How could I let this man go? He did things to me no other man ever could. The old addiction began to take over and I realised he was drawing me in, slowly and surely, like a fish on a line. I gazed into his eyes, aware of nothing but Jake. His lips, his hands, his smell, his passion smouldering beneath the surface.

"Right, folks, we're going to have a quick stop at the Botanical Gardens," announced Miranda. "Stacey has very kindly offered to take anyone who's interested into the Tropical Glasshouse, and there's a very nice tea room for those who'd like refreshments. Can I have you back here in around twenty minutes, please?"

Everyone disembarked. The majority, including Melvyn and his parents I was relieved to see, followed Stacey. Jake and I found the tearooms and ordered a pot of tea for two. He looked so tired I was beginning to question my decision to take the coach tour.

"Sorry, Jake. I thought we could just sit and listen. I didn't realise we'd be stopping off along the way."

"As long as we're together, I don't mind," he said, putting his hand over mine. "I thought I'd lost you. The thought of you being with someone else made me feel sick."

I looked into his eyes.

"You know I'd never do that, Jake. I could never be unfaithful to you."

I crossed the fingers of my other hand behind my back. There were some things on this holiday that needed to remain secret.

CHAPTER 28

"Our last stop is Fitzroy Gardens," Miranda informed us, when we were back on the coach. "It has several points of interest, including a carved fairytale tree, a miniature Tudor village and Captain Cook's cottage, which was moved lock, stock and barrel, in 1934, from Yorkshire in England and reassembled here. There's lots to see, folks, so we'll give you forty-five minutes to look around."

Dave parked the coach and we disembarked, Melvyn taking his parents in one direction, Ken and Stacey finding themselves once again at the centre of an enthusiastic crowd, and Jake looking bleary-eyed as jet lag took hold.

I looked around. This was where Rosalyn had done her fun run when I first arrived. It seemed a lifetime ago.

How strange my holiday had come full circle.

"Why don't we take a look at Captain Cook's Cottage?" I suggested.

"Whatever," said Jake, and so we set off, following the signposts until we found the picturesque little cottage, set amidst a well-stocked garden. We were about to step inside when Jake's phone rang. He made a face.

"Sorry, Abigail. It's Tiffany. I'd better take it."

He walked down the pathway, talking quietly and urgently into his phone.

Typical, I thought. He might have left her but it didn't change the fact she was having his child. Every time she snapped her fingers, he would come running. It was a timely phone-call and made me re-focus. Lust was all very well, but it wasn't a sound foundation on which to base a future life. Especially with a heavily pregnant wife in the background.

Sighing deeply, I wandered into the cottage. Inside, it was furnished in period style, with various ancient exhibits on display.

I spent a few minutes looking around disinterestedly

and was attempting to read a wall plaque when I heard a voice behind me.

"Abigail, we meet again."

I spun around and found myself staring into Bill's face.

"Oh my God. Bill, what are you doing here?"

"I could ask you the same thing."

"I'm on a coach tour of 'Melbourne's Gardens'." I felt myself going crimson, remembering our last meeting.

"And I'm doing research for the Gardens Tour. I take over next week."

He grinned lazily, eyeing me up and down. "I thought you might have gone home by now."

"A couple more days. Stop doing that, will you?"

"Doing what?"

"Mentally undressing me with your eyes. I can see what you're doing."

"Can you now?" he said, catching his hand round my waist and pulling me towards him.

I had no chance to stop him. The next second, his lips were on mine and he was kissing me hungrily. At the same time, I heard the door open behind us, and a woman shrieked loudly.

"Bill, what the hell d'you think you're doing?"

Bill broke away and I spun round, not knowing what to expect. To my horror, I saw Rosalyn advancing upon us, followed closely by Jake, a look of disbelief on his face.

"Abigail!" shrieked Rosalyn. "What are you doing with my boyfriend?"

"This better be good," said Jake over her shoulder.

"Your boyfriend?" I asked incredulously. "I don't think so. He was Miranda's boyfriend." Even as the words came out of my mouth, the truth hit me.

"It was you," I gasped. "It was you who was having the affair with him all along. You stole him from her. How could you do that? She was devastated."

I looked at Bill.

"So this is your mystery man? The one who won't commit, who's living in your apartment?"

"It was going nowhere with Miranda," she said angrily. "I didn't steal him. Bill was going to finish with her anyway. Isn't that right, Bill?"

Bill shrugged and grinned sheepishly.

"More to the point, what are you doing with Bill?" she demanded.

"My question exactly," said Jake.

"I turn my back for two minutes to find the ladies toilet," she continued, " and when I come back he's got his tongue down your throat. You obviously know each other very well. How long has this been going on for?"

I stayed silent, not knowing what to say.

"Bill?" she turned her fury on him.

"We met on the Dandenong Mountains trip, " he admitted.

"You did it, didn't you?" she demanded, turning to me. "You had sex with him. Don't forget, I know exactly what he's like. Can't keep it in his trousers."

"Is it true, Abigail?" asked Jake.

I turned on him. "If it is, what are you going to do about it, Jake? Now you know how it feels to have somebody screwing around behind your back. It hurts, doesn't it?"

"This is Jake?" asked Rosalyn in amazement. "You never said he was here in Melbourne. Oh my God, he's left his wife for you." She looked incredulous. "But if Jake's here, why are you messing round with Bill? I don't understand. Is one man not enough?"

"How could you, Abigail?" cried Jake, his face contorting in anger. "I trusted you."

"Well, maybe you shouldn't, Jake. Now you're getting a taste of your own medicine. And so are you, Rosalyn. Now, let me out. I'm going back to the coach."

I pushed past Rosalyn and Jake, not understanding how I'd become the bad guy in all this when their track record was just as bad, if not worse.

"Abigail, wait," called Jake.

I ignored him and ran out of the cottage, down the pathway in the direction of the coach. I needed some fresh air to clear my head and space to think.

Actually, I needed Melvyn. Dear, kind, funny, uncomplicated Melvyn, who came with a clean slate and no secret agenda. I was done with complicated relationships.

I arrived back at the coach and found Melvyn about to board with his parents.

"Melvyn," I gasped. "I'm sorry. Sorry I had to leave Sydney and sorry I didn't tell you how I feel. If you want to give it a go, then let's go for it."

He looked surprised and pleased, and I was aware of Daphne and Reggie exchanging hopeful looks.

"Abigail, this is out of the blue," said Melvyn, a big grin mushrooming over his face. "You're certainly full of surprises."

"Isn't she just?" said a voice over my shoulder. It was Rosalyn, followed closely by Jake and Bill.

"Turns out she's been screwing my boyfriend," Rosalyn hissed. "I don't think she's the kind of girl you want to be with, Melvyn."

"You're a fine one to speak, Rosalyn," I countered, "after what you've done."

"Can everyone board in an orderly fashion, please?" came Miranda's voice from inside the coach. "There's plenty of time, no need to rush."

"Can we talk, Melvyn?" I pleaded. "I need to explain."

"I think you'd better, Abigail," he said, frowning. "Just not when my parents are around, okay?"

"I'm sure there's a good explanation, dear," said Daphne. "She's such a nice girl. I can't see her 'screwing' someone else's boyfriend. Come on, Reggie, let's get on the coach."

"You don't want to let this one get away, son," advised Reggie, following his wife up the coach steps.

I watched as Melvyn and his parents made their way along the coach to their seats at the rear. Then I turned to Rosalyn.

"Why don't you just keep quiet, Rosalyn?" I pleaded. "What good is this doing? For any of us?"

But it was no use. Rosalyn was on a roll and all the frustration and heartache she'd been bottling up over the last few months came to a head. She snapped.

"You want me to keep quiet, Abigail? Well, tough. I'll show you how quiet I can be."

She stormed up the coach steps, surprising Miranda, who stood by the driver, welcoming people back on board.

"Hi, Rosalyn. Where did you come from? Are you going to join the trip?"

"No, I'm bloody well not," shouted Rosalyn. "Give me your microphone."

She snatched the microphone from Miranda's hand and began speaking in to it loudly.

"Can everybody hear me? I've got an announcement to make. Come on, Jake, get on the coach. And Bill… Isn't this cosy?"

Miranda stared aghast as Jake and Bill awkwardly climbed the steps, neither sure what to do about the mad woman before them.

"Bill?" said Miranda. "Oh my God, why are you here?"

"Hi Miranda," he smiled awkwardly. "Sorry about this."

"Sit down and make yourselves comfortable," Rosalyn instructed them, indicating two seats at the front.

They sat down, looking miserable.

"I think maybe I should go," suggested Bill.

"Shut up, Bill," commanded Rosalyn in a strange, high pitched voice. "Now, let's see exactly what's been going on. For those of you who don't know, this is my friend, Abigail from England."

She got hold of my arm and pulled me up the steps so everyone could see me.

"And this is Jake, her married lover, who has just left his pregnant wife for her. Not satisfied with wrecking one relationship, turns out she's also been sleeping with my boyfriend, Bill, sitting here. Actually, he's a pretty shitty boyfriend, because not only is he sleeping with me and Abigail, but any other girl he can get his hands on."

I didn't dare look at the back of the coach to see Melvyn's reaction. What was the point? Any chance of a relationship with him had just slipped well and truly away. And Jake's face was looking like thunder. After all, he'd travelled from the other side of the world to find I'd fallen well and truly off my pedestal. Only Ken and Stacey seemed to be enjoying themselves. Ken was grinning all over his face, loving every minute.

Now things took an ugly turn.

"Hang on there, Rosalyn," said Miranda, as she took stock of Rosalyn's words. "So you were the bitch who took Bill off me. Cheers, Bill. Sleeping with my housemate behind my back."

"Sorry, Miranda, it didn't mean anything," said Bill, with a hangdog expression. "I never meant for this to happen. I told her I couldn't offer her anything. She threatened to tell you unless I finished with you. I didn't have a choice."

"Shut up, scumbag," said Miranda. "You know what? You deserve each other. You're both spineless pieces of shit. And Rosalyn, this is for you, for nicking my boyfriend."

She pulled her fist back and landed a major punch in Rosalyn's face. Rosalyn went down like a ninepin, blood rushing from her nose. There was a collective intake of breath throughout the coach, then somebody cheered and shouted 'Way to go'. It could have been Ken.

Miranda turned to me.

"And you're no better, Abigail. You kept your liaison with Bill pretty quiet. I thought you were my friend. Turns out you're no better than her. Why don't you get back to your home-wrecking boyfriend? I reckon you two deserve each other. Don't worry, I'm not going to thump you. The damage was already done before you came along, thanks to Rosalyn."

She turned to the rest of the coach and picked up the microphone.

"Okay, folks, the show's over. And I for one am checking out. Have a good day."

As she turned off the microphone, the coach party burst into spontaneous applause. With a wry smile, she stepped over the prostrate Rosalyn, trying to stem the flow of blood with a handkerchief. Dusting her hands down, Miranda walked off the coach with her head held high.

"Great entertainment," called out Ken. "What's the encore?"

I gave him the finger.

Melvyn was not so easy to deal with. He walked down the aisle, with Daphne and Reggie following.

"I think it's time for us to check out, too," he said sadly. "Goodbye, Abigail. Looks like you have a few issues to sort out. This is all too complicated for me. Have a nice life."

"Goodbye, dear," said Daphne, looking philosophical. "It was nice meeting you. A word of advice, dear. Steer clear of married men. Somebody always gets hurt."

"Bye, dear," said Reggie, gazing through his thick lenses.

There was nothing I could say or do. I watched them go, leaving me with the mess of Rosalyn, Bill and Jake to sort out. In one fell swoop, I'd lost my oldest friend, my new friend, my lover and my potential new boyfriend.

It was a pretty spectacular fall from grace, by anyone's standards.

CHAPTER 29

Two days later I flew back to England.

I'd checked into a small bed and breakfast for the last two nights. Staying at the house was impossible. Miranda had nothing to say to me and Rosalyn had too much. I couldn't see the household arrangement lasting much longer. Ken was moving out to live with Stacey, Miranda couldn't trust herself to stay in control when Rosalyn was around, and Rosalyn was bereft now her affair with Bill was over. It was one huge mess and I seemed to be at the heart of it. There was nothing else to do but move out for the remainder of my holiday.

Jake and I talked for hours, but we were going round in circles. He couldn't forgive me for being unfaithful and didn't appear to see the irony of the situation. All he kept saying was: "I gave up everything for you and this is how you treat me", to the point when I couldn't stand it any more.

Eventually, I made a decision.

"Sorry, Jake, I can't do this any more. I know you left Tiffany for me and I know you flew ten thousand miles to be with me, but we're getting nowhere. How can we have a future together with all this baggage? It was a dream and now it's over. Go back to Tiffany. She needs you. Your son needs you. And your new baby will need you."

"But what about me?" he asked forlornly. "I need you."

"No you don't," I said firmly. "You'll survive without me. It's time to face up to your responsibilities. We had an amazing time together, and I'll never forget you, but it was a case of wrong time, wrong place."

I left him in his hotel room, tears streaming down his cheeks and that was the last I saw of him.

Three days later, I was back in England, battle weary and scarred, glad to be back in the sanctuary of my apartment to lick my wounds and think about all that had transpired.

But, of course, that wasn't the end of the story.

I'd only been back a couple of days when my intercom buzzed.

"Hello," I said, thinking it was the postman.

"Abigail?" said a female voice. "This is Tiffany, can you let me in?"

Aghast and with a beating heart, I pressed the button to open the downstairs door. I had about thirty seconds to compose myself.

I opened the front door of my apartment to find the small, pretty blonde woman I'd seen on Facebook, now heavily pregnant, standing in front of me.

"Hi Tiffany," I said. "D'you want to come in?"

She looked at me with huge, blue, watery eyes and silently stepped over the threshold.

"Er, d'you want a cup of coffee or anything?"

"No thanks," she said curtly. "I'd like to see Jake."

"Jake?" I asked stupidly.

"Yeah, Jake, my husband, the one you've been having an affair with for goodness knows how long. The one who left me and flew out to Australia to be with you. The one who abandoned me just as his second child is about to be born. Or am I living in an alternative universe and none of this ever happened?"

She stared at me icily.

"No you're not. It happened. And for what it's worth, I'm sorry. It was wrong. I thought it was all over between you and Jake, that's why I allowed myself to get involved."

"Oh, please," she looked at me disparagingly. "It was so 'over' between us we were having our second child together. Do you have any idea how pathetic you sound? You're a home-breaker, Abigail, there's no other word for it. You've deprived my children of their father, and you've taken my husband away from me. Now where is he?"

I looked at her perplexed.

"He's not here. We broke up in Australia. I told him to go back to you. Strange as it may seem, Tiffany, I do have a sense of decency and I realised we had no future together. I told him to face up to his responsibilities. Last time I saw him was in a hotel room in Melbourne."

"Save me the sordid details, please," she said coldly. "If he's not here, where is he?"

"I don't know. I arrived back in the UK two days ago. But I haven't seen anything of Jake. Maybe he stayed in Australia for a holiday, I don't know. Have you tried phoning him?"

"Of course. It just goes to voicemail. Are you sure he's not here?"

"You can search the place if you like. I've told you, it's over between us. I haven't seen him."

"Oh God, d'you think he's all right?" she stared at me with panic in her eyes, "You don't think he's done anything stupid?"

"No, of course not. Are you okay?"

Tiffany had begun holding her stomach and was grimacing in pain.

"The baby. I think the baby's coming."

Great. Just what I needed, Jake's wife was about to give birth in my appartment and he was nowhere to be seen. It was payback time.

"Hang on," I said, not having the slightest clue what to do. "Come and sit down. Breathe slowly. And keep your legs crossed."

I led her into the lounge, where she sat on the sofa, exhaling loudly with great long whooshing sounds.

"D'you want me to call an ambulance?" I said, feeling useless and out of my depth.

"I'm having a baby, not a heart attack," she said angrily. "Where the fuck is Jake? The best thing you can do is find him for me."

"I don't know where he is, Tiffany. I wouldn't know where to look."

She continued to exhale loudly.

"Please, let me get an ambulance for you."

"There's no time," she said. "The baby's head's engaged and my waters have just broken."

I stared in dismay at the large expanse of water seeping into my sofa.

"You'll have to take me to hospital," she said, "and quickly."

With no time to think, I grabbed my handbag and car keys, and helped her out of the flat, down the stairs and into my car, fortunately parked outside.

"Hold it in," I advised. "I'll have you at hospital in no time."

"Better hurry, Abigail," she gasped. "The contractions are coming thick and fast. I don't think it will be long."

"Okay, just hold on."

I drove like a maniac, grateful the hospital was close at hand. I found the signs to 'Maternity' and not caring whether I was clamped or fined, parked my car on double yellow lines and ran in to the hospital.

"Emergency!" I shouted. "There's a woman in my car having a baby. Can someone help, please?"

Immediately, two nurses appeared with a wheel chair and soon Tiffany was being wheeled in, huffing and puffing loudly.

"Do you want to come in with her?" asked one of the nurses.

"Me?" I asked fearfully. "Why would I want to do that?"

"You're her friend, aren't you? Doesn't she want you there?"

"It's coming," screamed Tiffany, and without further ado, they whisked her away, leaving me standing in the reception area, feeling like a fool.

Jake. I had to find Jake.

I sat in my car and dialled his number on my mobile. He answered immediately.

"Abby, is that you?"

"Yes. Where the hell are you?"

"I'm in a hotel."

"What, in Australia?"

"No, in Birmingham."

I mentally sighed in relief. "Thank God for that."

"Does this mean you want to see me?"

"No, it doesn't. It means your pregnant wife turned up on my doorstep and went into labour. She's now at my local hospital, giving birth. I thought you might want to be there."

"Oh, I see." There was silence on the line.

"Jake, did you hear me? Your child is about to be born, probably has by now, judging by the state she was in. You need to get here."

"But what about us, Abigail?"

"Jake, there is no 'us'. You have to forget me. Tiffany needs you. I don't."

"But I love you, Abigail. Can you truly tell me you don't love me any more?"

I took a deep breath and answered. "No, Jake, I don't love you any more. I'm sorry."

There was silence again. Then he spoke.

"Okay. Tell the hospital I'm on my way. Goodbye."

He hung up and I stared at the phone in my hand. It was one of the hardest things I'd ever had to do, because deep down there was a part of me that would always love Jake. He would always have part of my soul. It just wasn't enough to build a relationship on.

I went back to the reception area and asked them to tell Tiffany her husband was on his way. Then I got in my car and drove home.

Back in my apartment, I made a cup of coffee and attempted to dry out the sofa.

I needed someone to talk to. But who?

Miranda would have understood, but she was oceans away and, besides, she'd told me she never wanted to hear from me again. Was there any relationship I hadn't messed up?

Right on cue, the telephone rang. It was Edith.

"Hi Abigail, how are you? Glad to be back home?"

"Hi Edith. Feeling a bit flat. I don't know what to do with myself."

"Post holiday blues, gets me every time," she said cheerfully.

I couldn't tell her what had happened. For a start, she didn't know about Jake and would never have approved. And it was all too complicated to explain about events in Australia. When she and Derek had picked me up from the airport, I'd put on a brave face, telling them about all the amazing places I'd visited, making it sound like the trip of a lifetime. Which it was, I suppose.

It just didn't have the expected outcome.

"How are you, Edith?" I asked. "Isn't it time you kicked Derek into shape?"

"That's what I'm calling about," she said excitedly. "He's going to make an honest woman of me. Proposed last night."

"No way," I exclaimed. "That's fantastic news. The best thing I've heard in a long time. Congratulations. When's the wedding?"

"Can't come soon enough, actually."

"You mean…."

"Yep, confirmed yesterday. I'm expecting."

"Oh my God, a wedding and a baby. This is too much to take in. When's it due?"

"Well, it's early days yet, so I'd appreciate if you don't tell anyone, but if all goes well, should be due around the end of the year."

"Was it a romantic proposal?"

"Not exactly. You know Derek. His football team was playing and they were three nil up at half time. He was flushed with the excitement of it all and proposed over the washing up bowl. I said yes before he could retract. Just as well. His team ended up losing. If I'd waited, he might have changed his mind."

I let her babble on, feeling pleased for her, glad to be speaking to somebody and happy to hear about a relationship with a happy ending. After she'd hung up, I sat on my damp sofa, thinking about things.

I was genuinely happy to hear Edith's news, but it highlighted what I didn't have. I was sure Tiffany and Jake would work things out, once he'd grown up a bit, and I really did hope they'd make it together. But where did that leave me?

I was older, wiser, and still on my own, with no prospect of a relationship and a whole heap of emotional baggage to lug around. I was sad for what hadn't happened with Melvyn. I wasn't in love with him, but I'd liked him and felt more at ease with him than any other person I'd met. It was a relationship that had potential. At least it did, until I'd messed things up. What was wrong with me I wondered? Why couldn't I have a normal relationship like anyone else? Why did I have to pick the no-hopers and put off the good guys?

I felt a tear fall down my cheek. I didn't want to do the self-pity thing but surely I was allowed a little grieving? And so I sat and cried, mourning for what I'd had and lost with Jake and what had never come to pass with Melvyn.

Then with true British fortitude, I dusted myself down and looked forward. I may be temporarily down and out, but I wasn't beaten. As long as I drew breath, I still had hope.

EPILOGUE

August 21st 6 months later

The buzzer sounded and I rushed to answer.

"Abigail?" said a voice I recognised but couldn't quite place.

"Yes?"

"It's Rosalyn. Can you let me in?"

You could have knocked me down with a feather. This was unexpected.

"Yes. Come up."

I opened the front door and there she was, tall, suntanned and magnificent, white blonde hair pulled back in a ponytail, casually gorgeous in blue faded jeans and a blue printed top. If I wasn't mistaken, she'd put weight on.

"How are you?" I asked nervously, showing her into the lounge.

"I'm good," she answered. She showed me her ring finger. "Better than good. I'm engaged. To be married."

"Yeah, I worked that bit out," I said, genuinely shocked "Wow! Congratulations! Who to?"

"Who d'you think?" she asked.

"I don't know."

"Okay, don't be too shocked. Stuart."

"Stuart? Oh my God. I thought you weren't interested. You have a lot to tell me, Rosalyn. I'll put the kettle on."

Over a cup of tea, she told me what had happened.

"After you left, it was pretty bad. Miranda wouldn't speak to me. Bill moved out. My flat was repossessed and I had to find somewhere else to live. My aerobics classes were cancelled and it was all looking pretty bleak. No job, no man, nowhere to live. Then, who should come sailing to my rescue…?"

"Stuart," I answered. "I always knew he had a thing for you. It was just the time wasn't right. So how long have you been seeing him?"

"About four months. He proposed on 1st August, my birthday. We flew to Sydney for the weekend and he popped the question at the top of Sydney Tower. It was so romantic. Now, he's building a gym and fitness centre that I'm going to run for him."

"Wow, your life has really turned about," I said, bowled over by her massive life-style change. "Where will you live?"

"He has an apartment in Melbourne, plus the penthouse suite in Port Fairy for weekends. Although we'll probably buy a big house in the suburbs, you know, if we decide to have a family."

"A family?" I echoed in surprise. "I thought you hated the idea."

She wrinkled her nose.

"Well, I do, but you never know. I might just agree to it, with nannies and domestic help in place."

I couldn't help but smile. This was a totally different Rosalyn to the one I knew. This was one that had been seduced by lifestyle and money, but I had to say, it was a huge improvement on the manic, tortured soul I'd last encountered.

"I'm really pleased for you, Rosalyn," I said, and genuinely meant it. "I really like Stuart and you make a very attractive couple. When's the wedding?"

"We don't see any point in delaying, it's October. I was kind of hoping you might come, you know, as an olive branch. After all, you are my oldest friend."

I smiled at her.

"I'd be delighted."

"It's settled then, Matron of Honour. You could come over with mother and father. They're ecstatic about the news. Especially as Stuart's been nominated for Melbourne Businessman of the Year."

"It just gets better," I said. "I can't believe how life has changed for you. Any news of Ken and Miranda?"

"Ken struck gold with Stacey. They're inseparable. Had a civil ceremony at the beginning of July, so it's official now. And against everyone's better judgement, Miranda went back with Bill. Personally, I don't think it's a good idea, but she says he's changed and they're very happy. They're living together in a gorgeous apartment overlooking the river and she's been getting some good acting jobs, with the possibility of a regular gig on a soap. I think he genuinely loves her, so good luck to them. We'll never be friends again after everything that happened, but it seems we've moved on to better things. How about you, Abigail?"

I stared out of the window for a second.

"In a word, nothing. Same job, same apartment, same single status. No rich man on the horizon. In fact, no man on the horizon, full stop. Don't get me wrong, I'm not unhappy, just nothing to report."

"And Jake?" she asked.

"As far as I know, back with his wife. I haven't seen him since Australia. It wasn't right for us to be together. I'm hoping they've managed to patch things up. I heard he had a little girl. So much for the expected Baby Joey."

"So, you're on your own?" asked Rosalyn.

"Er, yes, I think I just said that."

"Good. That's the best news I could have heard."

"That's a bit harsh, isn't it, especially given your news?"

"Sorry, that came out wrong. I didn't mean it like that."

"What did you mean?"

"Before I say any more, I've brought someone with me. He's waiting in the car. I wanted to make sure everything was okay between us before he came in."

"Who? Stuart?"

She nodded. "I'll text him and tell him to come up."

She went to the front door, while I sat on the sofa, trying to take in all that she'd told me. It was a fairy tale ending for everyone. Except me. But I guess I didn't deserve it. I'd tweaked karmic law and now I was suffering the sting.

I heard voices on the landing, and Stuart and Rosalyn came into the lounge, holding hands and looking ecstatically happy. If possible, Stuart was even more handsome. He matched Rosalyn perfectly in a pale blue sweatshirt and dark blue chinos.

"Hi Abigail," he said, kissing my cheek. "Good to see you."

"Congratulations," I said. "You make a lovely couple. I'm really pleased for you."

"Thanks, Abigail, it means a lot to us that we have your blessing."

"Of course you have my blessing. I always told Rosalyn she should be with you. It'll be a marriage made in heaven. Now, who'd like a cup of tea?"

"Actually, we've brought some bubbly."

"Excellent. Let's celebrate. I'll get some glasses."

"Better get four," said Rosalyn.

"Four? There's only three of us."

"Actually, there's someone else. I hope you don't mind."

"Okay. The more the merrier, I guess. Who is it?"

"Okay, buddy, you can come in," called Stuart.

A familiar face appeared in the doorway and I had to pinch myself in disbelief. It was Melvyn.

Although not as I remembered him. It was a new, slimmed down version. He must have lost at least three stones.

"Melvyn!" I cried, not sure if I was more shocked by his presence in my apartment or his new slimline look. "Oh my God, you've changed."

"Lost a few pounds," he grinned. "How are you, Abigail? Good to see you."

"Good to see you, too. But how come you're here. I don't understand. How d'you know Rosalyn and Stuart?"

"Long story," said Melvyn. "To give you the abbreviated version, our company's been developing an ePOS software system for Stuart's new retail venture. We got to know each other and it turns out we have mutual acquaintances. I heard Stu and Rosalyn were coming over to see her parents, so thought I'd come along as well. See my Mum and Dad, and look you up at the same time. I hope you don't mind."

Did I mind? I was grinning from ear to ear.

"I couldn't have asked for a better surprise, Melvyn. I am so pleased to see you."

Stuart poured out the champagne and I raised my glass.

"Here's to the happy couple and to absent friends returning."

"Cheers," said Melvyn, raising his glass. "Hope you're free tonight, Abigail. I've booked a table for dinner. I just hope you don't blow me out this time."

"As if! I'd love to come. I promise, one hundred per cent, I'll be there."

Later that evening, Melvyn and I sat in a candlelit restaurant, enjoying a meal that I never imagined we would have. To celebrate, Melvyn ordered a bottle of Cristal champagne and we clinked glasses, toasting ourselves.

"You look great, Melvyn," I said, sipping my champagne. "How come you lost so much weight?"

He grimaced.

"I was a couch potato. Meeting you made me take a good long look at myself and I didn't like what I saw. After you left, I went on a health kick. I dieted, exercised, went running every morning. The weight soon fell off. What you see now is how I used to be."

I had to admit, he looked good.

Whereas previously he'd been cuddly, now he was just plain gorgeous. Dark hair, blue eyes, chiselled features and a great bod. I couldn't help but notice he was turning more than a few heads. But there was still something bothering me.

"Melvyn, I have to ask. I thought you never wanted to see me again. What changed?"

"Actually, nothing changed, Abigail," he said, sipping his champagne. "I fell for you the minute I saw you. There were just a lot of obstacles in the way. And you were involved with somebody else, so that didn't make it easy."

"I guess you've seen me at my worst," I said, thinking back to my time in Australia. "The drunkenness, the social ineptitude, the loose behaviour… Which means, on a positive note, I have absolutely nothing to hide. You've seen all the skeletons in my closet. It was an error of judgment getting involved with Jake, and it took meeting you to make me see that."

"Good," he said, placing his hand over mine. "I take it Jake's history?"

"Back with his wife, as far as I know. I haven't seen him since I got back."

"So, that leaves the way clear for me?" asked Melvyn, hopefully.

"It does. Apart from one rather major drawback."

"What's that?" he asked, frowning.

"We're live on different continents. It gives whole new meaning to the phrase 'distance relationship'."

He relaxed. "Oh, didn't I say? I'm being seconded to the UK in two months' time. There are problems with the Midlands office. They need a trouble-shooter."

"No, you left out that rather key fact," I said, unable to take the smile off my face. "That does rather change everything."

At last. It was my turn.

Thank you for reading Abigail's Affair

If you enjoyed reading Abigail's Affair, please leave a review on Amazon / Goodreads. Thank you! Pat Spence

Other titles by Pat Spence:

The Blue Crystal Trilogy:

Blue Moon (Book One)
True Blue (Book Two)
Into The Blue (Book 3) coming soon!

Re-Discover Your Razzle Dazzle:
The 30-day SPARKLE Programme
Self-help guide to looking good and feeling great.
Coming soon!

Follow Pat Spence:
On Facebook:
https://www.facebook.com/PatSpenceAuthor
On Twitter:
https://twitter.com/pat_spence

Follow The Blue Crystal Trilogy:
On Facebook:
https://www.facebook.com/bluecrystaltrilogy
On Twitter:
https://twitter.com/pat_spence

See the Blue Moon trailer:
https://www.youtube.com/watch?v=SFvsXlPem4Q

Titles to come
in the *'Looking For Love'* series:

Looking For Mr Blue Eyes
"I see you meeting a man with blue eyes and stooped posture," the clairvoyant said, staring into her crystal ball. The only trouble was, every man I met seemed to have blue eyes and varying degrees of stoop.
How did I know which was the right one? There was only one way to find out.

The Stepdaughter
Extended families are always difficult when you're the new wife. But to what lengths will your stepdaughter go to keep you away from her father. Especially when she's dead…

ABOUT THE AUTHOR

Pat Spence is a freelance writer and previously a magazine editor. She has also worked as a copywriter in advertising agencies, a freelance trainer in personal development and jobsearch skills, and a massage therapist/aromatherapist. She is married with one child, has a degree in English Literature, reads Tarot and is learning banjo.

Pat Spence

Made in the USA
Charleston, SC
04 April 2016